LOST HORIZON
and
GOOD-BYE,
MR. CHIPS

James Hilton

LOST HORIZON
and
GOOD-BYE,
MR. CHIPS

International Collectors Library
Garden City, New York

PUBLISHERS' NOTE—1957

WHEN James Hilton died in 1954 the world of arts and letters lost one of the really fine creative writers of our time.

The author's Preface that follows was written almost twenty-one years ago. If James Hilton were alive today to write a preface to celebrate this new edition of his most beloved novel, he would have to point out again that "its message of the peril of war to all that we mean by the word 'civilization'" is even more topical in 1957 than it was in 1936 or 1933. This fact undoubtedly explains in part why *Lost Horizon* lives on decade after decade.

If and when the day comes that we no longer face the possible destruction of civilization, and the topical interest in *Lost Horizon* is consequently diminished, the story's appeal will have to depend on the fact that it is one of the most original and one of the great imaginative stories of this century.

WILLIAM MORROW & COMPANY

PREFACE

Lost Horizon was first published on both sides of the Atlantic in the autumn of 1933. Its sale was slow at first, and though it had a few fervent and even notable admirers, by Christmas of that year one might have prophesied that even the ripple it had stirred was already stilled. As this happens to ninety-nine percent of novels, I was not enormously surprised, though I was—dare I now say it?—a little disappointed. But in June, 1934, the story received the Hawthornden Prize, which is given yearly in England for an imaginative work written by a British author under the age of forty-one. The result was in the nature of a resurrection; the sale of the original English edition began to gather momentum, while in America the publishers took the almost unique step of issuing the book afresh. Such a second chance was well taken, for during the past two years seventeen editions have been printed. This, the eighteenth, makes a permanent one.

I recount these details without vainglory, though I cannot pretend to be indifferent over them. There is certainly no book of mine whose success I ever desired more keenly, for *Lost Horizon* was, in part, the expression of a mood for which I had always hoped to find sympathizers. I found them in thousands, and now, through the medium of the screen version that Frank Capra has made, the same mood, I hope, will find them in millions.

Which leads me to a final remark about this mood. When *Lost Horizon* first appeared three years ago, its message of the peril of war to all that we mean by the word "civilization" was considered topical.

"It will be such a storm as the world has not seen before. There will be no safety by arms, no help from authority, no answer in science. It will rage till every flower of culture is trampled, and all human things are leveled in a vast chaos. . . . The Dark Ages that are to come will cover the whole world in a single pall; there will be neither escape nor sanctuary, save such as are too secret to be found or too humble to be noticed. . . ."

How much happier one would be to dismiss all this as thoroughly out-of-date, than to admit, as one must, that in 1936 it has become more terrifyingly up-to-date than ever!

James Hilton

London
August 4, 1936

Lost Horizon

PROLOGUE

CIGARS had burned low, and we were beginning to sample the disillusionment that usually afflicts old school friends who have met again as men and found themselves with less in common than they had believed they had. Rutherford wrote novels; Wyland was one of the Embassy secretaries; he had just given us dinner at Tempelhof—not very cheerfully, I fancied, but with the equanimity which a diplomat must always keep on tap for such occasions. It seemed likely that nothing but the fact of being three celibate Englishmen in a foreign capital could have brought us together, and I had already reached the conclusion that the slight touch of priggishness which I remembered in Wyland Tertius had not diminished with years and an M.V.O. Rutherford I liked more; he had ripened well out of the skinny, precocious infant whom I had once alternately bullied and patronized. The probability that he was making much more money and having a more interesting life than either of us, gave Wyland and me our one mutual emotion—a touch of envy.

The evening, however, was far from dull. We had a good view of the big Lufthansa machines as they arrived at the aerodrome from all parts of Central Europe, and towards dusk, when arc-flares were lighted, the scene took on a rich, theatrical brilliance. One of the planes was English, and its pilot, in full flying-kit, strolled past our table and saluted Wyland, who did not at first recognize him. When he, did so there were introductions all

around, and the stranger was invited to join us. He was a pleasant, jolly youth named Sanders. Wyland made some apologetic
remark about the difficulty of identifying people when they were
all dressed up in Sibleys and flying-helmets; at which Sanders
laughed and answered: "Oh, rather, I know that well enough.
Don't forget I was at Baskul." Wyland laughed also, but less
spontaneously, and the conversation then took other directions.

Sanders made an attractive addition to our small company,
and we all drank a great deal of beer together. About ten o'clock
Wyland left us for a moment to speak to some one at a table
near by, and Rutherford, into the sudden hiatus of talk, remarked: "Oh, by the way, you mentioned Baskul just now. I
know the place slightly. What was it you were referring to that
happened there?"

Sanders smiled rather shyly. "Oh, just a bit of excitement we
had once when I was in the Service." But he was a youth who
could not long refrain from being confidential. "Fact is, an
Afghan or an Afridi or somebody ran off with one of our buses,
and there was the very devil to pay afterwards, as you can imagine. Most impudent thing I ever heard of. The blighter waylaid
the pilot, knocked him out, pinched his kit, and climbed into the
cockpit without a soul spotting him. Gave the mechanics the
proper signals, too, and was up and away in fine style. The trouble was, he never came back."

Rutherford looked interested. "When did this happen?"

"Oh—must have been about a year ago. May, 'thirty-one. We
were evacuating civilians from Baskul to Peshawur owing to the
revolution—perhaps you remember the business. The place was
in a bit of an upset, or I don't suppose the thing could have happened. Still, it *did* happen—and it goes some way to show that
clothes make the man, doesn't it?"

Rutherford was still interested. "I should have thought you'd
have had more than one fellow in charge of a plane on an occasion like that?"

"We did, on all the ordinary troop-carriers, but this machine was a special one, built for some maharajah originally—quite a stunt kind of outfit. The Indian Survey people had been using it for high-altitude flights in Kashmir."

"And you say it never reached Peshawur?"

"Never reached there, and never came down anywhere else, so far as we could discover. That was the queer part about it. Of course, if the fellow was a tribesman he might have made for the hills, thinking to hold the passengers for ransom. I suppose they all got killed, somehow. There are heaps of places on the frontier where you might crash and not be heard of afterwards."

"Yes, I know the sort of country. How many passengers were there?"

"Four, I think. Three men and some woman missionary."

"Was one of the men, by any chance, named Conway?"

Sanders looked surprised. "Why, yes, as a matter of fact. 'Glory' Conway—did you know him?"

"He and I were at the same school," said Rutherford a little self-consciously, for it was true enough, yet a remark which he was aware did not suit him.

"He was a jolly fine chap, by all accounts of what he did at Baskul," went on Sanders.

Rutherford nodded. "Yes, undoubtedly . . . but how extraordinary . . . extraordinary . . ." He appeared to collect himself after a spell of mind-wandering. Then he said: "It was never in the papers, or I think I should have read about it. How was that?"

Sanders looked suddenly rather uncomfortable, and even, I imagined, was on the point of blushing. "To tell you the truth," he replied, "I seem to have let out more than I should have. Or perhaps it doesn't matter now—it must be stale news in every mess, let alone in the bazaars. It was hushed up, you see—I mean, about the way the thing happened. Wouldn't have sounded well. The Government people merely gave out that one of their machines was missing, and mentioned the names. Sort of

thing that didn't attract an awful lot of attention among outsiders."

At this point Wyland rejoined us, and Sanders turned to him
half apologetically. "I say, Wyland, these chaps have been talking about 'Glory' Conway. I'm afraid I spilled the Baskul yarn—
I hope you don't think it matters?"

Wyland was severely silent for a moment. It was plain that
he was reconciling the claims of compatriot courtesy and official
rectitude. "I can't help feeling," he said at length, "that it's a
pity to make a mere anecdote of it. I always thought you air
fellows were put on your honor not to tell tales out of school."
Having thus snubbed the youth, he turned, rather more graciously, to Rutherford. "Of course, it's all right in your case, but
I'm sure you realize that it's sometimes necessary for events up
on the Frontier to be shrouded in a little mystery."

"On the other hand," replied Rutherford dryly, "one has a curious itch to know the truth."

"It was never concealed from any one who had any real reason for wanting to know it. I was at Peshawur at the time, and I
can assure you of that. Did you know Conway well—since
schooldays, I mean?"

"Just a little at Oxford, and a few chance meetings since. Did
you come across him much?"

"At Angora, when I was stationed there, we met once or
twice."

"Did you like him?"

"I thought he was clever, but rather slack."

Rutherford smiled. "He was certainly clever. He had a most
exciting university career—until war broke out. Rowing Blue and
a leading light at the Union and prizeman for this, that, and the
other—also I reckon him the best amateur pianist I ever heard.
Amazingly many-sided fellow, the kind, one feels, that Jowett
would have tipped for a future premier. Yet, in point of fact, one
never heard much about him after those Oxford days. Of course

the War cut into his career. He was very young and I gather he
went through most of it."

"He was blown up or something," responded Wyland, "but
nothing very serious. Didn't do at all badly, got a D.S.O. in
France. Then I believe he went back to Oxford for a spell as a
sort of don. I know he went East in 'twenty-one. His Oriental
languages got him the job without any of the usual preliminaries.
He had several posts."

Rutherford smiled more broadly. "Then, of course, that accounts for everything. History will never disclose the amount of
sheer brilliance wasted in the routine of decoding F.O. chits and
handing round tea at Legation bun-fights."

"He was in the Consular Service, not the Diplomatic," said
Wyland loftily. It was evident that he did not care for chaff, and
he made no protest when, after a little more badinage of a similar kind, Rutherford rose to go. In any case it was getting late,
and I said I would go, too. Wyland's attitude as we made our
farewells was still one of official propriety suffering in silence,
but Sanders was very cordial and said he hoped to meet us again
sometime.

I was catching a transcontinental train at a very dismal hour of
the early morning, and, as we waited for a taxi, Rutherford asked
me if I would care to spend the interval at his hotel. He had a
sitting-room, he said, and we could talk. I said it would suit me
excellently, and he answered: "Good. We can talk about Conway, if you like, unless you're completely bored with his affairs."

I said that I wasn't, at all, though I had scarcely known him.
"He left at the end of my first term, and I never met him afterwards. But he was extraordinarily kind to me on one occasion. I
was a new boy and there was no earthly reason why he should
have done what he did. It was only a trivial thing, but I've always remembered it."

Rutherford assented. "Yes, I liked him a good deal too, though
I also saw surprisingly little of him, if you measure it in time."

And then there was a somewhat odd silence, during which it

was evident that we were both thinking of some one who had mattered to us far more than might have been judged from such casual contacts. I have often found since then that others who met Conway, even quite formally and for a moment, remembered him afterwards with great vividness. He was certainly remarkable as a youth, and to me, who had known him at the hero-worshiping age, his memory is still quite romantically distinct. He was tall and extremely good looking, and not only excelled at games but walked off with every conceivable kind of school prize. A rather sentimental headmaster once referred to his exploits as "glorious," and from that arose his nickname. Perhaps only he could have survived it. He gave a Speech Day oration in Greek, I recollect, and was outstandingly first-rate in school theatricals. There was something rather Elizabethan about him—his casual versatility, his good looks, that effervescent combination of mental with physical activities. Something a bit Philip-Sidneyish. Our civilization doesn't often breed people like that nowadays. I made a remark of this kind to Rutherford, and he replied: "Yes, that's true, and we have a special word of disparagement for them—we call them dilettanti. I suppose some people must have called Conway that, people like Wyland, for instance. I don't much care for Wyland. I can't stand his type— all that primness and mountainous self-importance. And the complete head-prefectorial mind, did you notice it? Little phrases about 'putting people on their honor' and 'telling tales out of school'—as though the bally Empire were the Fifth Form at St. Dominic's! But, then, I always fall foul of these sahib diplomats."

We drove a few blocks in silence, and then he continued: "Still, I wouldn't have missed this evening. It was a peculiar experience for me, hearing Sanders tell that story about the affair at Baskul. You see, I'd heard it before, and hadn't properly believed it. It was part of a much more fantastic story, which I saw no reason to believe at all, or well, only one very slight reason, anyway. *Now* there are *two* very slight reasons. I dare say you can guess that I'm not a particularly gullible person. I've spent a good deal of my life traveling about, and I know there are queer things in the world—if you see them yourself, that is, but not so often if you hear of them second-hand. And yet . . ."

He seemed suddenly to realize that what he was saying could not mean very much to me, and broke off with a laugh. "Well, there's one thing certain—I'm not likely to take Wyland into my confidence. It would be like trying to sell an epic poem to *Tit-Bits*. I'd rather try my luck with you."

"Perhaps you flatter me," I suggested.

"Your book doesn't lead me to think so."

I had not mentioned my authorship of that rather technical work (after all, a neurologist's is not everybody's "shop"), and I was agreeably surprised that Rutherford had even heard of it. I said as much, and he answered: "Well, you see, I was interested, because amnesia was Conway's trouble at one time."

We had reached the hotel and he had to get his key at the bureau. As we went up to the fifth floor he said: "All this is mere beating about the bush. The fact is, Conway isn't dead. At least he wasn't a few months ago."

This seemed beyond comment in the narrow space and time of an elevator ascent. In the corridor a few seconds later I responded: "Are you sure of that? How do you know?"

And he answered, unlocking his door: "Because I traveled with him from Shanghai to Honolulu in a Jap liner last November." He did not speak again till we were settled in armchairs and had fixed ourselves with drinks and cigars. "You see, I was in China in the autumn on a holiday. I'm always wandering about. I hadn't seen Conway for years. We never corresponded, and I can't say he was often in my thoughts, though his was one of the few faces that have always come to me quite effortlessly if I tried to picture it. I had been visiting a friend in Hankow and was returning by the Pekin express. On the train I chanced to get into conversation with a very charming Mother Superior of some French sisters of charity. She was traveling to Chung-

Kiang, where her convent was, and, because I knew a little French, she seemed to enjoy chattering to me about her work and affairs in general. As a matter of fact, I haven't much sympathy with ordinary missionary enterprise, but I'm prepared to admit, as many people are nowadays, that the Romans stand in a class by themselves, since at least they work hard and don't pose as commissioned officers in a world full of other ranks. Still, that's by the by. The point is that this lady, talking to me about the mission hospital at Chung-Kiang, mentioned a fever case that had been brought in some weeks back, a man who they thought must be a European, though he could give no account of himself and had no papers. His clothes were native, and of the poorest kind, and when taken in by the nuns he had been very ill indeed. He spoke fluent Chinese, as well as pretty good French, and my train companion assured me that before he realized the nationality of the nuns, he had also addressed them in English with a refined accent. I said I couldn't imagine such a phenomenon, and chaffed her gently about being able to detect a refined accent in a language she didn't know. We joked about these and other matters, and it ended by her inviting me to visit the mission if ever I happened to be thereabouts. This, of course, seemed then as unlikely as that I should climb Everest, and when the train reached Chung-Kiang I shook hands with genuine regret that our chance contact had come to an end. As it happened, though, I was back in Chung-Kiang within a few hours. The train broke down a mile or two further on, and with much difficulty pushed us back to the station, where we learned that a relief engine could not possibly arrive for twelve hours. That's the sort of thing that often happens on Chinese railways. So there was half a day to be lived through in Chung-Kiang—which made me decide to take the good lady at her word and call at the mission.

"I did so, and received a cordial, though naturally a somewhat astonished, welcome. I suppose one of the hardest things for a non-Catholic to realize is how easily a Catholic can combine official rigidity with non-official broad-mindedness. Is that too complicated? Anyhow, never mind, those mission people made quite delightful company. Before I'd been there an hour I found that a meal had been prepared, and a young Chinese Christian doctor sat down with me to it and kept up a conversation in a jolly mixture of French and English. Afterwards, he and the Mother Superior took me to see the hospital, of which they were very proud. I had told them I was a writer, and they were simple-minded enough to be a-flutter at the thought that I might put them all into a book. We walked past the beds while the doctor explained the cases. The place was spotlessly clean and looked to be very competently run. I had forgotten all about the mysterious patient with the refined English accent till the Mother Superior reminded me that we were just coming to him. All I could see was the back of the man's head; he was apparently asleep. It was suggested that I should address him in English, so I said 'Good afternoon,' which was the first and not very original thing I could think of. The man looked up suddenly and said 'Good afternoon' in answer. It was true; his accent was educated. But I hadn't time to be surprised at that, for I had already recognized him, despite his beard and altogether changed appearance and the fact that we hadn't met for so long. He was Conway. I was certain he was, and yet, if I'd paused to think about it, I might well have come to the conclusion that he couldn't possibly be. Fortunately I acted on the impulse of the moment. I called out his name and my own, and though he looked at me without any definite sign of recognition, I was positive I hadn't made any mistake. There was an odd little twitching of the facial muscles that I had noticed in him before, and he had the same eyes that at Balliol we used to say were so much more of a Cambridge blue than an Oxford. But besides all that, he was a man one simply didn't make mistakes about—to see him once was to know him always. Of course the doctor and the Mother Superior were greatly excited. I told them that I knew the man, that he was English, and a friend of mine, and that if he didn't recognize me, it could only be because he had completely lost his memory. They agreed, in a rather amazed way, and we had a long consultation about the case. They weren't able to make any suggestions as to how Conway could possibly have arrived at Chung-Kiang in his condition.

"To make the story brief, I stayed there over a fortnight, hoping that somehow or other I might induce him to remember things. I didn't succeed, but he regained his physical health, and we talked a good deal. When I told him quite frankly who I was and who he was, he was docile enough not to argue about it. He was quite cheerful, even, in a vague sort of way, and seemed glad enough to have my company. To my suggestion that I should take him home, he simply said that he didn't mind. It was a little unnerving, that apparent lack of any personal desire. As soon as I could I arranged for our departure. I made a confidant of an acquaintance in the consular office at Hankow, and thus the necessary passport and so on were made out without the fuss there might otherwise have been. Indeed, it seemed to me that for Conway's sake the whole business had better be kept free from publicity and newspaper headlines, and I'm glad to say I succeeded in that. It would have been jam, of course, for the press.

"Well, we made our exit from China in quite a normal way. We sailed down the Yangtze to Nanking, and then took train for Shanghai. There was a Jap liner leaving for 'Frisco that same night, so we made a great rush and got on board."

"You did a tremendous lot for him," I said.

Rutherford did not deny it. "I don't think I should have done quite as much for any one else," he answered. "But there was something about the fellow, and always had been—it's hard to explain, but it made one enjoy doing what one could."

"Yes," I agreed. "He had a peculiar charm, a sort of winsomeness that's pleasant to remember even now when I picture it, though, of course, I think of him still as a schoolboy in cricket flannels."

"A pity you didn't know him at Oxford. He was just brilliant—

there's no other word. After the War people said he was different. I, myself, think he was. But I can't help feeling that with all his gifts he ought to have been doing bigger work. All that Britannic Majesty stuff isn't my idea of a great man's career. And Conway was—or should have been—*great*. You and I have both known him, and I don't think I'm exaggerating when I say it's an experience we shan't ever forget. And even when he and I met in the middle of China, with his mind a blank and his past a mystery, there was still that queer core of attractiveness in him."

Rutherford paused reminiscently and then continued: "As you can imagine, we renewed our old friendship on the ship. I told him as much as I knew about himself, and he listened with an attention that might almost have seemed a little absurd. He remembered everything quite clearly since his arrival at Chung-Kiang, and another point that may interest you is that he hadn't forgotten languages. He told me, for instance, that he knew he must have had something to do with India, because he could speak Hindostani.

"At Yokohama the ship filled up, and among the new passengers was Sieveking, the pianist, *en route* for a concert tour in the States. He was at our dining table and sometimes talked with Conway in German. That will show you how outwardly normal Conway was. Apart from his loss of memory, which didn't show in ordinary intercourse, there couldn't have seemed much wrong with him.

"A few nights after leaving Japan, Sieveking was prevailed upon to give a piano recital on board, and Conway and I went to hear him. He played well, of course, some Brahms and Scarlatti, and a lot of Chopin. Once or twice I glanced at Conway and judged that he was enjoying it all, which appeared very natural, in view of his own musical past. At the end of the program the show lengthened out into an informal series of encores which Sieveking bestowed, very amiably, I thought, upon a few enthusiasts grouped round the piano. Again he played mostly Chopin; he rather specializes in it, you know. At last he left the piano and moved towards the door, still followed by admirers, but evidently feeling that he had done enough for them. In the meantime a rather odd thing was beginning to happen. Conway had sat down at the keyboard and was playing some rapid, lively piece that I didn't recognize, but which drew Sieveking back in great excitement to ask what it was. Conway, after a long and rather strange silence, could only reply that he didn't know. Sieveking exclaimed that that was incredible, and grew more excited still. Conway then made what appeared to be a tremendous physical and mental effort to remember, and said at last that the thing was a Chopin study. I didn't think myself it could be, and I wasn't surprised when Sieveking denied it absolutely. Conway, however, grew suddenly quite indignant about the matter—which startled me, because up to then he had shown so little emotion about anything. 'My dear fellow,' Sieveking remonstrated, 'I know everything of Chopin's that exists, and I can assure you that he never wrote what you have just played. He might well have done so, because it's utterly in his style, but he just didn't. I challenge you to show me the score in any of the editions.' To which Conway replied at length: 'Oh, yes, I remember now, it was never printed. I only know it myself from meeting a man who used to be one of Chopin's pupils. . . . Here's another unpublished thing I learned from him.'"

Rutherford steadied me with his eyes as he went on: "I don't know if you're a musician, but even if you're not, I dare say you'll be able to imagine something of Sieveking's excitement, and mine, too, as Conway continued to play. To me, of course, it was a sudden and quite mystifying glimpse into his past, the first clew of any kind that had escaped. Sieveking was naturally engrossed in the musical problem, which was perplexing enough, as you'll realize when I remind you that Chopin died in 1849.

"The whole incident was so unfathomable, in a sense, that perhaps I should add that there were at least a dozen witnesses of it, including a Californian university professor of some repute. Of course, it was easy to say that Conway's explanation was chronologically impossible, or almost so; but there was still the music itself to be explained. If it wasn't what Conway said it was, then what *was* it? Sieveking assured me that if those two pieces were published, they would be in every virtuoso's repertoire within six months. Even if this is an exaggeration, it shows Sieveking's opinion of them. After much argument at the time, we weren't able to settle anything, for Conway stuck to his story, and as he was beginning to look fatigued, I was anxious to get him away from the crowd and off to bed. The last episode was about making some phonograph records. Sieveking said he would fix up all arrangements as soon as he reached America, and Conway gave his promise to play before the microphone. I often feel it was a great pity, from every point of view, that he wasn't able to keep his word."

Rutherford glanced at his watch and impressed on me that I should have plenty of time to catch my train, since his story was practically finished. "Because that night—the night after the recital—he got back his memory. We had both gone to bed and I was lying awake, when he came into my cabin and told me. His face had stiffened into what I can only describe as an expression of overwhelming sadness—a sort of universal sadness, if you know what I mean—something remote or impersonal, a *Wehmut* or *Weltschmerz*, or whatever the Germans call it. He said he could call to mind everything, that it had begun to come back to him during Sieveking's playing, though only in patches at first. He sat for a long while on the edge of my bed, and I let him take his own time and make his own method of telling me. I said that I was glad his memory had returned, but sorry if he already wished that it hadn't. He looked up then and paid me what I shall always regard as a marvelously high compliment. 'Thank God, Rutherford,' he said, 'you are capable of imagining things.' After a while I dressed and persuaded him to do the same, and we walked up and down the boat deck. It was a calm night, starry and very warm, and the sea had a pale, sticky look, like condensed milk. Except for the vibration of the engines, we might have been pacing an esplanade. I let Conway go on in his own way, without questions at first. Somewhere about dawn he began to talk consecutively, and it was breakfast time and hot sunshine when he had finished. When I say 'finished' I don't mean that there was nothing more to tell me after that first confession. He filled in a good many important gaps during the next twenty-four hours. He was very unhappy, and couldn't have slept, so we talked almost constantly. About the middle of the following night the ship was due to reach Honolulu. We had drinks in my cabin the evening before; he left me about ten o'clock, and I never saw him again."

"You don't mean—" I had a picture in mind of a very calm, deliberate suicide I once saw on the mailboat from Holyhead to Kingstown.

Rutherford laughed. "Oh, Lord, no—he wasn't that sort. He just gave me the slip. It was easy enough to get ashore, but he must have found it hard to avoid being traced when I set people searching for him, as of course I did. Afterwards I learned that he'd managed to join the crew of a banana-boat going south to Fiji."

"How did you get to know that?"

"Quite straightforwardly. He wrote to me, three months later, from Bangkok, enclosing a draft to pay the expenses I'd been put to on his account. He thanked me and said he was very fit. He also said he was about to set out on a long journey—to the northwest. That was all."

"Where did he mean?"

"Yes, it's pretty vague, isn't it? A good many places must lie to the northwest of Bangkok. Even Berlin does, for that matter."

Rutherford paused and filled up my glass and his own. It had been a queer story—or else he had made it seem so; I hardly knew which. The music part of it, though puzzling, did not interest me so much as the mystery of Conway's arrival at that Chinese mission hospital; and I made this comment. Rutherford answered that in point of fact they were both parts of the same problem. "Well, how *did* he get to Chung-Kiang?" I asked. "I suppose he told you all about it that night on the ship?"

"He told me something about it, and it would be absurd of me, after letting you know so much, to be secretive about the rest. Only, to begin with, it's a longish sort of tale, and there wouldn't be time even to outline it before you'd have to be off for your train. And besides, as it happens, there's a more convenient way. I'm a little diffident about revealing the tricks of my dishonorable calling, but the truth is, Conway's story, as I pondered over it afterwards, appealed to me enormously. I had begun by making simple notes after our various conversations on the ship, so that I shouldn't forget details; later, as certain aspects of the thing began to grip me, I had the urge to do more, to fashion the written and recollected fragments into a single narrative. By that I don't mean that I invented or altered anything. There was quite enough material in what he told me: he was a fluent talker and had a natural gift for communicating an atmosphere. Also, I suppose, I felt I was beginning to understand the man himself." He went to an attaché-case and took out a bundle of typed manuscript. "Well, here it is, anyhow, and you can make what you like of it."

"By which I suppose you mean that I'm not expected to believe it?"

"Oh, hardly so definite a warning as that. But mind, if you *do* believe, it will be for Tertullian's famous reason—you remember? —*quia impossibile est.* Not a bad argument, maybe. Let me know what you think, at all events."

I took the manuscript away with me and read most of it on the Ostend express. I intended returning it with a long letter when I reached England, but there were delays, and before I could post it I got a short note from Rutherford to say that he was off on his wanderings again and would have no settled address for some months. He was going to Kashmir, he wrote, and thence "east." I was not surprised.

1

During that third week of May the situation in Baskul had become much worse and, on the 20th, Air Force machines arrived by arrangement from Peshawur to evacuate the white residents. These numbered about eighty, and most were safely transported across the mountains in troop-carriers. A few miscellaneous aircraft were also employed, among them being a cabin machine lent by the Maharajah of Chandapore. In this, about 10 A.M., four passengers embarked: Miss Roberta Brinklow, of the Eastern Mission; Henry D. Barnard, an American; Hugh Conway, H.M. Consul; and Captain Charles Mallinson, H.M. Vice-Consul.

These names are as they appeared later in Indian and British newspapers.

Conway was thirty-seven. He had been at Baskul for two years, in a job which now, in the light of events, could be regarded as a persistent backing of the wrong horse. A stage of his life was finished; in a few weeks' time, or perhaps after a few months' leave in England, he would be sent somewhere else. Tokio or Teheran, Manila or Muscat; people in his profession never knew what was coming. He had been ten years in the Consular Service, long enough to assess his own chances as shrewdly as he was apt to do those of others. He knew that the plums were not for him; but it was genuinely consoling, and not merely sour grapes, to reflect that he had no taste for plums. He preferred the less formal and more picturesque jobs that were on offer, and as these were often not good ones, it had doubtless seemed to others that he was playing his cards rather badly. Actually, he felt he had played them rather well; he had had a varied and moderately enjoyable decade.

He was tall, deeply bronzed, with brown, short cropped hair and slate-blue eyes. He was inclined to look severe and brooding until he laughed, and then (but it happened not so very often) he looked boyish. There was a slight nervous twitch near the left eye which was usually noticeable when he worked too hard or drank too much, and as he had been packing and destroying documents throughout the whole of the day and night preceding the evacuation, the twitch was very conspicuous when he climbed into the aeroplane. He was tired out, and overwhelmingly glad that he had contrived to be sent in the maharajah's luxurious air liner instead of in one of the crowded troopcarriers. He spread himself indulgently in the basket seat as the plane soared aloft. He was the sort of man who, being used to major hardships, expects minor comforts by way of compensation. Cheerfully he might endure the rigors of the road to Samarkand, but from London to Paris he would spend his last tenner on the Golden Arrow.

It was after the flight had lasted more than an hour that Mallinson said he thought the pilot wasn't keeping a straight course. Mallinson sat immediately in front. He was a youngster in his middle twenties, pink-cheeked, intelligent without being intellectual, beset with public school limitations, but also with their excellences. Failure to pass an examination was the chief cause of his being sent to Baskul, where Conway had had six months of his company and had grown to like him.

But Conway did not want to make the effort that an aeroplane conversation demands. He opened his eyes drowsily and replied that whatever the course taken, the pilot presumably knew best.

Half an hour later, when weariness and the drone of the engine had lulled him nearly to sleep, Mallinson disturbed him again. "I say, Conway, I thought Fenner was piloting us?"

"Well, isn't he?"

"The chap turned his head just now and I'll swear it wasn't he."

"It's hard to tell, through that glass panel."

"I'd know Fenner's face anywhere."

"Well, then, it must be some one else. I don't see that it matters."

"But Fenner told me definitely that he was taking this machine."

"They must have changed their minds and given him one of the others."

"Well, who is this man, then?"

"My dear boy, how should I know? You don't suppose I've memorized the face of every flight-lieutenant in the Air Force, do you?"

"I know a good many of them, anyway, but I don't recognize this fellow."

"Then he must belong to the minority whom you don't know." Conway smiled and added: "When we arrive in Peshawur very soon you can make his acquaintance and ask him all about himself."

"At this rate we shan't get to Peshawur at all. The man's right off his course. And I'm not surprised, either—flying so damned high he can't see where he is."

Conway was not bothering. He was used to air travel, and took things for granted. Besides, there was nothing particular he was eager to do when he got to Peshawur, and no one particular he was eager to see; so it was a matter of complete indifference to him whether the journey took four hours or six. He was unmarried; there would be no tender greetings on arrival. He had friends, and a few of them would probably take him to the club and stand him drinks; it was a pleasant prospect, but not one to sigh for in anticipation.

Nor did he sigh retrospectively, when he viewed the equally pleasant, but not wholly satisfying vista of the past decade. Changeable, fair intervals, becoming rather unsettled; it had been his own meteorological summary during that time, as well as the world's. He thought of Baskul, Pekin, Macao, and the other places—he had moved about pretty often. Remotest of all was Oxford, where he had had a couple of years of donhood after the War, lecturing on Oriental History, breathing dust in sunny libraries, cruising down the High on a push-bicycle. The vision attracted, but did not stir him; there was a sense in which he felt that he was still a part of all that he might have been.

A familiar gastric lurch informed him that the plane was beginning to descend. He felt tempted to rag Mallinson about his fidgets, and would perhaps have done so had not the youth risen abruptly, bumping his head against the roof, and waking Barnard, the American, who had been dozing in his seat at the other side of the narrow gangway. "My God!" Mallinson cried, peering through the window. "Look down there!"

Conway looked. The view was certainly not what he had expected, if, indeed, he had expected anything. Instead of the trim, geometrically laid-out cantonments and the larger oblongs of the hangars, nothing was visible but an opaque mist veiling an immense, sun-brown desolation. The plane, though descending rapidly, was still at a height unusual for ordinary flying. Long, corrugated mountain-ridges could be picked out, perhaps a mile or so closer than the cloudier smudge of the valleys. It was typical Frontier scenery, though Conway had never viewed it before from such an altitude. It was also, which struck him as odd, nowhere that he could imagine near Peshawur. "I don't recognize this part of the world," he commented. Then, more privately, for he did not wish to alarm the others, he added into Mallinson's ear: "Looks as if you're right. The man's lost his way."

The plane was swooping down at a tremendous speed, and as it did so, the air grew hotter; the scorched earth below was like an oven with the door suddenly opened. One mountain top after another lifted itself above the horizon in craggy silhouette; now the flight was along a curving valley, the base of which was strewn with rocks and the débris of dried-up watercourses. It looked like a floor littered with nutshells. The plane bumped and tossed in air pockets as uncomfortably as a rowboat in a swell. All four passengers had to hold on to their seats.

"Looks like he wants to land!" shouted the American hoarsely.

"He can't!" Mallinson retorted. "He'd be simply mad if he tried to! He'll crash and then—"

But the pilot did land. A small cleared space opened by the side of a gully, and with considerable skill the machine was jolted and heaved to a standstill. What happened after that, however, was more puzzling and less reassuring. A swarm of bearded and turbaned tribesmen came forward from all directions, surrounding the machine and effectively preventing any one from getting out of it except the pilot. The latter clambered to earth and held excited colloquy with them, during which proceeding it became clear that, so far from being Fenner, he was not an Englishman at all, and possibly not even a European. Meanwhile cans of gasoline were fetched from a dump close by, and emptied into the exceptionally capacious tanks. Grins and disregarding silence met the shouts of the four imprisoned passengers, while the slightest attempt to alight provoked a menacing movement from a score of rifles. Conway, who knew a little Pushtu, harangued the tribesmen as well as he could in that language, but without effect; while the pilot's sole retort to remarks addressed to him in any language was a significant flourish of his revolver. Midday sunlight, blazing on the roof of the cabin, grilled the air inside till the occupants were almost fainting with the heat and with the exertion of their protests. They were quite powerless; it had been a condition of the evacuation that they should carry no arms.

When the tanks were at last screwed up, a gasoline can filled with tepid water was handed through one of the cabin windows. No questions were answered, though it did not appear that the men were personally hostile. After a further parley the pilot climbed back into the cockpit, a Pathan clumsily swung the propeller, and the flight was resumed. The take-off, in that confined space and with the extra gasoline load, was even more skillful than the landing. The plane rose high into the hazy vapors; then turned east, as if setting a course. It was mid-afternoon.

A most extraordinary and bewildering business! As the cooler air refreshed them, the passengers could hardly believe that it had really happened; it was an outrage to which none could recall any parallel, or suggest any precedent, in all the turbulent records of the Frontier. It would have been incredible, indeed, had they not been victims of it themselves. It was quite natural that high indignation should follow incredulity, and anxious speculation only when indignation had worn itself out. Mallinson then developed the theory which, in the absence of any other, they found easiest to accept. They were being kidnaped for ransom. The trick was by no means new in itself, though this particular technique must be regarded as original. It was a little more comforting to feel that they were not making entirely virgin history; after all, there had been kidnapings before, and a good many of them had ended up all right. The tribesmen kept you in some lair in the mountains till the Government paid up and you were released. You were treated quite decently, and as the money that had to be paid wasn't your own, the whole business was only unpleasant while it lasted. Afterwards, of course, the Air people sent a bombing squadron, and you were left with one good story to tell for the rest of your life. Mallinson enunciated the proposition a shade nervously; but Barnard, the American, chose to be heavily facetious. "Well, gentlemen, I dare say this is a cute idea on somebody's part, but I can't exactly see that your Air Force has covered itself with glory. You Britishers make jokes about the hold-ups in Chicago and all that, but I don't recollect any instance of a gunman running off with one of Uncle Sam's aeroplanes. And I should like to know, by the way, what

this fellow did with the real pilot. Sandbagged him, I bet." He
yawned. He was a large, fleshy man, with a hard-bitten face in
which good-humored wrinkles were not quite offset by pessi-
mistic pouches. Nobody in Baskul had known much about him
except that he had arrived from Persia, where it was presumed
he had something to do with oil.

Conway meanwhile was busying himself with a very practical
task. He had collected every scrap of paper that they all had,
and was composing messages in various native languages to be
dropped to earth at intervals. It was a slender chance, in such
sparsely populated country, but worth taking.

The fourth occupant, Miss Brinklow, sat tight-lipped and
straight-backed, with few comments and no complaints. She was
a small, rather leathery woman, with an air of having been compelled to attend a party at which there were goings-on that she
could not wholly approve.

Conway had talked less than the two other men, for translating SOS messages into dialects was a mental exercise requiring
concentration. He had, however, answered questions when
asked, and had agreed, tentatively, with Mallinson's kidnaping
theory. He had also agreed, to some extent, with Barnard's stric-
tures on the Air Force. "Though one can see, of course, how it
may have happened. With the place in commotion as it was, one
man in flying-kit would look very much like another. No one
would think of doubting the *bona fides* of any man in the proper
clothes who looked as if he knew his job. And this fellow *must*
have known it—the signals, and so forth. Pretty obvious, too, that
he knows how to fly . . . still, I agree with you that it's the sort
of thing that some one ought to get into hot water about. And
somebody will, you may be sure, though I suspect he won't deserve it."

"Well, sir," responded Barnard, "I certainly do admire the
way you manage to see both sides of the question. It's the right
spirit to have, no doubt, even when you're being taken for a
ride."

Americans, Conway reflected, had the knack of being able to say patronizing things without being offensive. He smiled tolerantly, but did not continue the conversation. His tiredness was of a kind that no amount of possible peril could stave off. Towards late afternoon, when Barnard and Mallinson, who had been arguing, appealed to him on some point, it appeared that he had fallen asleep.

"Dead beat," Mallinson commented. "And I don't wonder at it, after these last few weeks."

"You're his friend?" queried Barnard.

"I've worked with him at the Consulate. I happen to know that he hasn't been in bed for the last four nights. As a matter of fact, we're damned lucky in having him with us in a tight corner like this. Apart from knowing the languages, he's got a sort of way with him in dealing with people. If any one can get us out of the mess, he'll do it. He's pretty cool about most things."

"Well, let him have his sleep, then," agreed Barnard.

Miss Brinklow made one of her rare remarks. "I think he *looks* like a very brave man," she said.

Conway was far less certain that he *was* a very brave man. He had closed his eyes in sheer physical fatigue, but without actually sleeping. He could hear and feel every movement of the plane, and he heard also, with mixed feelings, Mallinson's eulogy of himself. It was then that he had his doubts, recognizing a tight sensation in his stomach which was his own bodily reaction to a disquieting mental survey. He was not, as he knew well from experience, one of those persons who love danger for its own sake. There was an aspect of it which he sometimes enjoyed, an excitement, a purgative effect upon sluggish emotions, but he was far from fond of risking his life. Twelve years earlier he had grown to hate the perils of trench warfare in France, and had several times avoided death by declining to attempt valorous impossibilities. Even his D.S.O. had been won, not so much by physical courage, as by a certain hardly developed technique of endurance. And since the War, whenever there had been danger again, he had faced it with increasing lack of relish unless it promised extravagant dividends in thrills.

He still kept his eyes closed. He was touched, and a little dismayed, by what he had heard Mallinson say. It was his fate in life to have his equanimity always mistaken for pluck, whereas it was actually something much more dispassionate and much less virile. They were all in a damnably awkward situation, it seemed to him, and so far from being full of bravery about it, he felt chiefly an enormous distaste for whatever trouble might be in store. There was Miss Brinklow, for instance. He foresaw that in certain circumstances he would have to act on the supposition that because she was a woman she mattered far more than the rest of them put together, and he shrank from a situation in which such disproportionate behavior might be unavoidable.

Nevertheless, when he showed signs of wakefulness, it was to Miss Brinklow that he spoke first. He realized that she was neither young nor pretty—negative virtues, but immensely helpful ones in such difficulties as those in which they might soon find themselves. He was also rather sorry for her, because he suspected that neither Mallinson nor the American liked missionaries, especially female ones. He himself was unprejudiced, but he was afraid she would find his open mind a less familiar and therefore an even more disconcerting phenomenon. "We seem to be in a queer fix," he said, leaning forward to her ear, "but I'm glad you're taking it calmly. I don't really think anything dreadful is going to happen to us."

"I'm certain it won't if you can prevent it," she answered; which did not console him.

"You must let me know if there is anything we can do to make you more comfortable."

Barnard caught the word. "Comfortable?" he echoed raucously. "Why, of course we're comfortable. We're just enjoying the trip. Pity we haven't a pack of cards—we could play a rubber of bridge."

Conway welcomed the spirit of the remark, though he disliked bridge. "I don't suppose Miss Brinklow plays," he said, smiling. But the missionary turned round briskly to retort: "Indeed I do, and I could never see any harm in cards at all. There's nothing against them in the Bible."

They all laughed, and seemed obliged to her for providing an excuse. At any rate, Conway thought, she wasn't hysterical.

All afternoon the plane had soared through the thin mists of the upper atmosphere, far too high to give clear sight of what lay beneath. Sometimes, at longish intervals, the veil was torn for a moment, to display the jagged outline of a peak, or the glint of some unknown stream. The direction could be determined roughly from the sun; it was still east, with occasional twists to the north; but where it had led depended on the speed of travel, which Conway could not judge with any accuracy. It seemed likely, though, that the flight must already have exhausted a good deal of the gasoline; though that again depended on uncertain factors. Conway had no technical knowledge of aircraft, but he was sure that the pilot, whoever he might be, was altogether an expert. That halt in the rock-strewn valley had demonstrated it, and also other incidents since. And Conway could not repress a feeling that was always his in the presence of any superb and indisputable competence. He was so used to being appealed to for help that mere awareness of some one who would neither ask nor need it was slightly tranquilizing, even amidst the greater perplexities of the future. But he did not expect his companions to share such a tenuous emotion. He recognized that they were likely to have far more personal reasons for anxiety than he had himself. Mallinson, for instance, was engaged to a girl in England; Barnard might be married; Miss Brinklow had her work, vocation, or however she might regard it. Mallinson, incidentally, was by far the least composed; as the hours passed he showed himself increasingly excitable—apt, also, to resent to Conway's face the very coolness which he had praised behind his back. Once, above the roar of the engine, a sharp storm of argument arose. "Look here," Mallinson shouted angrily, "are we bound to sit here twiddling our thumbs while this maniac does everything he damn well wants? What's to prevent us from smashing that panel and having it out with him?"

"Nothing at all," replied Conway, "except that he's armed and we're not, and that in any case, none of us would know how to bring the machine to earth afterwards."

"It can't be very hard, surely. I dare say you could do it."

"My dear Mallinson, why is it always *me* you expect to perform these miracles?"

"Well, anyway, this business is getting hellishly on my nerves. Can't we *make* the fellow come down?"

"How do you suggest it should be done?"

Mallinson was becoming more and more agitated. "Well, he's *there*, isn't he? About six feet away from us, and we're three men to one! Have we got to stare at his damned back all the time? At least we might force him to tell us what the game is."

"Very well, we'll see." Conway took a few paces forward to the partition between the cabin and the pilot's cockpit, which was situated in front and somewhat above. There was a pane of glass, about six inches square and made to slide open, through which the pilot, by turning his head and stooping slightly, could communicate with his passengers. Conway tapped on this with his knuckles. The response was almost comically as he had expected. The glass panel slid sideways and the barrel of a revolver obtruded. Not a word; just that. Conway retreated without arguing the point, and the panel slid back again.

Mallinson, who had watched the incident, was only partly satisfied. "I don't suppose he'd have dared to shoot," he commented. "It's probably bluff."

"Quite," agreed Conway, "but I'd rather leave you to make sure."

"Well, I do feel we ought to put up some sort of a fight before giving in tamely like this."

Conway was sympathetic. He recognized the convention, with all its associations of red-coated soldiers and school history books, that Englishmen fear nothing, never surrender, and are never defeated. He said: "Putting up a fight without a decent chance of winning is a poor game, and I'm not that sort of hero."

"Good for you, sir," interposed Barnard heartily. "When somebody's got you by the short hairs you may as well give in pleasantly and admit it. For my part I'm going to enjoy life while it lasts and have a cigar. I hope you don't think a little bit of extra danger matters to us?"

"Not so far as I'm concerned, but it might bother Miss Brinklow."

Barnard was quick to make amends. "Pardon me, madam, but do you mind if I smoke?"

"Not at all," she answered graciously. "I don't do so myself, but I just love the smell of a cigar."

Conway felt that of all the women who could possibly have made such a remark, she was easily the most typical. Anyhow, Mallinson's excitement had calmed a little, and to show friendliness he offered him a cigarette, though he did not light one himself. "I know how you feel," he said gently. "It's a bad outlook, and it's all the worse, in some ways, because there isn't much we can do about it."

"And all the better, too, in other ways," he could not help adding to himself. For he was still immensely fatigued. There was also in his nature a trait which some people might have called laziness, though it was not quite that. No one was capable of harder work, when it had to be done, and few could better shoulder responsibility; but the facts remained that he was not passionately fond of activity, and did not enjoy responsibility at all. Both were included in his job, and he made the best of them, but he was always ready to give way to any one else who could function as well or better. It was partly this, no doubt, that had made his success in the Service less striking than it might have been. He was not ambitious enough to shove his way past others, or to make an important parade of doing nothing when there was really nothing doing. His despatches were sometimes laconic to the point of curtness, and his calm in emergencies, though admired, was often suspected of being too sincere. Authority likes to feel that a man is imposing some effort on himself, and that his apparent nonchalance is only a cloak to disguise an outfit of well-bred emotions. With Conway the dark suspicion had sometimes been current that he really was as unruffled as he looked, and that whatever happened, he did not give a damn. But this, too, like the laziness, was an imperfect interpretation. What most observers failed to perceive in him was something quite bafflingly simple—a love of quietness, contemplation, and being alone.

Now, since he was so inclined and there was nothing else to do, he leaned back in the basket chair and went definitely to sleep. When he woke he noticed that the others, despite their various anxieties, had likewise succumbed. Miss Brinklow was sitting bolt upright with her eyes closed, like some rather dingy and outmoded idol; Mallinson had lolled forward in his place with his chin in the palm of a hand. The American was even snoring. Very sensible of them all, Conway thought; there was no point in wearying themselves with shouting. But immediately he was aware of certain physical sensations in himself, slight dizziness and heart-thumping and a tendency to inhale sharply and with effort. He remembered similar symptoms once before—in the Swiss Alps.

Then he turned to the window and gazed out. The surrounding sky had cleared completely, and in the light of late afternoon there came to him a vision which, for the instant, snatched the remaining breath out of his lungs. Far away, at the very limit of distance, lay range upon range of snow peaks, festooned with glaciers, and floating, in appearance, upon vast levels of cloud. They compassed the whole arc of the circle, merging towards the west in a horizon that was fierce, almost garish in coloring, like an impressionist backdrop done by some half-mad genius.

And meanwhile, the plane, on that stupendous stage, was dron-
ing over an abyss in face of a sheer white wall that seemed part
of the sky itself until the sun caught it. Then, like a dozen piled-
up Jungfraus seen from Mürren, it flamed into superb and dazzling incandescence.

Conway was not apt to be easily impressed, and as a rule he
did not care for "views," especially the more famous ones for
which thoughtful municipalities provide garden seats. Once, on
being taken to Tiger Hill, near Darjeeling, to watch the sunrise
upon Everest, he had found the highest mountain in the world a
definite disappointment. But this fearsome spectacle beyond the
window pane was of different caliber; it had no air of posing to
be admired. There was something raw and monstrous about
those uncompromising ice-cliffs, and a certain sublime imperti-
nence in approaching them thus. He pondered, envisaging maps,
calculating distances, estimating times and speeds. Then he became aware that Mallinson had wakened also. He touched the
youth on the arm.

2

It was typical of Conway that he let the others waken for themselves, and made small response to their exclamations of astonishment; yet later, when Barnard sought his opinion, gave it with something of the detached fluency of a university professor elucidating a problem. He thought it likely, he said, that they were still in India; they had been flying east for several hours, too high to see much, but probably the course had been along some river valley, one stretching roughly east and west. "I wish I hadn't to rely on memory, but my impression is that the valley of the upper Indus fits in well enough. That would have brought us by now to a very spectacular part of the world, and, as you see, so it has."

"You know where we are, then?" Barnard interrupted.

"Well, no—I've never been anywhere near here before, but I wouldn't be surprised if that mountain is Nanga Parbat, the one Mummery lost his life on. In structure and general layout it seems in accord with all I've heard about it."

"You are a mountaineer yourself?"

"In my younger days I was keen. Only the usual Swiss climbs, of course."

Mallinson intervened peevishly: "There'd be more point in discussing where we're going to. I wish to God somebody could tell us."

"Well, it looks to me as if we're heading for that range yonder," said Barnard. "Don't you think so, Conway? You'll excuse me calling you that, but if we're all going to have a little adventure together, it's a pity to stand on ceremony."

Conway thought it very natural that any one should call him by his own name, and found Barnard's apologies for so doing a trifle needless. "Oh, certainly," he agreed, and added: "I think that range must be the Karakorams. There are several passes if our man intends to cross them."

"Our man?" exclaimed Mallinson. "You mean our maniac! I reckon it's time we dropped the kidnaping theory. We're far past the Frontier country by now, there aren't any tribes living around here. The only explanation I can think of is that the fellow's a raving lunatic. Would anybody except a lunatic fly into this sort of country?"

"I know that nobody except a damn fine airman *could,*" retorted Barnard. "I never was great at geography, but I understand that these are reputed to be the highest mountains in the world, and if that's so, it'll be a pretty first-class performance to cross them."

"And also the will of God," put in Miss Brinklow unexpectedly.

Conway did not offer his opinion. The will of God or the lunacy of man—it seemed to him that you could take your choice, if you wanted a good enough reason for most things. Or, alternatively (and he thought of it as he contemplated the small orderliness of the cabin against the window background of such frantic natural scenery), the will of man and the lunacy of God. It must be satisfying to be quite certain which way to look at it. Then, while he watched and pondered, a strange transformation took place. The light turned to bluish over the whole mountain, with the lower slopes darkening to violet. Something deeper than his usual aloofness rose in him—not quite excitement, still less fear, but a sharp intensity of expectation. He said: "You're quite right, Barnard, this affair grows more and more remarkable."

"Remarkable or not, I don't feel inclined to propose a vote of thanks about it," Mallinson persisted. "We didn't ask to be brought here, and Heaven knows what we shall do when we get *there,* wherever *there* is. And I don't see that it's any less of an outrage because the fellow happens to be a stunt flyer. Even if he is, he can be just as much a lunatic. I once heard of a pilot going mad in mid-air. This fellow must have been mad from the beginning. That's my theory, Conway."

Conway was silent. He found it irksome to be continually shouting above the roar of the machine, and after all, there was little point in arguing possibilities. But when Mallinson pressed for an opinion, he said: "Very well-organized lunacy, you know. Don't forget the landing for gasoline, and also that this was the only machine that could climb to such a height."

"That doesn't prove he isn't mad. He may have been mad enough to plan everything."

"Yes, of course, that's possible."

"Well, then, we've got to decide on a plan of action. What are we going to do when he comes to earth? If he doesn't crash and kill us all, that is. What are we going to *do?* Rush forward and congratulate him on his marvelous flight, I suppose."

"Not on your life," answered Barnard. "I'll leave you to do all the rushing forward."

Again Conway was loath to prolong the argument, especially since the American, with his level-headed banter, seemed quite capable of handling it himself. Already Conway found himself reflecting that the party might have been far less fortunately constituted. Only Mallinson was inclined to be cantankerous, and that might partly be due to the altitude. Rarefied air had different effects on people; Conway, for instance, derived from it a combination of mental clarity and physical apathy that was not unpleasant. Indeed, he breathed the clear cold air in little spasms of content. The whole situation, no doubt, was appalling, but he had no power at the moment to resent anything that proceeded so purposefully and with such captivating interest.

And there came over him, too, as he stared at that superb

mountain, a glow of satisfaction that there were such places still left on earth, distant, inaccessible, as yet unhumanized. The icy rampart of the Karakorams was now more striking than ever against the northern sky, which had become mouse-colored and sinister; the peaks had a chill gleam; utterly majestic and remote, their very namelessness had dignity. Those few thousand feet by which they fell short of the known giants might save them eternally from the climbing expedition; they offered a less tempting lure to the record-breaker. Conway was the antithesis of such a type; he was inclined to see vulgarity in the Western ideal of superlatives, and "the utmost for the highest" seemed to him a less reasonable and perhaps more commonplace proposition than "the much for the high." He did not, in fact, care for excessive striving, and he was bored by mere exploits.

While he was still contemplating the scene, twilight fell, steeping the depths in a rich, velvet gloom that spread upwards like a dye. Then the whole range, much nearer now, paled into fresh splendor; a full moon rose, touching each peak in succession like some celestial lamp-lighter, until the long horizon glittered against a blue-black sky. The air grew cold and a wind sprang up, tossing the machine uncomfortably. These new distresses lowered the spirits of the passengers; it had not been reckoned that the flight could go on after dusk, and now the last hope lay in the exhaustion of gasoline. That, however, was bound to come soon. Mallinson began to argue about it, and Conway, with some reluctance, for he really did not know, gave as his estimate that the utmost distance might be anything up to a thousand miles, of which they must already have covered most. "Well, where would that bring us?" queried the youth miserably.

"It's not easy to judge, but probably some part of Tibet. If these are the Karakorams, Tibet lies beyond. One of the crests, by the way, must be K2, which is generally counted the second highest mountain in the world."

"Next on the list after Everest," commented Barnard. "Gee, this is some scenery."

"And from a climber's point of view much stiffer than Everest. The Duke of Abruzzi gave it up as an absolutely impossible peak."

"*Oh, God!*" muttered Mallinson testily, but Barnard laughed. "I guess you must be the official guide on this trip, Conway, and I'll admit that if I only had a flask of café cognac I wouldn't care if it's Tibet or Tennessee."

"But what are we going to do about it?" urged Mallinson again. "Why are we here? What can be the point of it all? I don't see how you can make jokes about it."

"Well, it's as good as making a scene about it, young fellow. Besides, if the man *is* off his nut, as you've suggested, there probably *isn't* any point."

"He *must* be mad. I can't think of any other explanation. Can you, Conway?"

Conway shook his head.

Miss Brinklow turned round as she might have done during the interval of a play. "As you haven't asked my opinion, perhaps I oughtn't to give it," she began, with shrill modesty, "but I should like to say that I agree with Mr. Mallinson. I'm sure the poor man can't be quite right in his head. The pilot, I mean, of course. There would be no excuse for him, anyhow, if he were *not mad.*" She added, shouting confidentially above the din: "And do you know, this is my first trip in the air! My very first! Nothing would ever induce me to do it before, though a friend of mine tried her very best to persuade me to fly from London to Paris."

"And now you're flying from India to Tibet instead," said Barnard. "That's the way things happen."

She went on: "I once knew a missionary who had been to Tibet. He said the Tibetans were very odd people. They believe we are descended from monkeys."

"Real smart of 'em."

"Oh, dear, no, I don't mean in the modern way. They've had the belief for hundreds of years; it's only one of their superstitions. Of course I'm against all of it myself, and I think Darwin was far worse than any Tibetan. I take my stand on the Bible."

"Fundamentalist, I suppose?"

But Miss Brinklow did not appear to understand the term. "I used to belong to the L.M.S.," she shrieked, "but I disagreed with them about infant baptism."

Conway continued to feel that this was a rather comic remark long after it had occurred to him that the initials were those of the London Missionary Society. Still picturing the inconveniences of holding a theological argument at Euston Station, he began to think that there was something slightly fascinating about Miss Brinklow. He even wondered if he could offer her any article of his clothing for the night, but decided at length that her constitution was probably wirier than his. So he huddled up, closed his eyes, and went quite easily and peacefully to sleep.

And the flight proceeded.

Suddenly they were all wakened by a lurch of the machine. Conway's head struck the window, dazing him for the moment; a returning lurch sent him floundering between the two tiers of seats. It was much colder. The first thing he did, automatically, was to glance at his watch; it showed half-past one; he must have been asleep for some time. His ears were full of a loud, flapping sound, which he took to be imaginary until he realized that the engine had been shut off and that the plane was rushing against a gale. Then he stared through the window and could see the earth quite close, vague and snail-gray, scampering underneath. "He's going to land!" Mallinson shouted; and Barnard, who had also been flung out of his seat, responded with a saturnine: "If he's lucky." Miss Brinklow, whom the entire commotion seemed to have disturbed least of all, was adjusting her hat as calmly as if Dover Harbor were just in sight.

Presently the plane touched ground. But it was a bad landing this time—"Oh, my God, damned bad, *damned* bad!" Mallinson

groaned as he clutched at his seat during ten seconds of crashing
and swaying. Something was heard to strain and snap, and one
of the tires exploded. "That's done it," he added in tones of an-
guished pessimism. "A broken tail skid; we'll have to stay where
we are now, that's certain."

Conway, never talkative at times of crisis, stretched his
stiffened legs and felt his head where it had banged against the
window. A bruise, nothing much. He must do something to help
these people. But he was the last of the four to stand up when
the plane came to rest. "Steady," he called out as Mallinson
wrenched open the door of the cabin and prepared to make the
jump to earth; and eerily, in the comparative silence, the youth's
answer came: "No need to be steady—this looks like the end of
the world—there's not a soul about, anyhow."

A moment later, chilled and shivering, they were all aware
that this was so. With no sound in their ears save the fierce gusts
of wind and their own crunching footsteps, they felt themselves
at the mercy of something dour and savagely melancholy—a
mood in which both earth and air were saturated. The moon
looked to have disappeared behind clouds, and starlight illu-
mined a tremendous emptiness heaving with wind. Without
thought or knowledge, one could have guessed that this bleak
world was mountain-high, and that the mountains rising from it
were mountains on top of mountains. A range of them gleamed
on a far horizon like a row of dog teeth.

Mallinson, feverishly active, was already making for the cockpit. "I'm not scared of the fellow on land, whoever he is," he
cried. "I'm going to tackle him right away. . . ."

The others watched apprehensively, hypnotized by the spectacle of such energy. Conway sprang after him, but too late to prevent the investigation. After a few seconds, however, the youth
dropped down again, gripping his arm and muttering in a
hoarse, sobered staccato: "I say, Conway, it's queer. . . . I think
the fellow's ill or dead or something. . . . I can't get a word

out of him. Come up and look. . . . I took his revolver, at any rate."

"Better give it to me," said Conway, and though still rather dazed by the recent blow on his head, he nerved himself for action. Of all times and places and situations on earth, this seemed to him to combine the most hideous discomforts. He hoisted himself stiffly into a position from which he could see, not very well, into the enclosed cockpit. There was a strong smell of gasoline, so he did not risk striking a match. He could just discern the pilot, huddled forward, his head sprawling over the controls. He shook him, unfastened his helmet, and loosened the clothes round his neck. A moment later he turned round to report: "Yes, something's happened to him. We must get him out." But an observer might have added that something had happened to Conway as well. His voice was sharper, more incisive; no longer did he sound as if hovering on the brink of some profound doubtfulness. The time, the place, the cold, his fatigue, were now of less account; there was a job that simply had to be done, and the more conventional part of him was uppermost and preparing to do it.

With Barnard and Mallinson assisting, the pilot was extracted from his seat and lifted to the ground. He was unconscious, not dead. Conway had no particular medical knowledge, but, as to most men who have lived in outlandish places, the phenomena of illness were mostly familiar. "Possibly a heart attack brought on by the high altitude," he diagnosed, stooping over the unknown man. "We can do very little for him out here—there's no shelter from this infernal wind. Better get him inside the cabin, and ourselves too. We haven't an idea where we are, and it's hopeless to make a move until daylight."

The verdict and the suggestion were both accepted without dispute. Even Mallinson concurred. They carried the man into the cabin and laid him full-length along the gangway between the seats. The interior was no warmer than outside, but offered a screen to the flurries of wind. It was the wind, before much time had passed, that became the central preoccupation of them all—the leitmotif, as it were, of the whole mournful night. It was not an ordinary wind. It was not merely a strong wind or a cold wind. It was somehow a frenzy that lived all around them, a master stamping and ranting over his own domain. It tilted the loaded machine and shook it viciously, and when Conway glanced through the windows it seemed as if the same wind were whirling splinters of light out of the stars.

The stranger lay inert, while Conway, with difficulty in the dimness and confined space, made what examination he could by the light of matches. But it did not reveal much. "His heart's faint," he said at last, and then Miss Brinklow, after groping in her handbag, created a small sensation. "I wonder if this would be of any use to the poor man," she proffered condescendingly. "I never touch a drop myself, but I always carry it with me in case of accidents. And this *is* a sort of accident, isn't it?"

"I should say it was," replied Conway with grimness. He unscrewed the bottle, smelt it, and poured some of the brandy into the man's mouth. "Just the stuff for him. Thanks." After an interval the slightest movement of eyelids was visible. Mallinson suddenly became hysterical. "I can't help it," he cried, laughing wildly. "We all look such a lot of damn fools striking matches over a corpse. . . . And he isn't much of a beauty, is he? Chink, I should say, if he's anything at all."

"Possibly." Conway's voice was level and rather severe. "But he's not a corpse yet. With a bit of luck we may bring him round."

"Luck? It'll be his luck, not ours."

"Don't be too sure. And shut up for the time being, anyhow."

There was enough of the schoolboy still in Mallinson to make him respond to the curt command of a senior, though he was obviously in poor control of himself. Conway, though sorry for him, was more concerned with the immediate problem of the pilot, since he, alone of them all, might be able to give some explanation of their plight. Conway had no desire to discuss the matter further in a merely speculative way; there had been enough of that during the journey. He was uneasy now beyond his continuing mental curiosity, for he was aware that the whole situation had ceased to be excitingly perilous and was threatening to become a trial of endurance ending in catastrophe. Keeping vigil throughout that gale-tormented night, he faced facts none the less frankly because he did not trouble to enunciate them to the others. He guessed that the flight had progressed far beyond the western range of the Himalaya towards the less known heights of the Kuen-Lun. In that event they would by now have reached the loftiest and least hospitable part of the earth's surface, the Tibetan plateau, two miles high even in its lowest valleys, a vast, uninhabited, and largely unexplored region of wind-swept upland. Somewhere they were, in that forlorn country, marooned in far less comfort than on most desert islands. Then abruptly, as if to answer his curiosity by increasing it, a rather awe-inspiring change took place. The moon, which he had thought to be hidden by clouds, swung over the lip of some shadowy eminence and, whilst still not showing itself directly, unveiled the darkness ahead. Conway could see the outline of a long valley, with rounded, sad-looking low hills on either side, jet-black against the deep electric blue of the night-sky. But it was to the head of the valley that his eyes were led irresistibly, for there, soaring into the gap, and magnificent in the full shimmer of moonlight, appeared what he took to be the loveliest mountain on earth. It was an almost perfect cone of snow, simple in outline as if a child had drawn it, and impossible to classify as to size, height, or nearness. It was so radiant, so serenely poised, that he wondered for a moment if it were real at all. Then, while he gazed, a tiny puff clouded the edge of the pyramid, giving life to the vision before the faint rumble of the avalanche confirmed it.

He had an impulse to rouse the others to share the spectacle, but decided after consideration that its effect might not be tranquilizing. Nor was it so, from a common sense viewpoint; such virgin splendors merely emphasized the facts of isolation and danger. There was quite a probability that the nearest human settlement was hundreds of miles away. And they had no food; they were unarmed except for one revolver; the aeroplane was damaged and almost fuelless, even if any one had known how to fly. They had no clothes suited to the terrific chills and winds; Mallinson's motoring-coat and his own ulster were quite inadequate, and even Miss Brinklow, woolied and muffled as for a polar expedition (ridiculous, he had thought, on first beholding her), could not be feeling happy. They were all, too, except himself, affected by the altitude. Even Barnard had sunk into melancholy under the strain. Mallinson was muttering to himself; it was clear what would happen to him if these hardships went on for long. In face of such distressful prospects Conway found himself quite unable to restrain an admiring glance at Miss Brinklow. She was not, he reflected, a normal person; no woman who taught Afghans to sing hymns could be considered so. But she was, after every calamity, still normally abnormal, and he was deeply obliged to her for it. "I hope you're not feeling too bad?" he said sympathetically, when he caught her eye.

"The soldiers during the War had to suffer worse things than this," she replied.

The comparison did not seem to Conway a very valuable one. In point of fact, he had never spent a night in the trenches quite so thoroughly unpleasant, though doubtless many others had. He concentrated his attention on the pilot, now breathing fitfully and sometimes slightly stirring. Probably Mallinson was right in guessing the man Chinese. He had the typical Mongol nose and cheekbones, despite his successful impersonation of a British flight-lieutenant. Mallinson had called him ugly, but Conway, who had lived in China, thought him a fairly passable specimen, though now, in the burnished circle of match-flame, his pallid skin and gaping mouth were not pretty.

The night dragged on, as if each minute were something heavy and tangible that had to be pushed to make way for the next. Moonlight faded after a time, and with it that distant specter of the mountain; then the triple mischiefs of darkness, cold, and wind increased until dawn. As though at its signal, the wind dropped, leaving the world in compassionate quietude. Framed in the pale triangle ahead, the mountain showed again, gray at first, then silver, then pink as the earliest sun rays caught the summit. In the lessening gloom the valley itself took shape, revealing a floor of rock and shingle sloping upwards. It was not a friendly picture, but to Conway, as he surveyed, there came a queer perception of fineness in it, of something that had no romantic appeal at all, but a steely, almost an intellectual quality. The white pyramid in the distance compelled the mind's assent as passionlessly as a Euclidean theorem, and when at last the sun rose into a sky of deep delphinium blue, he felt only a little less than comfortable again.

As the air grew warmer the others wakened, and he suggested carrying the pilot into the open, where the sharp dry air and the sunlight might help to revive him. This was done, and they began a second and pleasanter vigil. Eventually the man opened his eyes and began to speak convulsively. His four passengers stooped over him, listening intently to sounds that were meaningless except to Conway, who occasionally made answers. After some time the man became weaker, talked with increasing difficulty, and finally died. That was about mid-morning.

Conway then turned to his companions. "I'm sorry to say he told me very little—little, I mean, compared with what we should like to know. Merely that we are in Tibet, which is obvious. He didn't give any coherent account of why he had brought us here, but he seemed to know the locality. He spoke a kind of Chinese that I don't understand very well, but I think he said something about a lamasery near here, along the valley, I gathered, where we could get food and shelter. Shangri-La, he called it. *La* is Tibetan for mountain pass. He was most emphatic that we should go there."

"Which doesn't seem to me any reason at all why we should,"

said Mallinson. "After all, he was probably off his head. Wasn't he?"

"You know as much about that as I do. But if we don't go to this place, where else are we to go?"

"Anywhere you like, I don't care. All I'm certain of is that this Shangri-La, if it's in that direction, must be a few extra miles from civilization. I should feel happier if we were lessening the distance, not increasing it. Damnation, man, aren't you going to get us back?"

Conway replied patiently: "I don't think you properly understand the position, Mallinson. We're in a part of the world that no one knows very much about, except that it's difficult and dangerous, even for a fully equipped expedition. Considering that hundreds of miles of this sort of country probably surround us on all sides, the notion of walking back to Peshawur doesn't strike me as very hopeful."

"I don't think I could possibly manage it," said Miss Brinklow seriously.

Barnard nodded. "It looks as if we're darned lucky, then, if this lamasery *is* round the corner."

"Comparatively lucky, maybe," agreed Conway. "After all, we've no food, and as you can see for yourselves, the country isn't the kind it would be easy to live on. In a few hours we shall all be famished. And then to-night, if we were to stay here, we should have to face the wind and the cold again. It's not a pleasant prospect. Our only chance, it seems to me, is to find some other human beings, and where else should we begin looking for them except where we've been told they exist?"

"And what if it's a trap?" asked Mallinson, but Barnard supplied an answer. "A nice warm trap," he said. "With a piece of cheese in it, would suit me down to the ground."

They laughed, except Mallinson, who looked distraught and nerve-racked. Finally Conway went on: "I take it, then, that we're all more or less agreed? There's an obvious way along the valley; it doesn't look too steep, though we shall have to take it slowly. In any case, we could do nothing here. We couldn't even bury this man without dynamite. Besides, the lamasery people may be able to supply us with porters for the journey back. We shall need them. I suggest we start at once, so that if we don't locate the place by late afternoon we shall have time to return for another night in the cabin."

"And supposing we *do* locate it?" queried Mallinson, still intransigeant. "Have we any guarantee that we shan't be murdered?"

"None at all. But I think it is a lesser, and perhaps also a preferable, risk than being starved or frozen to death." He added, feeling that such chilly logic might not be entirely suited for the occasion: "As a matter of fact, murder is the very last thing one would expect in a Buddhist monastery. It would be rather less likely than being killed in an English cathedral."

"Like Saint Thomas of Canterbury," said Miss Brinklow, nodding an emphatic agreement, but completely spoiling his point. Mallinson shrugged his shoulders and responded with melancholy irritation: "Very well, then, we'll be off to Shangri-La. Wherever and whatever it is, we'll try it. But let's hope it's not halfway up that mountain."

The remark served to fix their glances on the glittering cone towards which the valley pointed. Sheerly magnificent it looked in the full light of day; and then their gaze turned to a stare, for they could see, far away and approaching them down the slope, the figures of men. "Providence!" whispered Miss Brinklow.

3

Part of Conway was always an onlooker, however active might be the rest. Just now, while waiting for the strangers to come nearer, he refused to be fussed into deciding what he might or mightn't do in any number of possible contingencies. And this was not bravery, or coolness, or any especially sublime confidence in his own power to make decisions on the spur of the moment. It was, if the worst view be taken, a form of indolence, an unwillingness to interrupt his mere spectator's interest in what was happening.

As the figures moved down the valley they revealed themselves to be a party of a dozen or more, carrying with them a hooded chair. In this, a little later, could be discerned a person robed in blue. Conway could not imagine where they were all going, but it certainly seemed providential, as Miss Brinklow had said, that such a detachment should chance to be passing just there and then. As soon as he was within hailing distance he left his own party and walked ahead, though not hurriedly, for he knew that Orientals enjoy the ritual of meeting and like to take their time over it. Halting when a few yards off, he bowed with due courtesy. Much to his surprise the robed figure stepped from the chair, came forward with dignified deliberation, and held out his hand. Conway responded, and observed an old or elderly Chinese, gray-haired, clean-shaven, and rather pallidly decorative in a silk embroidered gown. He in his turn appeared to be submitting Conway to the same kind of ready reckoning. Then, in precise and perhaps too accurate English, he said: "I am from the lamasery of Shangri-La."

Conway bowed again, and after a suitable pause began to explain briefly the circumstances that had brought him and his three companions to such an unfrequented part of the world. At the end of the recital the Chinese made a gesture of understanding. "It is indeed remarkable," he said, and gazed reflectively at the damaged aeroplane. Then he added: "My name is Chang, if you would be so good as to present me to your friends."

Conway managed to smile urbanely. He was rather taken with this latest phenomenon, a Chinese who spoke perfect English and observed the social formalities of Bond Street amidst the wilds of Tibet. He turned to the others, who had by this time caught up and were regarding the encounter with varying degrees of astonishment. "Miss Brinklow . . . Mr. Barnard, who is an American . . . Mr. Mallinson . . . and my own name is Conway. We are all glad to see you, though the meeting is almost as puzzling as the fact of our being here at all. Indeed, we were just about to make our way to your lamasery, so it is doubly fortunate. If you could give us directions for the journey—"

"There is no need for that. I shall be delighted to act as your guide."

"But I could not think of putting you to such trouble. It is exceedingly kind of you, but if the distance is not far—"

"It is not far, but it is not easy, either. I shall esteem it an honor to accompany you and your friends."

"But really—"

"I must insist."

Conway thought that the argument, in its context of place and circumstance, was in some danger of becoming ludicrous. "Very well," he responded. "I'm sure we are all most obliged."

Mallinson, who had been somberly enduring these pleasantries, now interposed with something of the shrill acerbity of the barrack-square. "Our stay won't be long," he announced curtly. "We shall pay for anything we have, and we should like to hire some of your men to help us on our journey back. We want to return to civilization as soon as possible."

"And are you so very certain that you are away from it?"

The query, delivered with much suavity, only stung the youth to further sharpness. "I'm quite sure I'm far away from where I want to be, and so are we all. We shall be grateful for temporary shelter, but we shall be more grateful still if you'll provide means for us to return. How long do you suppose the journey to India will take?"

"I really could not say at all."

"Well, I hope we're not going to have any trouble about it. I've had some experience of hiring native porters, and we shall expect you to use your influence to get us a square deal."

Conway felt that most of all this was rather needlessly truculent, and he was just about to intervene when the reply came, still with immense dignity: "I can only assure you, Mr. Mallinson, that you will be honorably treated and that ultimately you will have no regrets."

"*Ultimately?*" Mallinson exclaimed, pouncing on the word, but there was greater ease in avoiding a scene since wine and fruit were now on offer, having been unpacked by the marching party, stocky Tibetans in sheepskins, fur hats, and yak-skin boots. The wine had a pleasant flavor, not unlike a good hock, while the fruit included mangoes, perfectly ripened and almost painfully delicious after so many hours of fasting. Mallinson ate and drank with incurious relish; but Conway, relieved of immediate worries and reluctant to cherish distant ones, was wondering how mangoes could be cultivated at such an altitude. He was also interested in the mountain beyond the valley; it was a sensational peak, by any standards, and he was surprised that some traveler had not made much of it in the kind of book that a journey in Tibet invariably elicits. He climbed it in mind as he gazed, choosing a route by *col* and *couloir* until an exclamation from Mallinson drew his attention back to earth; he looked round then and saw that the Chinese had been earnestly regarding him. "You were contemplating the mountain, Mr. Conway?" came the enquiry.

"Yes. It's a fine sight. It has a name, I suppose?"

"It is called Karakal."

"I don't think I ever heard of it. Is it very high?"

"Over twenty-eight thousand feet."

"Indeed? I didn't realize there would be anything on that scale outside the Himalaya. Has it been properly surveyed? Whose are the measurements?"

"Whose would you expect, my dear sir? Is there anything incompatible between monasticism and trigonometry?"

Conway savored the phrase and replied: "Oh, not at all—not at all." Then he laughed politely. He thought it a poorish joke, but one perhaps worth making the most of. Soon after that the journey to Shangri-La was begun.

All morning the climb proceeded, slowly and by easy gradients; but at such height the physical effort was considerable, and none had energy to spare for talk. The Chinese traveled luxuriously in his chair, which might have seemed unchivalrous had it not been absurd to picture Miss Brinklow in such a regal setting. Conway, whom the rarefied air troubled less than the rest, was at pains to catch the occasional chatter of the chair-bearers. He knew a very little Tibetan, just enough to gather that the men were glad to be returning to the lamasery. He could not, even had he wished, have continued converse with their leader, since the latter, with eyes closed and face half hidden behind curtains, appeared to have the knack of instant and well-timed sleep.

Meanwhile the sun was warm; hunger and thirst had been appeased, if not satisfied; and the air, clean as from another planet, was more precious with every intake. One had to breathe consciously and deliberately, which, though disconcerting at first, induced after a time an almost ecstatic tranquillity of mind. The whole body moved in a single rhythm of breathing, walking, and thinking; the lungs, no longer discrete and automatic, were disciplined to harmony with mind and limb. Conway, in whom a mystical strain ran in curious consort with skepticism, found himself not unhappily puzzled over the sensation. Once or twice he spoke a cheerful word to Mallinson, but the youth was laboring under the strain of the ascent. Barnard also gasped asthmatically, while Miss Brinklow was engaged in some grim pulmonary warfare which for some reason she made efforts to conceal. "We're nearly at the top," Conway said encouragingly.

"I once ran for a train and felt just like this," she answered.

So also, Conway reflected, there were people who considered cider was just like champagne. It was a matter of palate.

He was surprised to find that beyond his puzzlement he had few misgivings, and none at all on his own behalf. There were moments in life when one opened wide one's soul just as one might open wide one's purse if an evening's entertainment were proving unexpectedly costly but also unexpectedly novel. Conway, on that breathless morning in sight of Karakal, made just such a willing, relieved, yet not excited response to the offer of new experience. After ten years in various parts of Asia he had attained to a somewhat fastidious valuation of places and happenings; and this, he was bound to admit, promised unusual.

About a couple of miles along the valley the ascent grew steeper, but by this time the sun was overclouded and a silvery mist obscured the view. Thunder and avalanches resounded from the snow fields above; the air took chill, and then, with the sudden changefulness of mountain regions, became bitterly cold. A flurry of wind and sleet drove up, drenching the party and adding immeasurably to their discomfort; even Conway felt at one moment that it would be impossible to go much further. But shortly afterwards it seemed that the summit of the ridge had been reached, for the chair-bearers halted to readjust their burden. The condition of Barnard and Mallinson, who were both suffering severely, led to continued delay; but the Tibetans were clearly anxious to press on, and made signs that the rest of the journey would be less fatiguing.

After these assurances it was disappointing to see them uncoiling ropes. "Do they mean to hang us already?" Barnard managed to exclaim, with desperate facetiousness; but the guides soon showed that their less sinister intention was merely to link the party together in ordinary mountaineering fashion. When they observed that Conway was familiar with ropecraft, they became much more respectful and allowed him to dispose the party in his own way. He put himself next to Mallinson, with Tibetans ahead and to the rear, and with Barnard and Miss Brinklow and more Tibetans further back still. He was prompt to notice that the men, during their leader's continuing sleep, were inclined to let him deputize. He felt a familiar quickening of authority; if there were to be any difficult business he would give what he knew was his to give—confidence and command. He had been a first-class mountaineer in his time, and was still, no doubt, pretty good. "You've got to look after Barnard," he told Miss Brinklow, half jocularly, half meaning it; and she answered, with the coyness of an eagle: "I'll do my best, but you know, I've never been roped before."

But the next stage, though occasionally exciting, was less arduous than he had been prepared for, and a relief from the lung-bursting strain of the ascent. The track consisted of a traverse cut along the flank of a rock wall whose height above them the mist obscured. Perhaps mercifully it also obscured the abyss on the other side, though Conway, who had a good eye for heights, would have liked to see where he was. The path was scarcely more than two feet wide in places, and the manner in which the bearers maneuvered the chair at such points drew his admiration almost as strongly as did the nerves of the occupant who could manage to sleep through it all. The Tibetans were reliable enough, but they seemed happier when the path widened and became slightly downhill. Then they began to sing amongst themselves, lilting barbaric tunes that Conway could imagine orchestrated by Massenet for some Tibetan ballet. The rain ceased and the air grew warmer. "Well, it's quite certain we could never have found our way here by ourselves," said Conway, intending to be cheerful, but Mallinson did not find the remark very comforting. He was, in fact, acutely terrified, and in more danger of showing it now that the worst was over. "Should we be missing much?" he retorted bitterly. The track went on, more sharply downhill, and at one spot Conway found some edelweiss, the first welcome sign of more hospitable levels. But this, when he announced it, consoled Mallinson even less. "Good God, Conway, d'you fancy you're pottering about the Alps? What sort of hell's kitchen are we making for, that's what I'd like to know? And what's our plan of action when we get to it? *What are we going to do?*"

Conway said quietly: "If you'd had all the experiences I've had, you'd know that there are times in life when the most comfortable thing is to do nothing at all. Things happen to you and you just let them happen. The War was rather like that. One is fortunate if, as on this occasion, a touch of novelty seasons the unpleasantness."

"You're too confoundedly philosophic for me. That wasn't your mood during the trouble at Baskul."

"Of course not, because then there was a chance that I could alter events by my own actions. But now, for the moment at least, there's no such chance. We're here because we're here, if you want a reason. I've usually found it a soothing one."

"I suppose you realize the appalling job we shall have to get back by the way we've come. We've been slithering along the face of a perpendicular mountain for the last hour—I've been taking notice."

"So have I."

"Have you?" Mallinson coughed excitedly. "I dare say I'm being a nuisance, but I can't help it. I'm suspicious about all this.

I feel we're doing far too much what these fellows want us to. They're getting us into a corner."

"Even if they are, the only alternative was to stay out of it and perish."

"I know that's logical, but it doesn't seem to help. I'm afraid I don't find it as easy as you do to accept the situation. I can't forget that two days ago we were in the consulate at Baskul. To think of all that has happened since is a bit overwhelming to me. I'm sorry. I'm overwrought. It makes me realize how lucky I was to miss the War; I suppose I should have got hysterical about things. The whole world seems to have gone completely mad all round me. I must be pretty wild myself to be talking to you like this."

Conway shook his head. "My dear boy, not at all. You're twenty-four years old, and you're somewhere about two and a half miles up in the air: those are reasons enough for anything you may happen to feel at the moment. I think you've come through a trying ordeal extraordinarily well, better than I should at your age."

"But don't *you* feel the madness of it all? The way we flew over those mountains and that awful waiting in the wind and the pilot dying and then meeting these fellows, doesn't it all seem nightmarish and incredible when you look back on it?"

"It does, of course."

"Then I wish I knew how you manage to keep so cool about everything."

"Do you really wish that? I'll tell you if you like, though you'll perhaps think me cynical. It's because so much else that I can look back on seems nightmarish too. This isn't the only mad part of the world, Mallinson. After all, if you *must* think of Baskul, do you remember just before we left how the revolutionaries were torturing their captives to get information? An ordinary washing-mangle, quite effective, of course, but I don't think I ever saw anything more comically dreadful. And do you recollect the last message that came through before we were cut off? It was a circular from a Manchester textile firm asking if we knew of any trade openings in Baskul for the sale of corsets! Isn't that mad enough for you? Believe me, in arriving here the worst that can have happened is that we've exchanged one form of lunacy for another. And as for the War, if you'd been in it you'd have done the same as I did, learned how to funk with a stiff lip."

They were still conversing when a sharp but brief ascent robbed them of breath, inducing in a few paces all their earlier strain. Presently the ground leveled, and they stepped out of the mist into clear, sunny air. Ahead, and only a short distance away, lay the lamasery of Shangri-La.

To Conway, seeing it first, it might have been a vision fluttering out of that solitary rhythm in which lack of oxygen had encompassed all his faculties. It was, indeed, a strange and half-incredible sight. A group of colored pavilions clung to the mountainside with none of the grim deliberation of a Rhineland castle, but rather with the chance delicacy of flower petals impaled upon a crag. It was superb and exquisite. An austere emotion carried the eye upward from milk-blue roofs to the gray rock bastion above, tremendous as the Wetterhorn above Grindelwald. Beyond that, in a dazzling pyramid, soared the snow slopes of Karakal. It might well be, Conway thought, the most terrifying mountainscape in the world, and he imagined the immense stress of snow and glacier against which the rock functioned as a gigantic retaining wall. Someday, perhaps, the whole mountain would split, and a half of Karakal's icy splendor come toppling into the valley. He wondered if the slightness of the risk combined with its fearfulness might even be found agreeably stimulating.

Hardly less an enticement was the downward prospect, for the mountain wall continued to drop, nearly perpendicularly, into a cleft that could only have been the result of some cataclysm in the far past. The floor of the valley, hazily distant, welcomed the eye with greenness; sheltered from winds, and surveyed rather than dominated by the lamasery, it looked to Conway a delightfully favored place, though if it were inhabited its community must be completely isolated by the lofty and sheerly unscalable ranges on the further side. Only to the lamasery did there appear to be any climbable egress at all. Conway experienced, as he gazed, a slight tightening of apprehension; Mallinson's misgivings were not, perhaps, to be wholly disregarded. But the feeling was only momentary, and soon merged in the deeper sensation, half mystical, half visual, of having reached at last some place that was an end, a finality.

He never exactly remembered how he and the others arrived at the lamasery, or with what formalities they were received, unroped, and ushered into the precincts. That thin air had a dream-like texture, matching the porcelain-blue of the sky; with every breath and every glance he took in a deep anesthetizing tranquillity that made him impervious alike to Mallinson's uneasiness, Barnard's witticisms, and Miss Brinklow's coy portrayal of a lady well prepared for the worst. He vaguely recollected surprise at finding the interior spacious, well warmed, and quite clean; but there was no time to do more than notice these qualities, for the Chinese had left his hooded chair and was already leading the way through various antechambers. He was quite affable now. "I must apologize," he said, "for leaving you to yourselves on the way, but the truth is, journeys of that kind don't suit me, and I have to take care of myself. I trust you were not too fatigued?"

"We managed," replied Conway with a wry smile.

"Excellent. And now, if you will come with me, I will show you to your apartments. No doubt you would like baths. Our accommodation is simple, but I hope adequate."

At this point Barnard, who was still affected by shortness of breath, gave vent to an asthmatic chuckle. "Well," he gasped, "I can't say I like your climate yet—the air seems to stick on my chest a bit—but you've certainly got a darned fine view out of your front windows. Do we all have to line up for the bathroom, or is this an American hotel?"

"I think you will find everything quite satisfactory, Mr. Barnard."

Miss Brinklow nodded primly. "I should hope so, indeed."

"And afterwards," continued the Chinese, "I should be greatly honored if you will all join me at dinner."

Conway replied courteously. Only Mallinson had given no sign of his attitude in the face of these unlooked-for amenities. Like Barnard, he had been suffering from the altitude, but now, with an effort, he found breath to exclaim: "And afterwards also, if you don't mind, we'll make our plans for getting away. The sooner the better, so far as I'm concerned."

4

"So you see," Chang was saying, "We are less barbarian than you
expected. . . ."

Conway, later that evening, was not disposed to deny it. He
was enjoying that pleasant mingling of physical ease and mental
alertness which seemed to him, of all sensations, the most truly
civilized. So far, the appointments of Shangri-La had been all
that he could have wished, certainly more than he could ever
have expected. That a Tibetan monastery should possess a system of central heating was not, perhaps, so very remarkable in
an age that supplied even Lhasa with telephones; but that it
should combine the mechanics of Western hygiene with so much
else that was Eastern and traditional, struck him as exceedingly
singular. The bath, for instance, in which he had recently lux-
uriated, had been of a delicate green porcelain, a product, according to inscription, of Akron, Ohio. Yet the native attendant
had valeted him in Chinese fashion, cleansing his ears and nos-
trils, and passing a thin, silk swab under his lower eyelids. He
had wondered at the time if and how his three companions were
receiving similar attentions.

Conway had lived for nearly a decade in China, not wholly in
the bigger cities; and he counted it, all things considered, the
happiest part of his life. He liked the Chinese, and felt at home
with Chinese ways. In particular he liked Chinese cooking, with
its subtle undertones of taste; and his first meal at Shangri-La

had therefore conveyed a welcome familiarity. He suspected, too, that it might have contained some herb or drug to relieve respiration, for he not only felt a difference himself, but could observe a greater ease among his fellow guests. Chang, he noticed, ate nothing but a small portion of green salad, and took no wine. "You will excuse me," he had explained at the outset, "but my diet is very restricted; I am obliged to take care of myself."

It was the reason he had given before, and Conway wondered by what form of invalidism he was afflicted. Regarding him now more closely, he found it difficult to guess his age; his smallish and somehow undetailed features, together with the moist clay texture of his skin, gave him a look that might either have been that of a young man prematurely old or of an old man remarkably well preserved. He was by no means without attractiveness of a kind; a certain stylized courtesy hung about him in a fragrance too delicate to be detected till one had ceased to think about it. In his embroidered gown of blue silk, with the usual side-slashed skirt and tight-ankled trousers, all the hue of water color skies, he had a cold metallic charm which Conway found pleasing, though he knew it was not everybody's taste.

The atmosphere, in fact, was Chinese rather than specifically Tibetan; and this in itself gave Conway an agreeable sensation of being at home, though again it was one that he could not expect the others to share. The room, too, pleased him; it was admirably proportioned, and sparingly adorned with tapestries and one or two fine pieces of lacquer. Light was from paper lanterns, motionless in the still air. He felt a soothing comfort of mind and body, and his renewed speculations as to some possible drug were hardly apprehensive. Whatever it was, if it existed at all, it had relieved Barnard's breathlessness and Mallinson's truculence; both had dined well, finding satisfaction in eating rather than talk. Conway also had been hungry enough, and was not sorry that etiquette demanded gradualness in approaching matters of importance. He had never cared for hurrying a situation that was itself enjoyable, so that the technique well suited him.

Not, indeed, until he had begun a cigarette did he give a gentle lead to his curiosity; he remarked then, addressing Chang: "You seem a very fortunate community, and most hospitable to strangers. I don't imagine, though, that you receive them often."

"Seldom indeed," replied the Chinese, with measured stateliness. "It is not a traveled part of the world."

Conway smiled at that. "You put the matter mildly. It looked to me, as I came, the most isolated spot I ever set eyes on. A separate culture might flourish here without contamination from the outside world."

"Contamination, would you say?"

"I use the word in reference to dance bands, cinemas, electric signs, and so on. Your plumbing is quite rightly as modern as you can get it, the only certain boon, to my mind, that the East can take from the West. I often think that the Romans were fortunate; their civilization reached as far as hot baths without touching the fatal knowledge of machinery."

Conway paused. He had been talking with an impromptu fluency which, though not insincere, was chiefly designed to create and control an atmosphere. He was rather good at that sort of thing. Only a willingness to respond to the superfine courtesy of the occasion prevented him from being more openly curious.

Miss Brinklow, however, had no such scruples. "Please," she said, though the word was by no means submissive, "will you tell us about the monastery?"

Chang raised his eyebrows in very gentle deprecation of such immediacy. "It will give me the greatest of pleasure, madam, so far as I am able. What exactly do you wish to know?"

"First of all, how many are there of you here, and what nationality do you belong to?" It was clear that her orderly mind was functioning no less professionally than at the Baskul mission-house.

Chang replied: "Those of us in full lamahood number about fifty, and there are a few others, like myself, who have not yet attained to complete initiation. We shall do so in due course, it is to be hoped. 'Till then we are half-lamas, postulants, you might say. As for our racial origins, there are representatives of a great many nations among us, though it is perhaps natural that Tibetans and Chinese make up the majority."

Miss Brinklow would never shirk a conclusion, even a wrong one. "I see. It's really a native monastery, then. Is your head lama a Tibetan or a Chinese?"

"No."

"Are there any English?"

"Several."

"Dear me, that seems very remarkable." Miss Brinklow paused only for breath before continuing: "And now, tell me what you all believe in."

Conway leaned back with somewhat amused expectancy. He had always found pleasure in observing the impact of opposite mentalities; and Miss Brinklow's girl-guide forthrightness applied to lamaistic philosophy promised to be entertaining. On the other hand, he did not wish his host to take fright. "That's rather a big question," he said, temporizingly.

But Miss Brinklow was in no mood to temporize. The wine, which had made the others more reposeful, seemed to have given her an extra liveliness. "Of course," she said with a gesture of magnanimity, "I believe in the true religion, but I'm broad-minded enough to admit that other people, foreigners, I mean, are quite often sincere in their views. And naturally in a monastery I wouldn't expect to be agreed with."

Her concession evoked a formal bow from Chang. "But why not, madam?" he replied in his precise and flavored English. "Must we hold that because one religion is true, all others are bound to be false?"

"Well, of course, that's rather obvious, isn't it?"

Conway again interposed. "Really, I think we had better not argue. But Miss Brinklow shares my own curiosity about the motive of this unique establishment."

Chang answered rather slowly and in scarcely more than a whisper: "If I were to put it into a very few words, my dear sir, I should say that our prevalent belief is in moderation. We inculcate the virtue of avoiding excess of all kinds—even including, if you will pardon the paradox, excess of virtue itself. In the valley which you have seen, and in which there are several thousand inhabitants living under the control of our order, we have found that the principle makes for a considerable degree of happiness. We rule with moderate strictness, and in return we are satisfied with moderate obedience. And I think I can claim that our people are moderately sober, moderately chaste, and moderately honest."

Conway smiled. He thought it well expressed, besides which it made some appeal to his own temperament. "I think I understand. And I suppose the fellows who met us this morning belonged to your valley people?"

"Yes. I hope you had no fault to find with them during the journey?"

"Oh, no, none at all. I'm glad they were more than moderately sure-footed, anyhow. You were careful, by the way, to say that the rules of moderation applied to *them*—am I to take it that it does not apply to your priesthood also?"

But at that Chang could only shake his head. "I regret, sir, that you have touched upon a matter which I may not discuss. I can only add that our community has various faiths and usages, but we are most of us moderately heretical about them. I am deeply grieved that at the moment I cannot say more."

"Please don't apologize. I am left with the pleasantest of speculations." Something in his own voice, as well as in his bodily sensations, gave Conway a renewed impression that he had been very slightly doped. Mallinson appeared to have been similarly affected, though he seized the present chance to remark: "All this has been very interesting, but I really think it's time we began to discuss our plans for getting away. We want to return to India as soon as possible. How many porters can we be supplied with?"

The question, so practical and uncompromising, broke through the crust of suavity to find no sure foothold beneath. Only after a longish interval came Chang's reply: "Unfortunately, Mr. Mallinson, I am not the proper person to approach. But in any case, I hardly think the matter could be arranged immediately."

"But something has *got* to be arranged! We've all got our work to return to, and our friends and relatives will be worrying about us. We simply *must* return. We're obliged to you for receiving us like this, but we really can't slack about here doing nothing. If it's at all feasible, we should like to set out not later than to-morrow. I expect there are a good many of your people who would volunteer to escort us—we should make it well worth their while, of course."

Mallinson ended nervously, as if he had hoped to be answered before saying so much; but he could extract from Chang no more than a quiet and almost reproachful: "But all this, you know, is scarcely in my province."

"Isn't it? Well, perhaps you can do *something*, at any rate. If you could get us a large scale map of the country, it would help. It looks as if we shall have a long journey, and that's all the more reason for making an early start. You have maps, I suppose?"

"Yes, we have a great many."

"We'll borrow some of them, then, if you don't mind. We can return them to you afterwards. I suppose you must have communications with the outer world from time to time. And it would be a good idea to send messages ahead, also, to reassure our friends. How far away is the nearest telegraph line?"

Chang's wrinkled face seemed to have acquired a look of infinite patience, but he did not reply.

Mallinson waited a moment and then continued: "Well, where do you send to when you want anything? Anything civilized, I mean." A touch of scaredness began to appear in his eyes and voice. Suddenly he thrust back his chair and stood up. He was pale, and passed his hand wearily across his forehead. "I'm so tired," he stammered, glancing round the room. "I don't feel that any of you are really trying to help me. I'm only asking a simple question. It's obvious you must know the answer to it. When you had all these modern baths installed, how did they get here?"

There followed another silence.

"You won't tell me, then? It's part of the mystery of everything else, I suppose. Conway, I must say I think you're damned slack. Why don't *you* get at the truth? I'm all in, for the time being—but—to-morrow, mind—we *must* get away to-morrow—it's essential—"

He would have slid to the floor had not Conway caught him and helped him to a chair. Then he recovered a little, but did not speak.

"To-morrow he will be much better," said Chang gently. "The air here is difficult for the stranger at first, but one soon becomes acclimatized."

Conway felt himself waking from a trance. "Things have been a little trying for him," he commented with rather rueful mildness. He added, more briskly: "I expect we're all feeling it somewhat. I think we'd better adjourn this discussion and go to bed. Barnard, will you look after Mallinson? And I'm sure *you're* in need of sleep too, Miss Brinklow." There had been some signal given, for at that moment a servant appeared. "Yes, we'll get along—good night—good night—I shall soon follow." He almost pushed them out of the room, and then, with a scantness of ceremony that was in marked contrast with his earlier manner, turned to his host. Mallinson's reproach had spurred him.

"Now, sir, I don't want to detain you long, so I'd better come to the point. My friend is impetuous, but I don't blame him, he's quite right to make things clear. Our return journey has to be arranged, and we can't do it without help from you or from others in this place. Of course, I realize that leaving to-morrow is impossible, and for my own part I hope to find a minimum stay quite interesting. But that, perhaps, is not the attitude of my companions. So if it's true, as you say, that you can do nothing for us yourself, please put us in touch with some one else who can."

The Chinese answered: "You are wiser than your friends, my dear sir, and therefore you are less impatient. I am glad."

"That's not an answer."

Chang began to laugh, a jerky, high pitched chuckle so obviously forced that Conway recognized in it the polite pretense of seeing an imaginary joke with which the Chinese "saves face" at awkward moments. "I feel sure you have no cause to worry about the matter," came the reply, after an interval. "No doubt in due course we shall be able to give you all the help you need. There are difficulties, as you can imagine, but if we all approach the problem sensibly, and without undue haste—"

"I'm not suggesting haste. I'm merely seeking information about porters."

"Well, my dear sir, that raises another point. I very much doubt whether you will easily find men willing to undertake such a journey. They have their homes in the valley, and they don't care for leaving them to make long and arduous trips outside."

"They can be prevailed upon to do so, though, or else why and where were they escorting you this morning?"

"This morning? Oh, that was quite a different matter."

"In what way? Weren't you setting out on a journey when I and my friends chanced to come across you?"

There was no response to this, and presently Conway continued in a quieter voice: "I understand. Then it was *not* a chance meeting. I had wondered all along, in fact. So you came there deliberately to intercept us. That suggests you must have known of our arrival beforehand. And the interesting question is, *How?*"

His words laid a note of stress amidst the exquisite quietude of the scene. The lantern light showed up the face of the Chinese; it was calm and statuesque. Suddenly, with a small gesture of the hand, Chang broke the strain; pulling aside a silken tapestry he undraped a window leading to a balcony. Then, with a touch upon Conway's arm, he led him into the cold crystal air. "You are clever," he said dreamily, "but not entirely correct. For that reason I should counsel you not to worry your friends by these abstract discussions. Believe me, neither you nor they are in any danger at Shangri-La."

"But it isn't danger we're bothering about. It's delay."

"I realize that. And of course there *may* be a certain delay, quite unavoidably."

"If it's only for a short time, and genuinely unavoidable, then naturally we shall have to put up with it as best we can."

"How very sensible, for we desire nothing more than that you and your companions should enjoy every moment of your stay here."

"That's all very well, and as I told you, in a personal sense I can't say I shall mind a great deal. It's a new and interesting experience, and in any case, we need some rest."

He was gazing upward to the gleaming pyramid of Karakal. At that moment, in bright moonlight, it seemed as if a hand reached high might just touch it, it was so brittle-clear against the blue immensity beyond.

"To-morrow," said Chang, "you may find it even more interesting. And as for rest, if you are fatigued, there are not many better places in the world."

Indeed, as Conway continued to gaze, a deeper repose overspread him, as if the spectacle were as much for the mind as for the eye. There was hardly any stir of wind, in contrast to the upland gales that had raged the night before; the whole valley, he perceived, was a landlocked harbor, with Karakal brooding over it, lighthouse-fashion. The simile grew as he considered it, for there was actually light on the summit, an ice blue gleam that matched the splendor it reflected. Something prompted him then to enquire the literal interpretation of the name, and Chang's answer came as a whispered echo of his own musing.

"Karakal, in the valley patois, means Blue Moon," said the Chinese.

Conway did not pass on his conclusion that the arrival of himself and party at Shangri-La had been in some way expected by its inhabitants. He had had it in mind that he must do so, and he was aware that the matter was important; but when morning came his awareness troubled him so little, in any but a theoretical sense, that he shrank from being the cause of greater concern in others. One part of him insisted that there was something distinctly queer about the place, that the attitude of Chang on the previous evening had been far from reassuring, and that the party were virtually prisoners unless and until the authorities chose to do more for them. And it was clearly his duty to compel them to do this. After all, he was a representative of the British Government, if nothing else; it was iniquitous that the inmates of a Tibetan monastery should refuse him any proper request. . . . That, no doubt, was the normal official view that would be taken; and part of Conway was both normal and official. No one could better play the strong man on occasions; during those final difficult days before the evacuation he had behaved in a manner which (he reflected wryly) should earn him nothing less than a knighthood and a Henty school prize novel entitled *With Conway at Baskul.* To have taken on himself the leadership of some scores of mixed civilians, including women and children, to have sheltered them all in a small consulate during a hot-blooded revolution led by anti-foreign agitators, and to have bullied and cajoled the revolutionaries into permitting a wholesale evacuation by air, it was not, he felt, a bad achievement. Perhaps by pulling wires and writing interminable reports, he could wangle something out of it in the next New Year Honors. At any rate it had won him Mallinson's fervent admiration. Unfortunately, the youth must now be finding him so much more of a disappointment. It was a pity, of course, but Conway had grown used to people liking him only because they misunderstood him. He was not genuinely one of those resolute, strong-jawed, hammer-and-tongs empire builders; the semblance he had given was merely a little one-act play, repeated from time to time by arrangement with fate and the Foreign Office, and for a salary which any one could turn up in the pages of Whitaker.

The truth was, the puzzle of Shangri-La, and of his own arrival there, was beginning to exercise over him a rather charming fascination. In any case he found it hard to feel any personal misgivings. His official job was always liable to take him into odd parts of the world, and the odder they were, the less, as a rule, he suffered from boredom; why, then, grumble because accident, instead of a chit from Whitehall, had sent him to this oddest place of all?

He was, in fact, very far from grumbling. When he rose in the morning and saw the soft lapis blue of the sky through his window, he would not have chosen to be elsewhere on earth either in Peshawur or Piccadilly. He was glad to find that on the others, also, a night's repose had had a heartening effect. Barnard was able to joke quite cheerfully about beds, baths, breakfasts, and other hospitable amenities. Miss Brinklow admitted that the most strenuous search of her apartment had failed to reveal any of the drawbacks she had been well prepared for. Even Mallinson had acquired a touch of half sulky complacency. "I suppose we shan't get away to-day after all," he muttered, "unless somebody looks pretty sharp about it. These fellows are typically Oriental, you can't get them to do anything quickly and efficiently."

Conway accepted the remark. Mallinson had been out of England just under a year; long enough, no doubt, to justify a generalization which he would probably still repeat when he had been out for twenty. And it was true, of course, in some degree. Yet to Conway it did not appear that the Eastern races were abnormally dilatory, but rather that Englishmen and Americans charged about the world in a state of continual and rather preposterous fever-heat. It was a point of view that he hardly expected any fellow Westerner to share, but he was more faithful to it as he grew older in years and experience. On the other hand, it was true enough that Chang was a subtle quibbler and that there was much justification for Mallinson's impatience. Conway had a slight wish that he could feel impatient too; it would have been so much easier for the boy.

He said: "I think we'd better wait and see what to-day brings. It was perhaps too optimistic to expect them to do anything last night."

Mallinson looked up sharply. "I suppose you think I made a fool of myself, being so urgent? I couldn't help it; I thought that Chinese fellow was damned fishy, and I do still. Did you succeed in getting any sense out of him after I'd gone to bed?"

"We didn't stay talking long. He was rather vague and non-committal about most things."

"We shall jolly well have to keep him up to scratch to-day."

"No doubt," agreed Conway, without marked enthusiasm for the prospect. "Meanwhile this is an excellent breakfast." It consisted of pomelo, tea, and chupatties, perfectly prepared and served. Towards the finish of the meal Chang entered and with a little bow began the exchange of politely conventional greetings which, in the English language, sounded just a trifle unwieldy. Conway would have preferred to talk in Chinese, but so far he had not let it be known that he spoke any Eastern tongue; he felt it might be a useful card up his sleeve. He listened gravely to Chang's courtesies, and gave assurances that he had slept well and felt much better. Chang expressed his pleasure at that, and added: "Truly, as your national poet says, 'Sleep knits up the raveled sleeve of care.'"

This display of erudition was not too well received. Mallinson answered with that touch of scorn which any healthy-minded young Englishman must feel at the mention of poetry. "I suppose you mean Shakespeare, though I don't recognize the quotation. But I know another one that says 'Stand not upon the order of your going, but go at once.' Without being impolite, that's rather what we should all like to do. And I want to hunt round for those porters right away, this morning, if you've no objection."

The Chinese received the ultimatum impassively, replying at length: "I am sorry to tell you that it would be of little use. I fear we have no men available who would be willing to accompany you so far from their homes."

"But good God, man, you don't suppose we're going to take that for an answer, do you?"

"I am sincerely regretful, but I can suggest no other."

"You seem to have figgered it all out since last night," put in Barnard. "You weren't nearly so dead sure of things then."

"I did not wish to disappoint you when you were so tired from your journey. Now, after a refreshing night, I am in hope that you will see matters in a more reasonable light."

"Look here," intervened Conway briskly, "this sort of vagueness and prevarication won't do. You know we can't stay here indefinitely. It's equally obvious that we can't get away by ourselves. What, then, do you propose?"

Chang smiled with a radiance that was clearly for Conway alone. "My dear sir, it is a pleasure to make the suggestion that is in my mind. To your friend's attitude there was no answer, but to the demand of a wise man there is always a response. You may recollect that it was remarked yesterday, again by your friend, I believe, that we are bound to have occasional communication with the outside world. That is quite true. From time to time we require certain things from distant *entrepôts*, and it is our habit to obtain them in due course, by what methods and with what formalities I need not trouble you. The point of importance is that such a consignment is expected to arrive shortly, and as the men who make delivery will afterwards return, it seems to me that you might manage to come to some arrangement with them. Indeed I cannot think of a better plan, and I hope, when they arrive—"

"When *do* they arrive?" interrupted Mallinson bluntly.

"The exact date is, of course, impossible to forecast. You have

yourself had experience of the difficulty of movement in this part
of the world. A hundred things may happen to cause uncer-
tainty, hazards of weather—"

Conway again intervened. "Let's get this clear. You're suggesting that we should employ as porters the men who are shortly
due here with some goods. That's not a bad idea as far as it goes,
but we must know a little more about it. First, as you've already
been asked, when are these people expected? And second, where
will they take us?"

"That is a question you would have to put to them."

"Would they take us to India?"

"It is hardly possible for me to say."

"Well, let's have an answer to the other question. When will
they be here? I don't ask for a date, I just want some idea
whether it's likely to be next week or next year."

"It might be about a month from now. Probably not more
than two months."

"Or three, four, or five months," broke in Mallinson hotly.
"And you think we're going to wait here for this convoy or cara-
van or whatever it is to take us God knows where at some completely vague time in the distant future?"

"I think, sir, the phrase 'distant future' is hardly appropriate.
Unless something unforeseen occurs, the period of waiting
should not be longer than I have said."

"But *two months!* Two months in this place! It's preposterous!
Conway, you surely can't contemplate it! Why, two weeks would
be the limit!"

Chang gathered his gown about him in a little gesture of
finality. "I am sorry. I did not wish to offend. The lamasery con-
tinues to offer all of you its utmost hospitality for as long as you
have the misfortune to remain. I can say no more."

"You don't need to," retorted Mallinson furiously. "And if you
think you've got the whip hand over us, you'll soon find you're
damn well mistaken! We'll get all the porters we want, don't
worry. You can bow and scrape and say what you like—"

Conway laid a restraining hand on his arm. Mallinson in a temper presented a childlike spectacle; he was apt to say anything that came into his head, regardless alike of point and decorum. Conway thought it readily forgivable in one so constituted and circumstanced, but he feared it might affront the more delicate susceptibilities of a Chinese. Fortunately Chang had ushered himself out, with admirable tact, in good time to escape the worst.

5

THEY SPENT the rest of the morning discussing the matter. It was certainly a shock for four persons who in the ordinary course should have been luxuriating in the clubs and mission houses of Peshawur, to find themselves faced instead with the prospect of two months in a Tibetan monastery. But it was in the nature of things that the initial shock of their arrival should have left them with slender reserves either of indignation or astonishment; even Mallinson, after his first outburst, subsided into a mood of half-bewildered fatalism. "I'm past arguing about it, Conway," he said, puffing at a cigarette with nervous irritability. "You know how I feel. I've said all along that there's something queer about this business. It's crooked. I'd like to be out of it this minute."

"I don't blame you for that," replied Conway. "Unfortunately, it's not a question of what any of us would like, but of what we've all got to put up with. Frankly, if these people say they won't or can't supply us with the necessary porters, there's nothing for it but to wait till the other fellows come. I'm sorry to admit that we're so helpless in the matter, but I'm afraid it's the truth."

"You mean we've got to stay here for two months?"

"I don't see what else we can do."

Mallinson flicked his cigarette ash with a gesture of forced nonchalance. "All right, then. Two months it is. And now let's all shout hooray about it."

Conway went on: "I don't see why it should be much worse than two months in any other isolated part of the world. People in our jobs are used to being sent to odd places; I think I can say that of us all. Of course, it's bad for those of us who have friends and relatives. Personally, I'm fortunate in that respect, I can't think of any one who'll worry over me acutely, and my work, whatever it might have been, can easily be done by somebody else."

He turned to the others as if inviting them to state their own cases. Mallinson proffered no information, but Conway knew roughly how he was situated. He had parents and a girl in England; it made things hard.

Barnard, on the other hand, accepted the position with what Conway had learned to regard as an habitual good humor. "Well, I guess I'm pretty lucky, for that matter, two months in the penitentiary won't kill me. As for the folks in my home town, they won't bat an eye. I've always been a bad letter writer."

"You forget that our names will be in the papers," Conway reminded him. "We shall all be posted missing, and people will naturally assume the worst."

Barnard looked startled for the moment; then he replied, with a slight grin: "Oh, yes, that's true, but it don't affect me, I assure you."

Conway was glad it didn't, though the matter remained a little puzzling. He turned to Miss Brinklow, who till then had been remarkably silent; she had not offered any opinion during the interview with Chang. He imagined that she too might have comparatively few personal worries. She said brightly: "As Mr. Barnard says, two months here is nothing to make a fuss about. It's all the same, wherever one is, when one's in the Lord's service. Providence has sent me here. I regard it as a call."

Conway thought the attitude a very convenient one, in the circumstances. "I'm sure," he said encouragingly, "you'll find your mission society pleased with you when you *do* return. You'll be able to give much useful information. We'll all of us have had an experience, for that matter. That should be a small consolation."

The talk then became general. Conway was rather surprised at the ease with which Barnard and Miss Brinklow had accommodated themselves to the new prospect. He was relieved, however, as well; it left him with only one disgruntled person to deal with. Yet even Mallinson, after the strain of all the arguing, was experiencing a reaction; he was still perturbed, but more willing to look at the brighter side of things. "Heaven knows what we shall find to do with ourselves," he exclaimed, but the mere fact of making such a remark showed that he was trying to reconcile himself.

"The first rule must be to avoid getting on each other's nerves," replied Conway. "Happily, the place seems big enough, and by no means overpopulated. Except for servants, we've only seen one of its inhabitants so far."

Barnard could find another reason for optimism. "We won't starve, at any rate, if our meals up to now are a fair sample. You know, Conway, this place isn't run without plenty of hard cash. Those baths, for instance, they cost real money. And I can't see that anybody earns anything here, unless those chaps in the valley have jobs, and even then, they wouldn't produce enough for export. I'd like to know if they work any minerals."

"The whole place is a confounded mystery," responded Mallinson. "I dare say they've got pots of money hidden away, like the Jesuits. As for the baths, probably some millionaire supporter presented them. Anyhow, it won't worry me, once I get away. I must say, though, the view *is* rather good, in its way. Fine winter sport center if it were in the right spot. I wonder if one could get any skiing on some of those slopes up yonder?"

Conway gave him a searching and slightly amused glance. "Yesterday, when I found some edelweiss, you reminded me that I wasn't in the Alps. I think it's my turn to say the same thing now. I wouldn't advise you to try any of your Wengen-Scheidegg tricks in this part of the world."

"I don't suppose anybody here has ever seen a ski jump."

"Or even an ice-hockey match," responded Conway banter-ingly. "You might try to raise some teams. What about 'Gentle-men *v*. Lamas'?"

"It would certainly teach them to play the game," Miss Brink-low put in with sparkling seriousness.

Adequate comment upon this might have been difficult, but there was no necessity, since lunch was about to be served, and its character and promptness combined to make an agreeable im-pression. Afterwards, when Chang entered, there was small dis-position to continue the squabble. With great tactfulness the Chinese assumed that he was still on good terms with every-body, and the four exiles allowed the assumption to stand. In-deed, when he suggested that they might care to be shown a lit-tle more of the lamasery buildings, and that if so, he would be pleased to act as guide, the offer was readily accepted. "Why, surely," said Barnard. "We may as well give the place the once-over while we're here. I reckon it'll be a long time before any of us pay a second visit."

Miss Brinklow struck a more thought-giving note. "When we left Baskul in that aeroplane I'm sure I never dreamed we should ever get to a place like this," she murmured as they all moved off under Chang's escort.

"And we don't know yet why we have," answered Mallinson unforgetfully.

Conway had no race or color prejudice, and it was an affecta-tion for him to pretend, as he sometimes did in clubs and first-class railway carriages, that he set any particular store on the "whiteness" of a lobster-red face under a topee. It saved trouble to let it be so assumed, especially in India, and Conway was a conscientious trouble-saver. But in China it had been less neces-sary; he had had many Chinese friends, and it had never oc-curred to him to treat them as inferiors. Hence, in his intercourse with Chang, he was sufficiently unpreoccupied to see in him a mannered old gentleman who might not be entirely trustworthy, but who was certainly of high intelligence. Mallinson, on the other hand, tended to regard him through the bars of an imaginary cage; Miss Brinklow was sharp and sprightly, as with the heathen in his blindness; while Barnard's wise-cracking *bonhomie* was of the kind he would have cultivated with a butler.

Meanwhile the grand tour of Shangri-La was interesting enough to transcend these attitudes. It was not the first monastic institution Conway had inspected, but it was easily the largest and, apart from its situation, the most remarkable. The mere procession through rooms and courtyards was an afternoon's exercise, though he was aware of many apartments passed by, indeed, of whole buildings into which Chang did not offer admission. The party were shown enough, however, to confirm the impressions each one of them had formed already. Barnard was more certain than ever that the lamas were rich; Miss Brinklow discovered abundant evidence that they were immoral. Mallinson, after the first novelty had worn off, found himself no less fatigued than on many sight-seeing excursions at lower altitudes; the lamas, he feared, were not likely to be his heroes.

Conway alone submitted to a rich and growing enchantment. It was not so much any individual thing that attracted him as the gradual revelation of elegance, of modest and impeccable taste, of harmony so fragrant that it seemed to gratify the eye without arresting it. Only indeed by a conscious effort did he recall himself from the artist's mood to the connoisseur's, and then he recognized treasures that museums and millionaires alike would have bargained for, exquisite pearl blue Sung ceramics, paintings in tinted inks preserved for more than a thousand years, lacquers in which the cold and lovely detail of fairyland was not so much depicted as orchestrated. A world of incomparable refinements still lingered tremulously in porcelain and varnish, yielding an instant of emotion before its dissolution into purest thought. There was no boastfulness, no striving after effect, no concentrated attack upon the feelings of the beholder. These delicate perfections had an air of having fluttered into existence like petals from a flower. They would have maddened a collector, but Conway did not collect; he lacked both money and the acquisitive instinct. His liking for Chinese art was an affair of the mind; in a world of increasing noise and hugeness, he turned in private to gentle, precise, and miniature things. And as he passed through room after room, a certain pathos touched him remotely at the thought of Karakal's piled immensity over against such fragile charms.

The lamasery, however, had more to offer than a display of Chinoiserie. One of its features, for instance, was a very delightful library, lofty and spacious, and containing a multitude of books so retiringly housed in bays and alcoves that the whole atmosphere was more of wisdom than of learning, of good manners rather than seriousness. Conway, during a rapid glance at some of the shelves, found much to astonish him; the world's best literature was there, it seemed, as well as a great deal of abstruse and curious stuff that he could not appraise. Volumes in English, French, German, and Russian abounded, and there were vast quantities of Chinese and other Eastern scripts. A section which interested him particularly was devoted to Tibetiana, if it might be so called; he noticed several rarities, among them the *Novo Descubrimento de grao catayo ou dos Regos de Tibet*, by Antonio de Andrada (Lisbon, 1626); Athanasius Kircher's *China* (Antwerp, 1667); Thevenot's *Voyage à la Chine des Pères Grueber et d'Orville;* and Beligatti's *Relazione Inedita di un Viaggio al Tibet*. He was examining the last named when he noticed Chang's eyes fixed on him in suave curiosity. "You are a scholar, perhaps?" came the enquiry.

Conway found it hard to reply. His period of donhood at Oxford gave him some right to assent, but he knew that the word, though the highest of compliments from a Chinese, had yet a faintly priggish sound for English ears, and chiefly out of consideration for his companions he demurred to it. He said: "I enjoy reading, of course, but my work during recent years hasn't supplied many opportunities for the studious life."

"Yet you wish for it?"

"Oh, I wouldn't say all that, but I'm certainly aware of its attractions."

Mallinson, who had picked up a book, interrupted: "Here's something for your studious life, Conway. It's a map of the country."

"We have a collection of several hundreds," said Chang. "They are all open to your inspection, but perhaps I can save you trouble in one respect. You will not find Shangri-La marked on any."

"Curious," Conway made comment. "I wonder why?"

"There is a very good reason, but I am afraid that is all I can say."

Conway smiled, but Mallinson looked peevish again. "Still piling up the mystery," he said. "So far we haven't seen much that any one need bother to conceal."

Suddenly Miss Brinklow came to life out of a mute preoccupation. "Aren't you going to show us the lamas at work?" she fluted, in the tone which one felt had intimidated many a Cook's man. One felt, too, that her mind was probably full of hazy visions of native handicrafts, prayer-mat weaving, or something picturesquely primitive that she could talk about when she got home. She had an extraordinary knack of never seeming very much surprised, yet of always seeming very slightly indignant, a combination of fixities which was not in the least disturbed by Chang's response: "I am sorry to say it is impossible. The lamas are never, or perhaps I should say only very rarely, seen by those outside the lamahood."

"I guess we'll have to miss 'em then," agreed Barnard. "But I do think it's a real pity. You've no notion how much I'd like to have shaken the hand of your head-man."

Chang acknowledged the remark with benign seriousness. Miss Brinklow, however, was not yet to be side-tracked. "What do the lamas do?" she continued.

"They devote themselves, madam, to contemplation and to the pursuit of wisdom."

"But that isn't *doing* anything."

"Then, madam, they do nothing."

"I thought as much." She found occasion to sum up. "Well, Mr. Chang, it's a pleasure being shown all these things, I'm sure, but you won't convince me that a place like this does any real good. I prefer something more practical."

"Perhaps you would like to take tea?"

Conway wondered at first if this were intended ironically, but it soon appeared not; the afternoon had passed swiftly, and Chang, though frugal in eating, had the typical Chinese fondness for tea-drinking at frequent intervals. Miss Brinklow, too, confessed that visiting art galleries and museums always gave her a touch of headache. The party, therefore, fell in with the suggestion, and followed Chang through several courtyards to a scene of quite sudden and unmatched loveliness. From a colonnade steps descended to a garden, in which a lotus-pool lay entrapped, the leaves so closely set that they gave an impression of a floor of moist green tiles. Fringing the pool were posed a brazen menagerie of lions, dragons, and unicorns, each offering a stylized ferocity that emphasized rather than offended the surrounding peace. The whole picture was so perfectly proportioned that the eye was entirely unhastened from one part to another; there was no vying or vanity, and even the summit of Karakal, peerless above the blue tiled roofs, seemed to have surrendered within the framework of an exquisite artistry. "Pretty little place," commented Barnard, as Chang led the way into an open pavilion which, to Conway's further delight, contained a harpsichord and a modern grand piano. He found this in some ways the crowning astonishment of a rather astonishing afternoon. Chang answered all his questions with complete candour up to a point; the lamas, he explained, held Western music in high esteem, particularly that of Mozart; they had a collection of all the great European compositions, and some were skilled performers on various instruments.

Barnard was chiefly impressed by the transport problem. "D'you mean to tell me that this pi-anno was brought here by the route we came along yesterday?"

"There is no other."

"Well, that certainly beats everything! Why, with a phonograph and a radio you'd be all fixed complete! Perhaps, though, you aren't yet acquainted with up-to-date music?"

"Oh, yes, we have had reports, but we are advised that the mountains would make wireless reception impossible, and as for a phonograph, the suggestion has already come before the authorities, but they have felt no need to hurry in the matter."

"I'd believe that even if you hadn't told me," Barnard retorted. "I guess that must be the slogan of your society, 'No hurry.'" He laughed loudly and then went on: "Well, to come down to details, suppose in due course your bosses decide that they *do* want a phonograph, what's the procedure? The makers wouldn't deliver here, that's a sure thing. You must have an agent in Pekin or Shanghai or somewhere, and I'll bet everything costs plenty by the time you handle it."

But Chang was no more to be drawn than on a previous occasion. "Your surmises are intelligent, Mr. Barnard, but I fear I cannot discuss them."

So there they were again, Conway reflected, edging the invisible border line between what might and might not be revealed. He thought he could soon begin to map out that line in imagination, though the impact of a new surprise deferred the matter. For servants were already bringing in the shallow bowls of scented tea, and along with the agile, lithe-limbed Tibetans there had also entered, quite inconspicuously, a girl in Chinese dress. She went directly to the harpsichord and began to play a gavotte by Rameau. The first bewitching twang stirred in Conway a pleasure that was beyond amazement; those silvery airs of eighteenth-century France seemed to match in elegance the

Sung vases and exquisite lacquers and the lotus-pool beyond; the same death-defying fragrance hung about them, lending immortality through an age to which their spirit was alien. Then he noticed the player. She had the long, slender nose, high cheekbones, and eggshell pallor of the Manchu; her black hair was drawn tightly back and braided; she looked very finished and miniature. Her mouth was like a little pink convolvulus, and she was quite still, except for her long-fingered hands. As soon as the gavotte was ended, she made a little obeisance and went out.

Chang smiled after her and then, with a touch of personal triumph, upon Conway. "You are pleased?" he queried.

"Who is she?" asked Mallinson, before Conway could reply.

"Her name is Lo-Tsen. She has much skill with Western keyboard music. Like myself, she has not yet attained the full initiation."

"I should think not, indeed!" exclaimed Miss Brinklow. "She looks hardly more than a child. So you have women lamas, then?"

"There are no sex distinctions among us."

"Extraordinary business, this lamahood of yours," Mallinson commented loftily, after a pause. The rest of the tea-drinking proceeded without conversation; echoes of the harpsichord seemed still in the air, imposing a strange spell. Presently, leading the departure from the pavilion, Chang ventured to hope that the tour had been enjoyable. Conway, replying for the others, seesawed with the customary courtesies. Chang then assured them of his own equal enjoyment, and hoped they would consider the resources of the music room and library wholly at their disposal throughout their stay. Conway, with some sincerity, thanked him again. "But what about the lamas?" he added. "Don't they ever want to use them?"

"They yield place with much gladness to their honored guests."

"Well, that's what I call real handsome," said Barnard. "And what's more, it shows that the lamas do really know we exist.

That's a step forward, anyhow, makes me feel much more at home. You've certainly got a swell outfit here, Chang, and that little girl of yours plays the pi-anno very nicely. How old would she be, I wonder?"

"I am afraid I cannot tell you."

Barnard laughed. "You don't give away secrets about a lady's age, is that it?"

"Precisely," answered Chang with a faintly shadowing smile.

That evening, after dinner, Conway made occasion to leave the others and stroll out into the calm, moon-washed courtyards. Shangri-La was lovely then, touched with the mystery that lies at the core of all loveliness. The air was cold and still; the mighty spire of Karakal looked nearer, much nearer than by daylight. Conway was physically happy, emotionally satisfied, and mentally at ease; but in his intellect, which was not quite the same thing as mind, there was a little stir. He was puzzled. The line of secrecy that he had begun to map out grew sharper, but only to reveal an inscrutable background. The whole amazing series of events that had happened to him and his three chance companions swung now into a sort of focus; he could not yet understand them, but he believed they were somehow to be understood.

Passing along a cloister, he reached the terrace leaning over the valley. The scent of tuberose assailed him, full of delicate associations; in China it was called "the smell of moonlight." He thought whimsically that if moonlight had a sound also, it might well be the Rameau gavotte he had heard so recently; and that set him thinking of the little Manchu. It had not occurred to him to picture women at Shangri-La; one did not associate their presence with the general practice of monasticism. Still, he reflected, it might not be a disagreeable innovation; indeed, a female harpsichordist might be an asset to any community that permitted itself to be (in Chang's words) "moderately heretical."

He gazed over the edge into the blue-black emptiness. The

drop was phantasmal; perhaps as much as a mile. He wondered if he would be allowed to descend it and inspect the valley civilization that had been talked of. The notion of this strange culture-pocket, hidden amongst unknown ranges, and ruled over by some vague kind of theocracy, interested him as a student of history, apart from the curious though perhaps related secrets of the lamasery.

Suddenly, on a flutter of air, came sounds from far below. Listening intently, he could hear gongs and trumpets and also (though perhaps only in imagination) the massed wail of voices. The sounds faded on a veer of the wind, then returned to fade again. But the hint of life and liveliness in those veiled depths served only to emphasize the austere serenity of Shangri-La. Its forsaken courts and pale pavilions simmered in repose from which all the fret of existence had ebbed away, leaving a hush as if moments hardly dared to pass. Then, from a window high above the terrace, he caught the rose-gold of lantern light; was it there that the lamas devoted themselves to contemplation and the pursuit of wisdom, and were those devotions now in progress? The problem seemed one that he could solve merely by entering at the nearest door and exploring through gallery and corridor until the truth were his; but he knew that such freedom was illusory, and that in fact his movements were watched. Two Tibetans had padded across the terrace and were idling near the parapet. Good-humored fellows they looked, shrugging their colored cloaks negligently over naked shoulders. The whisper of gongs and trumpets uprose again, and Conway heard one of the men question his companion. The answer came: "They have buried Talu." Conway, whose knowledge of Tibetan was very slight, hoped they would continue talking; he could not gather much from a single remark. After a pause the questioner, who was inaudible, resumed the conversation, and obtained answers which Conway overheard and loosely understood as follows:

"He died outside."

"He obeyed the high ones of Shangri-La."

"He came through the air over the great mountains with a bird to hold him."

"Strangers he brought, also."

"Talu was not afraid of the outside wind, nor of the outside cold."

"Though he went outside long ago, the valley of Blue Moon remembers him still."

Nothing more was said that Conway could interpret, and after waiting for some time he went back to his own quarters. He had heard enough to turn another key in the locked mystery, and it fitted so well that he wondered he had failed to supply it by his own deductions. It had, of course, crossed his mind, but a certain initial and fantastic unreasonableness about it had been too much for him. Now he perceived that the unreasonableness, however fantastic, was to be swallowed. That flight from Baskul had *not* been the meaningless exploit of a madman. It had been something planned, prepared, and carried out at the instigation of Shangri-La. The dead pilot was known by name to those who lived there; he had been one of them, in some sense; his death was mourned. Everything pointed to a high directing intelligence bent upon its own purposes; there had been, as it were, a single arch of intention spanning the inexplicable hours and miles. But what *was* that intention? For what possible reason could four chance passengers in a British Government aeroplane be whisked away to these trans-Himalayan solitudes?

Conway was somewhat aghast at the problem, but by no means wholly displeased with it. It challenged him in the only way in which he was readily amenable to challenge—by touching a certain clarity of brain that only demanded a sufficient task. One thing he decided instantly; the cold thrill of discovery must not yet be communicated, neither to his companions, who could not help him, nor to his hosts, who doubtless would not.

6

"I RECKON some folks have to get used to worse places," Barnard remarked towards the close of his first week at Shangri-La, and it was doubtless one of the many lessons to be drawn. By that time the party had settled themselves into something like a daily routine, and with Chang's assistance the boredom was no more acute than on many a planned holiday. They had all become acclimatized to the atmosphere, finding it quite invigorating so long as heavy exertion was avoided. They had learned that the days were warm and the nights cold, that the lamasery was almost completely sheltered from winds, that avalanches on Karakal were most frequent about midday, that the valley grew a good brand of tobacco, that some foods and drinks were more pleasant than others, and that each one of themselves had personal tastes and peculiarities. They had, in fact, discovered as much about each other as four new pupils of a school from which every one else was mysteriously absent. Chang was tireless in his efforts to make smooth the rough places. He conducted excursions, suggested occupations, recommended books, talked with his slow, careful fluency whenever there was an awkward pause at meals, and was on every occasion benign, courteous, and resourceful. The line of demarcation was so marked between information willingly supplied and politely declined that the latter ceased to stir resentment, except fitfully from Mallinson. Conway was content to take note of it, adding another fragment to his constantly accumulating data. Barnard even "jollied" the Chinese after the manner and traditions of a Middle West Rotary convention. "You know, Chang, this is a damned bad hotel. Don't you have any newspapers sent here ever? I'd give all the books in your library for this morning's *Herald Tribune*." Chang's replies were always serious, though it did not necessarily follow that he took every question seriously. "We have the files of *The Times*, Mr. Barnard, up to a few years ago. But only, I regret to say, the London *Times*."

Conway was glad to find that the valley was not to be "out of bounds," though the difficulties of the descent made unescorted visits impossible. In company with Chang they all spent a whole day inspecting the green floor that was so pleasantly visible from the cliff edge, and to Conway, at any rate, the trip was of absorbing interest. They traveled in bamboo sedan chairs, swinging perilously over precipices while their bearers in front and to the rear picked a way nonchalantly down the steep track. It was not a route for the squeamish, but when at last they reached the lower levels of forest and foothill the supreme good fortune of the lamasery was everywhere to be realized. For the valley was nothing less than an enclosed paradise of amazing fertility, in which the vertical difference of a few thousand feet spanned the whole gulf between temperate and tropical. Crops of unusual diversity grew in profusion and contiguity, with not an inch of ground untended. The whole cultivated area stretched for perhaps a dozen miles, varying in width from one to five, and though narrow, it had the luck to take sunlight at the hottest part of the day. The atmosphere, indeed, was pleasantly warm even out of the sun, though the little rivulets that watered the soil were ice-cold from the snows. Conway felt again, as he gazed up at the stupendous mountain wall, that there was a superb and exquisite peril in the scene; but for some chance-placed barrier, the whole valley would clearly have been a lake, nourished continually from the glacial heights around it. Instead of which, a few streams dribbled through to fill reservoirs and irrigate fields and plantations with a disciplined conscientiousness worthy of a sanitary engineer. The whole design was almost uncannily fortunate, so long as the structure of the frame remained unmoved by earthquake or landslide.

But even such vaguely future fears could only enhance the total loveliness of the present. Once again Conway was captivated, and by the same qualities of charm and ingenuity that had made his years in China happier than others. The vast encircling *massif* made perfect contrast with the tiny lawns and weedless gardens, the painted tea-houses by the stream, and the frivolously toy-like houses. The inhabitants seemed to him a very successful blend of Chinese and Tibetan; they were cleaner and handsomer than the average of either race, and seemed to have suffered little from the inevitable inbreeding of such a small society. They smiled and laughed as they passed the chaired strangers, and had a friendly word for Chang; they were good-humored and mildly inquisitive, courteous and carefree, busy at innumerable jobs but not in any apparent hurry over them. Altogether Conway thought it one of the pleasantest communities he had ever seen, and even Miss Brinklow, who had been watching for symptoms of pagan degradation, had to admit that everything looked very well "on the surface." She was relieved to find the natives "completely" clothed, even though the women did wear ankle-tight Chinese trousers; and her most imaginative scrutiny of a Buddhist temple revealed only a few items that could be regarded as somewhat doubtfully phallic. Chang explained that the temple had its own lamas, who were under loose control from Shangri-La, though not of the same order. There were also, it appeared, a Taoist and a Confucian temple further along the valley. "The jewel has facets," said the Chinese, "and it is possible that many religions are moderately true."

"I agree with that," said Barnard heartily. "I never did believe in sectarian jealousies. Chang, you're a philosopher, I must remember that remark of yours. 'Many religions are moderately true.' You fellows up on the mountain must be a lot of wise guys to have thought that out. You're right, too, I'm dead certain of it."

"But we," responded Chang dreamily, "are only *moderately* certain."

Miss Brinklow could not be bothered with all that, which seemed to her a sign of mere laziness. In any case she was preoccupied with an idea of her own. "When I get back," she said with tightening lips, "I shall ask my society to send a missionary here. And if they grumble at the expense, I shall just bully them until they agree."

That, clearly, was a much healthier spirit, and even Mallinson, little as he sympathized with foreign missions, could not forbear his admiration. "They ought to send *you*," he said. "That is, of course, if you'd like a place like this."

"It's hardly a question of *liking* it," Miss Brinklow retorted. "One wouldn't like it, naturally—how could one? It's a matter of what one feels one ought to do."

"I think," said Conway, "if I were a missionary I'd choose this rather than quite a lot of other places."

"In that case," snapped Miss Brinklow, "there would be no merit in it, obviously."

"But I wasn't thinking of merit."

"More's the pity, then. There's no good in doing a thing because you like doing it. Look at these people here!"

"They all seem very happy."

"*Exactly,*" she answered with a touch of fierceness. She added: "Anyhow, I don't see why I shouldn't make a beginning by studying the language. Can you lend me a book about it, Mr. Chang?"

Chang was at his most mellifluous. "Most certainly, madam, with the greatest of pleasure. And, if I may say so, I think the idea an excellent one."

When they ascended to Shangri-La that evening he treated the matter as one of immediate importance. Miss Brinklow was at first a little daunted by the massive volume compiled by an industrious nineteenth-century German (she had more probably imagined some slighter work of a "Brush up your Tibetan" type), but with help from the Chinese and encouragement from Conway she made a good beginning and was soon observed to be extracting grim satisfaction from her task.

Conway, too, found much to interest him, apart from the engrossing problem he had set himself. During the warm, sunlit days he made full use of the library and music room, and was confirmed in his impression that the lamas were of quite exceptional culture. Their taste in books was catholic, at any rate; Plato in Greek touched Omar in English; Nietzsche partnered Newton; Thomas More was there, and also Hannah More, Thomas Moore, George Moore, and even Old Moore. Altogether Conway estimated the number of volumes at between twenty and thirty thousand; and it was tempting to speculate upon the method of selection and acquisition. He sought also to discover how recently there had been additions, but he did not come across anything later than a cheap reprint of *Im Westen Nichts Neues*. During a subsequent visit, however, Chang told him that there were other books published up to about the middle of 1930 which would doubtless be added to the shelves eventually; they had already arrived at the lamasery. "We keep ourselves fairly up-to-date, you see," he commented.

"There are people who would hardly agree with you," replied Conway with a smile. "Quite a lot of things have happened in the world since last year, you know."

"Nothing of importance, my dear sir, that could not have been foreseen in 1920, or that will not be better understood in 1940."

"You're not interested, then, in the latest developments of the world crisis?"

"I shall be very deeply interested—in due course."

"You know, Chang, I believe I'm beginning to understand you. You're geared differently, that's what it is. Time means less to you than it does to most people. If I were in London I wouldn't always be eager to see the latest hour-old newspaper, and you at Shangri-La are no more eager to see a year-old one. Both attitudes seem to me quite sensible. By the way, how long is it since you last had visitors here?"

"That, Mr. Conway, I am unfortunately unable to say."

It was the usual ending to a conversation, and one that Conway found less irritating than the opposite phenomenon from which he had suffered much in his time—the conversation which, try as he would, seemed never to end. He began to like Chang rather more as their meetings multiplied, though it still puzzled him that he met so few of the lamasery personnel; even assuming that the lamas themselves were unapproachable, were there not other postulants besides Chang?

There was, of course, the little Manchu. He saw her sometimes when he visited the music room; but she knew no English, and he was still unwilling to disclose his own Chinese. He could not quite determine whether she played merely for pleasure, or was in some way a student. Her playing, as indeed her whole behavior, was exquisitely formal, and her choice lay always among the more patterned compositions—those of Bach, Corelli, Scarlatti, and occasionally Mozart. She preferred the harpsichord to the piano, but when Conway went to the latter she would listen with grave and almost dutiful appreciation. It was impossible to know what was in her mind; it was difficult even to guess her age. He would have doubted her being over thirty or under thirteen; and yet, in a curious way, such manifest unlikelihoods could neither of them be ruled out as wholly impossible.

Mallinson, who sometimes came to listen to the music for want of anything better to do, found her a very baffling proposition. "I can't think what she's doing here," he said to Conway more than once. "This lama business may be all right for an old fellow like Chang, but what's the attraction in it for a girl? How long has she been here, I wonder?"

"I wonder too, but it's one of those things we're not likely to be told."

"Do you suppose she *likes* being here?"

"I'm bound to say she doesn't appear to *dis*like it."

"She doesn't appear to have feelings at all, for that matter. She's like a little ivory doll more than a human being."

"A charming thing to be like, anyhow."

"As far as it goes."

Conway smiled. "And it goes pretty far, Mallinson, when you come to think about it. After all, the ivory doll has manners, good taste in dress, attractive looks, a pretty touch on the harpsichord, and she doesn't move about a room as if she were playing hockey. Western Europe, so far as I recollect it, contains an exceptionally large number of females who lack those virtues."

"You're an awful cynic about women, Conway."

Conway was used to the charge. He had not actually had a great deal to do with the other sex, and during occasional leaves in Indian hill-stations the reputation of cynic had been as easy to sustain as any other. In truth he had had several delightful friendships with women who would have been pleased to marry him if he had asked them—but he had not asked them. He had once got nearly as far as an announcement in the *Morning Post,* but the girl did not want to live in Pekin and he did not want to live at Tunbridge Wells, mutual reluctances which proved impossible to dislodge. So far as he had had experience of women at all, it had been tentative, intermittent, and somewhat inconclusive. But he was not, for all that, a cynic about them.

He said with a laugh: "I'm thirty-seven—you're twenty-four. That's all it amounts to."

After a pause Mallinson asked suddenly: "Oh, by the way, how old should you say Chang is?"

"Anything," replied Conway lightly, "between forty-nine and a hundred and forty-nine."

Such information, however, was less trustworthy than much else that was available to the new arrivals. The fact that their curiosities were sometimes unsatisfied tended to obscure the really vast quantity of data which Chang was always willing to outpour. There were no secrecies, for instance, about the customs and habits of the valley population, and Conway, who was interested, had talks which might have been worked up into a quite serviceable degree thesis. He was particularly interested, as a student of affairs, in the way the valley population was governed; it appeared, on examination, to be a rather loose and elastic autocracy, operated from the lamasery with a benevolence that was almost casual. It was certainly an established success, as every descent into that fertile paradise made more evident. Conway was puzzled as to the ultimate basis of law and order; there appeared to be neither soldiers nor police, yet surely some provision must be made for the incorrigible? Chang replied that crime was very rare, partly because only serious things were considered crimes, and partly because every one enjoyed a sufficiency of everything he could reasonably desire. In the last resort the personal servants of the lamasery had power to expel an offender from the valley—though this, which was considered an extreme and dreadful punishment, had only very occasionally to be imposed. But the chief factor in the government of Blue Moon, Chang went on to say, was the inculcation of good manners, which made men feel that certain things were "not done," and that they lost caste by doing them. "You English inculcate the same feeling," said Chang, "in your public schools, but not, I fear, in regard to the same things. The inhabitants of our valley, for instance, feel that it is 'not done' to be inhospitable to strangers, to dispute acrimoniously, or to strive for priority amongst one another. The idea of enjoying what your English headmasters call the mimic warfare of the playing-field would seem to them entirely barbarous—indeed, a sheerly wanton stimulation of all the lower instincts."

Conway asked if there were never disputes about women.

"Only very rarely, because it would not be considered good manners to take a woman that another man wanted."

"Supposing somebody wanted her so badly that he didn't care a damn whether it was good manners or not?"

"Then, my dear sir, it would be good manners on the part of the other man to let him have her, and also on the part of the woman to be equally agreeable. You would be surprised, Conway, how the application of a little courtesy all round helps to smooth out these problems."

Certainly during visits to the valley Conway found a spirit of good will and contentment that pleased him all the more because he knew that of all the arts that of government has been brought least to perfection. When he made some complimentary remark, however, Chang responded: "Ah, but you see, we believe that to govern perfectly it is necessary to avoid governing too much."

"Yet you don't have any democratic machinery—voting, and so on?"

"Oh, no. Our people would be quite shocked by having to declare that one policy was completely right and another completely wrong."

Conway smiled. He found the attitude a curiously sympathetic one.

Meanwhile, Miss Brinklow derived her own kind of satisfaction from a study of Tibetan; meanwhile, also, Mallinson fretted and groused, and Barnard persisted in an equanimity which seemed almost equally remarkable, whether it were real or simulated.

"To tell you the truth," said Mallinson, "the fellow's cheerfulness is just about getting on my nerves. I can understand him trying to keep a stiff lip, but that continual joking of his begins to upset me. He'll be the life and soul of the party if we don't watch him."

Conway too had once or twice wondered at the ease with which the American had managed to settle down. He replied: "Isn't it rather lucky for us he *does* take things so well?"

"Personally, I think it's damned peculiar. What do you *know* about him, Conway? I mean who he is, and so on."

"Not much more than you do. I understood he came from Persia and was supposed to have been oil-prospecting. It's his way to take things easily—when the air evacuation was arranged I had quite a job to persuade him to join us at all. He only agreed when I told him that an American passport wouldn't stop a bullet."

"By the way, did you ever see his passport?"

"Probably I did, but I don't remember. Why?"

Mallinson laughed. "I'm afraid you'll think I haven't exactly been minding my own business. Why should I, anyhow? Two months in this place ought to reveal all our secrets, if we have any. Mind you, it was a sheer accident, in the way it happened, and I haven't let slip a word to any one else, of course. I didn't think I'd tell even you, but now we've got on to the subject I may as well."

"Yes, of course, but I wish you'd let me know what you're talking about."

"Just this. Barnard was traveling on a forged passport and he isn't Barnard at all."

Conway raised his eyebrows with an interest that was very much less than concern. He liked Barnard, so far as the man stirred him to any emotion at all; but it was quite impossible for him to care intensely who he really was or wasn't. He said: "Well, who do you think he is, then?"

"He's Chalmers Bryant."

"The deuce he is! What makes you think so?"

"He dropped a pocketbook this morning and Chang picked it up and gave it to me, thinking it was mine. I couldn't help seeing it was stuffed with newspaper clippings—some of them fell out as I was handling the thing, and I don't mind admitting that I looked at them. After all, newspaper clippings aren't private, or shouldn't be. They were all about Bryant and the search for him, and one of them had a photograph which was absolutely like Barnard except for a mustache."

"Did you mention your discovery to Barnard himself?"

"No, I just handed him his property without any comment."

"So the whole thing rests on your identification of a newspaper photograph?"

"Well, so far, yes."

"I don't think I'd care to convict any one on that. Of course you might be right—I don't say he couldn't *possibly* be Bryant. If he were, it would account for a good deal of his contentment at being here—he could hardly have found a better place to hide."

Mallinson seemed a trifle disappointed by this casual reception of news which he evidently thought highly sensational. "Well, what are you going to do about it?" he asked.

Conway pondered a moment and then answered: "I haven't much of an idea. Probably nothing at all. What *can* one do, in any case?"

"But dash it all, if the man *is* Bryant—"

"My dear Mallinson, if the man were Nero it wouldn't have to matter to us for the time being! Saint or crook, we've got to make what we can of each other's company as long as we're here, and I can't see that we shall help matters by striking any attitudes. If I'd suspected who he was at Baskul, of course, I'd have tried to get in touch with Delhi about him—it would have been merely a public duty. But now I think I can claim to be *off* duty."

"Don't you think that's rather a slack way of looking at it?"

"I don't care if it's slack so long as it's sensible."

"I suppose that means your advice to me is to forget what I've found out?"

"You probably can't do that, but I certainly think we might both of us keep our own counsel about it. Not in consideration for Barnard or Bryant or whoever he is, but to save ourselves the deuce of an awkward situation when we get away."

"You mean we ought to let him go?"

"Well, I'll put it a bit differently and say we ought to give somebody else the pleasure of catching him. When you've lived quite sociably with a man for a few months, it seems a little out of place to call for the handcuffs."

"I don't think I agree. The man's nothing but a large-scale thief—I know plenty of people who've lost their money through him."

Conway shrugged his shoulders. He admired the simple black-and-white of Mallinson's code; the public school ethic might be crude, but at least it was downright. If a man broke the law, it was every one's duty to hand him over to justice—always provided that it was the kind of law one was not allowed to break. And the law pertaining to checks and shares and balance-sheets was decidedly that kind. Bryant had transgressed it, and though Conway had not taken much interest in the case, he had an impression that it was a fairly bad one of its kind. All he knew was that the failure of the giant Bryant group in New York had resulted in losses of about a hundred million dollars—a record crash, even in a world that exuded records. In some way or other (Conway was not a financial expert) Bryant had been monkeying on Wall Street, and the result had been a warrant for his arrest, his escape to Europe, and extradition orders against him in half a dozen countries.

Conway said finally: "Well, if you take my tip you'll say nothing about it—not for his sake but for ours. Please yourself, of course, so long as you don't forget the possibility that he mayn't be the fellow at all."

But he was, and the revelation came that evening after dinner. Chang had left them; Miss Brinklow had turned to her Tibetan grammar; the three male exiles faced each other over coffee and cigars. Conversation during the meal would have languished more than once but for the tact and affability of the Chinese; now, in his absence, a rather unhappy silence supervened. Barnard was for once without jokes. It was clear to Conway that it lay beyond Mallinson's power to treat the American as if nothing had happened, and it was equally clear that Barnard was shrewdly aware that something *had* happened.

Suddenly the American threw away his cigar. "I guess you all know who I am," he said.

Mallinson colored like a girl, but Conway replied in the same quiet key: "Yes, Mallinson and I think we do."

"Darned careless of me to leave those clippings lying about."

"We're all apt to be careless at times."

"Well, you're mighty calm about it, that's something."

There was another silence, broken at length by Miss Brinklow's shrill voice: "I'm sure *I* don't know who you are, Mr. Barnard, though I must say I guessed all along you were traveling *incognito*." They all looked at her enquiringly and she went on: "I remember when Mr. Conway said we should all have our names in the papers, you said it didn't affect you. I thought then that Barnard probably wasn't your real name."

The culprit gave a slow smile as he lit himself another cigar. "Madam," he said eventually, "you're not only a smart detective, but you've hit on a really polite name for my present position. I'm traveling *incognito*. You've said it, and you're dead right. As for you boys, I'm not sorry in a way that you've found me out. So long as none of you had an inkling, we could all have managed, but considering how we're fixed it wouldn't seem very neighborly to play the high hat with you now. You folks have been so darned nice to me that I don't want to make a lot of trouble. It looks as if we were all going to be joined together for better or worse for some little time ahead, and it's up to us to help one another out as far as we can. As for what happens afterwards, I reckon we can leave that to settle itself."

All this appeared to Conway so eminently reasonable that he gazed at Barnard with considerably greater interest, and even—though it was perhaps odd at such a moment—a touch of genuine appreciation. It was curious to think of that heavy, fleshy, good-humored, rather paternal-looking man as the world's hugest swindler. He looked far more the type that, with a little extra education, would have made a popular headmaster of a prep school. Behind his joviality there were signs of recent strains and worries, but that did not mean that the joviality was forced. He obviously was what he looked—a "good fellow" in the world's sense, by nature a lamb and only by profession a shark.

Conway said: "Yes, that's very much the best thing, I'm certain."

Then Barnard laughed. It was as if he possessed even deeper reserves of good humor which he could only now draw upon. "Gosh, but it's mighty queer," he exclaimed, spreading himself in his chair. "The whole darned business, I mean. Right across Europe, and on through Turkey and Persia to that little one-horse burg! Police after me all the time, mind you—they nearly got me in Vienna! It's pretty exciting at first, being chased, but it gets on your nerves after a bit. I got a good rest at Baskul, though—I thought I'd be safe in the midst of a revolution."

"And so you were," said Conway with a slight smile, "except from bullets."

"Yeah, and that's what bothered me at the finish. I can tell you it was a mighty hard choice—whether to stay in Baskul and get plugged, or accept a trip in your Government's aeroplane and find the bracelets waiting at the other end. I wasn't exactly keen to do either."

"I remember you weren't."

Barnard laughed again. "Well, that's how it was, and you can figger it out for yourself that the change of plan which brought me here, don't worry me an awful lot. It's a first-class mystery, but, speaking personally, there couldn't have been a better one. It isn't my way to grumble as long as I'm satisfied."

Conway's smile became more definitely cordial. "A very sensible attitude, though I think you rather overdid it. We were all beginning to wonder how you managed to be so contented."

"Well, I *was* contented. This ain't a bad place, when you get used to it. The air's a bit snappy at first, but you can't have everything. And it's nice and quiet for a change. Every fall I go down to Palm Beach for a rest cure, but they don't give it you, those places—you're in the racket just the same. But here I guess I'm having just what the doctor ordered, and it certainly feels grand to me. I'm on a different diet, I can't look at the tape, and my broker can't get me on the telephone."

"I dare say he wishes he could."

"Sure. There'll be a tidy-sized mess to clear up, and I know it."

He said this with such simplicity that Conway could not help responding: "I'm not much of an authority on what people call high finance."

It was a lead, and the American accepted it without the slightest reluctance. "High finance," he said, "is mostly a lot of bunk."

"So I've often suspected."

"Look here, Conway, I'll put it like this. A feller does what he's been doing for years, and what lots of other fellers have been doing, and suddenly the market goes against him. He can't help it, but he braces up and waits for the turn. But somehow the turn don't come as it always used to, and when he's lost ten million dollars or so he reads in some paper that a Swede professor thinks it's the end of the world. Now I ask you, does that sort of thing help markets? Of course, it gives him a bit of a shock, but he still can't help it. And there he is till the cops come—if he waits for 'em. I didn't."

"You claim it was all just a run of bad luck, then?"

"Well, I certainly had a large packet."

"You also had other people's money," put in Mallinson sharply.

"Yeah, I did. And why? Because they all wanted something for nothing and hadn't the brains to get it for themselves."

"I don't agree. It was because they trusted you and thought their money was safe."

"Well, it wasn't safe. It couldn't be. There isn't safety anywhere, and those who thought there was were like a lot of saps trying to hide under an umbrella in a typhoon."

Conway said pacifyingly: "Well, we'll all admit you couldn't help the typhoon."

"I couldn't even pretend to help it—any more than you could help what happened after we left Baskul. The same thing struck me then as I watched you in the aeroplane keeping dead calm while Mallinson here had the fidgets. You knew you couldn't do anything about it, and you weren't caring two hoots. Just like I felt myself when the crash came."

"That's nonsense!" cried Mallinson. "Any one can help swindling. It's a matter of playing the game according to the rules."

"Which is a darned difficult thing to do when the whole game's going to pieces. Besides, there isn't a soul in the world who knows what the rules are. All the professors of Harvard and Yale couldn't tell you 'em."

Mallinson replied rather scornfully: "I'm referring to a few quite simple rules of everyday conduct."

"Then I guess your everyday conduct doesn't include managing trust companies."

Conway made haste to intervene. "We'd better not argue. I don't object in the least to the comparison between your affairs and mine. No doubt we've all been flying blind lately, both literally and in other ways. But we're here now, that's the important thing, and I agree with you that we could easily have had more to grumble about. It's curious, when you come to think about it, that out of four people picked up by chance and kidnaped a thousand miles, three should be able to find some consolation in the business. You want a rest cure and a hiding place; Miss Brinklow feels a call to evangelize the heathen Tibetan."

"Who's the third person you're counting?" Mallinson interrupted. "Not me, I hope?"

"I was including myself," answered Conway. "And my own reason is perhaps the simplest of all—I just rather like being here."

Indeed, a short time later, when he took what had come to be his usual solitary evening stroll along the terrace or beside the lotus-pool, he felt an extraordinary sense of physical and mental settlement. It was perfectly true; he just rather liked being at Shangri-La. Its atmosphere soothed while its mystery stimulated, and the total sensation was agreeable. For some days now he had been reaching, gradually and tentatively, a curious conclusion about the lamasery and its inhabitants; his brain was still busy with it, though in a deeper sense he was unperturbed. He was like a mathematician with an abstruse problem—worrying over it, but worrying very calmly and impersonally.

As for Bryant, whom he decided he would still think of and address as Barnard, the question of his exploits and identity faded instantly into the background, save for a single phrase of his—"the whole game's going to pieces." Conway found himself remembering and echoing it with a wider significance than the American had probably intended; he felt it to be true of more than American banking and trust company management. It fitted Baskul and Delhi and London, war making and empire building, consulates and trade concessions and dinner parties at Government House; there was a reek of dissolution over all that recollected world, and Barnard's cropper had only, perhaps, been better dramatized than his own. The whole game *was* doubtless going to pieces, but fortunately the players were not as a rule put on trial for the pieces they failed to save. In that respect financiers were unlucky.

But here, at Shangri-La, all was in deep calm. In a moonless sky the stars were lit to the full, and a pale blue sheen lay upon the dome of Karakal. Conway realized then that if by some change of plan the porters from the outside world were to arrive immediately, he would not be completely overjoyed at being spared the interval of waiting. And neither would Barnard, he reflected with an inward smile. It was amusing, really; and then suddenly he knew that he still liked Barnard, or he wouldn't have found it amusing. Somehow the loss of a hundred million dollars was too much to bar a man for; it would have been easier if he had only stolen one's watch. And after all, how *could* any one lose a hundred millions? Perhaps only in the sense in which a cabinet minister might airily announce that he had been "given India."

And then again he thought of the time when he would leave Shangri-La with the returning porters. He pictured the long, arduous journey, and that eventual moment of arrival at some planter's bungalow in Sikkim or Baltistan—a moment which ought, he felt, to be deliriously cheerful, but which would probably be slightly disappointing. Then the first hand-shakings and self-introductions; the first drinks on clubhouse verandas; sunbronzed faces staring at him in barely concealed incredulity. At Delhi, no doubt, interviews with the Viceroy and the C.I.C.; salaams of turbaned menials; endless reports to be prepared and sent off. Perhaps even a return to England and Whitehall; deck games on the P. & O.; the flaccid palm of an under-secretary; newspaper interviews; hard, mocking, sex-thirsty voices of women—"And is it really true, Mr. Conway, that when you were in Tibet . . . ?" There was no doubt of one thing: he would be able to dine out on his yarn for at least a season. But would he enjoy it? He recalled a sentence penned by Gordon during the last days at Khartoum—"I would sooner live like a Dervish with the Mahdi than go out to dinner every night in London." Conway's aversion was less definite—a mere anticipation that to tell his story in the past tense would bore him a great deal as well as sadden him a little.

Abruptly, in the midst of his reflections, he was aware of Chang's approach. "Sir," began the Chinese, his slow whisper slightly quickening as he spoke, "I am proud to be the bearer of important news. . . ."

So the porters *had* come before their time, was Conway's first thought; it was odd that he should have been thinking of it so recently. And he felt the pang that he was half prepared for. "Well?" he queried.

Chang's condition was as nearly that of excitement as seemed physically possible for him. "My dear sir, I congratulate you," he continued. "And I am happy to think that I am in some measure responsible—it was after my own strong and repeated recommendations that the High Lama made his decision. He wishes to see you immediately."

Conway's glance was quizzical. "You're being less coherent than usual, Chang. What has happened?"

"The High Lama has sent for you."

"So I gather. But why all the fuss?"

"Because it is extraordinary and unprecedented—even I who urged it did not expect it to happen yet. A fortnight ago you had not arrived, and now you are about to be received by *him!* Never before has it occurred so soon!"

"I'm still rather fogged, you know. I'm to see your High Lama—I realize that all right. But is there anything else?"

"Is it not enough?"

Conway laughed. "Absolutely, I assure you—don't imagine I'm being discourteous. As a matter of fact, something quite different was in my head at first. However, never mind about that now. Of course, I shall be both honored and delighted to meet the gentleman. When is the appointment?"

"Now. I have been sent to bring you to him."

"Isn't it rather late?"

"That is of no consequence. My dear sir, you will understand many things very soon. And may I add my own personal pleasure that this interval—always an awkward one—is now at an end. Believe me, it has been irksome to me to have to refuse you information on so many occasions—extremely irksome. I am joyful in the knowledge that such unpleasantness will never again be necessary."

"You're a queer fellow, Chang," Conway responded. "But let's be going, don't bother to explain any more. I'm perfectly ready and I appreciate your nice remarks. Lead the way."

7

CONWAY was quite unruffled, but his demeanor covered an eagerness that grew in intensity as he accompanied Chang across the empty courtyards. If the words of the Chinese meant anything, he was on the threshold of discovery; soon he would know whether his theory, still half formed, were less impossible than it appeared.

Apart from this, it would doubtless be an interesting interview. He had met many peculiar potentates in his time; he took a detached interest in them, and was shrewd as a rule in his assessments. Without self-consciousness he had also the valuable knack of being able to say polite things in languages of which he knew very little indeed. Perhaps, however, he would be chiefly a listener on this occasion. He noticed that Chang was taking him through rooms he had not seen before, all of them rather dim and lovely in lantern light. Then a spiral staircase climbed to a door at which the Chinese knocked, and which was opened by a Tibetan servant with such promptness that Conway suspected he had been stationed behind it. This part of the lamasery, on a higher storey, was no less tastefully embellished than the rest, but its most immediately striking feature was a dry, tingling warmth, as if all the windows were tightly closed and some kind of steam heating plant were working at full pressure. The airlessness increased as he passed on, until at last Chang paused before a door which, if bodily sensation could have been trusted, might well have admitted to a Turkish bath.

"The High Lama," whispered Chang, "will receive you alone." Having opened the door for Conway's entrance, he closed it afterwards so silently that his own departure was almost imperceptible. Conway stood hesitant, breathing an atmosphere that was not only sultry, but full of dusk, so that it was several seconds before he could accustom his eyes to the gloom. Then he slowly built up an impression of a dark-curtained, low-roofed apartment, simply furnished with table and chairs. On one of these sat a small, pale, and wrinkled person, motionlessly shadowed, and yielding an effect as of some fading, antique portrait in chiaroscuro. If there were such a thing as presence divorced from actuality, here it was, adorned with a classic dignity that was more an emanation than an attribute. Conway was curious about his own intense perception of all this, and wondered if it were dependable or merely his reaction to the rich, crepuscular warmth; he felt dizzy under the gaze of those ancient eyes, took a few forward paces, and then halted. The occupant of the chair grew now less vague in outline, but scarcely more corporeal; he was a little old man in Chinese dress, its folds and flounces loose against a flat, emaciated frame. "You are Mr. Conway?" he whispered in excellent English.

The voice was pleasantly soothing, and touched with a very gentle melancholy that fell upon Conway with strange beatitude; though once again the skeptic in him was inclined to hold the temperature responsible.

"I am," he answered.

The voice went on. "It is a pleasure to see you, Mr. Conway. I sent for you because I thought we should do well to have a talk together. Please sit down beside me and have no fear. I am an old man and can do no one any harm."

Conway answered: "I feel it a signal honor to be received by you."

"I thank you, my dear Conway—I shall call you that, according to your English fashion. It is, as I said, a moment of great pleasure for me. My sight is poor, but believe me, I am able to see you in my mind, as well as with my eyes. I trust you have been comfortable at Shangri-La since your arrival?"

"Extremely so."

"I am glad. Chang has done his best for you, no doubt. It has been a great pleasure to him also. He tells me you have been asking many questions about our community and its affairs?"

"I am certainly interested in them."

"Then if you can spare me a little time, I shall be pleased to give you a brief account of our foundation."

"There is nothing I should appreciate more."

"That is what I had thought—and hoped. . . . But first of all, before our discourse . . ."

He made the slightest stir of a hand, and immediately, by what technique of summons Conway could not detect, a servant entered to prepare the elegant ritual of tea-drinking. The little eggshell bowls of almost colorless fluid were placed on a lacquered tray; Conway, who knew the ceremony, was by no means contemptuous of it. The voice resumed: "Our ways are familiar to you, then?"

Obeying an impulse which he could neither analyze nor find desire to control, Conway answered: "I lived in China for some years."

"You did not tell Chang."

"No."

"Then why am I so honored?"

Conway was rarely at a loss to explain his own motives, but on this occasion he could not think of any reason at all. At length he replied: "To be quite candid, I haven't the slightest idea, except that I must have wanted to tell you."

"The best of all reasons, I am sure, between those who are to become friends. . . . Now tell me, is this not a delicate aroma? The teas of China are many and fragrant, but this, which is a special product of our own valley, is in my opinion their equal."

Conway lifted the bowl to his lips and tasted. The savor was slender, elusive, and recondite, a ghostly bouquet that haunted rather than lived on the tongue. He said: "It is very delightful, and also quite new to me."

"Yes, like a great many of our valley herbs, it is both unique and precious. It should be tasted, of course, very slowly—not only in reverence and affection, but to extract the fullest degree of pleasure. This is a famous lesson that we may learn from Kou Kai Tchou, who lived some fifteen centuries ago. He would always hesitate to reach the succulent marrow when he was eating a piece of sugar-cane, for, as he explained—'I introduce myself gradually into the region of delights.' Have you studied any of the great Chinese classics?"

Conway replied that he was slightly acquainted with a few of them. He knew that the allusive conversation would, according to etiquette, continue until the tea-bowls were taken away; but he found it far from irritating, despite his keenness to hear the history of Shangri-La. Doubtless there was a certain amount of Kou Kai Tchou's reluctant sensibility in himself.

At length the signal was given, again mysteriously, the servant padded in and out, and with no more preamble the High Lama of Shangri-La began:

"Probably you are familiar, my dear Conway, with the general outline of Tibetan history. I am informed by Chang that you have made ample use of our library here, and I doubt not that you have studied the scanty but exceedingly interesting annals of these regions. You will be aware, anyhow, that Nestorian Christianity was widespread throughout Asia during the Middle Ages, and that its memory lingered long after its actual decay. In the seventeenth century a Christian revival was impelled directly from Rome through the agency of those heroic Jesuit missionaries whose journeys, if I may permit myself the remark, are so much more interesting to read of than those of St. Paul. Gradually the Church established itself over an immense area, and it is a remarkable fact, not realized by many Europeans to-day,

that for thirty-eight years there existed a Christian mission in
Lhasa itself. It was not, however, from Lhasa but from Pekin, in
the year 1719, that four Capuchin friars set out in search of any
remnants of the Nestorian faith that might still be surviving in
the hinterland.

"They traveled southwest for many months, by Lanchow and
the Koko-Nor, facing hardships which you will well imagine.
Three died on the way, and the fourth was not far from death
when by accident he stumbled into the rocky defile that remains
to-day the only practical approach to the valley of Blue Moon.
There, to his joy and surprise, he found a friendly and prosper-
ous population who made haste to display what I have always
regarded as our oldest tradition—that of hospitality to strangers.
Quickly he recovered health and began to preach his mission.
The people were Buddhists, but willing to hear him, and he had
considerable success. There was an ancient lamasery existing
then on this same mountain-shelf, but it was in a state of decay
both physical and spiritual, and as the Capuchin's harvest increased, he conceived the idea of setting up on the same
magnificent site a Christian monastery. Under his surveillance
the old buildings were repaired and largely reconstructed, and
he himself began to live here in the year 1734, when he was fifty-
three years of age.

"Now let me tell you more about this man. His name was Perrault, and he was by birth a Luxembourger. Before devoting
himself to Far Eastern missions he had studied at Paris, Bologna,
and other universities; he was something of a scholar. There are
few existing records of his early life, but it was not in any way
unusual for one of his age and profession. He was fond of music
and the arts, had a special aptitude for languages, and before he
was sure of his vocation he had tasted all the familiar pleasures
of the world. Malplaquet was fought when he was a youth, and
he knew from personal contact the horrors of war and invasion.
He was physically sturdy; during his first years here he labored
with his hands like any other man, tilling his own garden, and

learning from the inhabitants as well as teaching them. He found gold deposits along the valley, but they did not tempt him; he was more deeply interested in local plants and herbs. He was humble and by no means bigoted. He deprecated polygamy, but he saw no reason to inveigh against the prevalent fondness for the *tangatse* berry, to which were ascribed medicinal properties, but which was chiefly popular because its effects were those of a mild narcotic. Perrault, in fact, became somewhat of an addict himself; it was his way to accept from native life all that it offered which he found harmless and pleasant, and to give in return the spiritual treasure of the West. He was not an ascetic; he enjoyed the good things of the world, and was careful to teach his converts cooking as well as catechism. I want you to have an impression of a very earnest, busy, learned, simple, and enthusiastic person who, along with his priestly functions, did not disdain to put on a mason's overall and help in the actual building of these very rooms. That was, of course, a work of immense difficulty, and one which nothing but his pride and steadfastness could have overcome. Pride, I say, because it was undoubtedly a dominant motive at the beginning—the pride in his own Faith that made him decide that if Gautama could inspire men to build a temple on the ledge of Shangri-La, Rome was capable of no less.

"But time passed, and it was not unnatural that this motive should yield place gradually to more tranquil ones. Emulation is, after all, a young man's spirit, and Perrault, by the time his monastery was well established, was already full of years. You must bear in mind that he had not, from a strict point of view, been acting very regularly; though some latitude must surely be extended to one whose ecclesiastical superiors are located at a distance measurable in years rather than miles. But the folk of the valley and the monks themselves had no misgivings; they loved and obeyed him, and as years went on, came to venerate him also. At intervals it was his custom to send reports to the Bishop of Pekin, but often they never reached him, and as it was to be presumed that the bearers had succumbed to the perils of the journey, Perrault grew more and more unwilling to hazard their lives, and after about the middle of the century he gave up the practice. Some of his earlier messages, however, must have got through, and a doubt of his activities have been aroused, for in the year 1769 a stranger brought a letter written twelve years before, summoning Perrault to Rome.

"He would have been over seventy had the command been received without delay; as it was, he had turned eighty-nine. The long trek over mountain and plateau was unthinkable; he could never have endured the scouring gales and fierce chills of the wilderness outside. He sent, therefore, a courteous reply explaining the situation, but there is no record that his message ever passed the barrier of the great ranges.

"So Perrault remained at Shangri-La, not exactly in defiance of superior orders, but because it was physically impossible for him to fulfill them. In any case he was an old man, and death would probably soon put an end both to him and his irregularity. By this time the institution he had founded had begun to undergo a subtle change. It might be deplorable, but it was not really very astonishing; for it could hardly be expected that one man unaided should uproot permanently the habits and traditions of an epoch. He had no Western colleagues to hold firm when his own grip relaxed; and it had perhaps been a mistake to build on a site that held such older and differing memories. It was asking too much; but was it not asking even more to expect a white-haired veteran, just entering the nineties, to realize the mistake that he had made? Perrault, at any rate, did not then realize it. He was far too old and happy. His followers were devoted even when they forgot his teaching, while the people of the valley held him in such reverent affection that he forgave with ever-increasing ease their lapse into former customs. He was still active, and his faculties had remained exceptionally keen. At the age of ninety-eight he began to study the Buddhist writings that had been left at Shangri-La by its previous occupants, and his intention was then to devote the rest of his life to the composition of a book attacking Buddhism from the standpoint of orthodoxy. He actually finished this task (we have his manuscript complete), but the attack was very gentle, for he had by that time reached the round figure of a century—an age at which even the keenest acrimonies are apt to fade.

"Meanwhile, as you may suppose, many of his early disciples had died, and as there were few replacements, the number resident under the rule of the old Capuchin steadily diminished. From over eighty at one time, it dwindled to a score, and then to a mere dozen, most of them very aged themselves. Perrault's life at this time grew to be a very calm and placid waiting for the end. He was far too old for disease and discontent; only the everlasting sleep could claim him now, and he was not afraid. The valley people, out of kindness, supplied food and clothing; his library gave him work. He had become rather frail, but still kept energy to fulfill the major ceremonial of his office; the rest of the tranquil days he spent with his books, his memories, and the mild ecstasies of the narcotic. His mind remained so extraordinarily clear that he even embarked upon a study of certain mystic practices that the Indians called *yoga*, and which are based upon various special methods of breathing. For a man of such an age the enterprise might well have seemed hazardous, and it was certainly true that soon afterwards, in that memorable year 1789, news descended to the valley that Perrault was dying at last.

"He lay in this room, my dear Conway, where he could see from the window the white blurr that was all his failing eyesight gave him of Karakal; but he could see with his mind also; he could picture the clear and matchless outline that he had first glimpsed half a century before. And there came to him, too, the strange parade of all his many experiences, the years of travel across desert and upland, the great crowds in Western cities, the clang and glitter of Marlborough's troops. His mind had straitened to a snow-white calm; he was ready, willing, and glad to

die. He gathered his friends and servants round him and bade
them all farewell; then he asked to be left alone awhile. It was
during such a solitude, with his body sinking and his mind lifted
to beatitude, that he had hoped to give up his soul . . . but it
did not happen so. He lay for many weeks without speech or
movement, and then he began to recover. He was a hundred and
eight."

The whispering ceased for a moment, and to Conway, stirring
slightly, it appeared that the High Lama had been translating,
with fluency, out of a remote and private dream. At length he
went on:

"Like others who have waited long on the threshold of death,
Perrault had been granted a vision of some significance to take
back with him into the world; and of this vision more must be
said later. Here I will confine myself to his actions and behavior,
which were indeed remarkable. For instead of convalescing idly,
as might have been expected, he plunged forthwith into rigorous
self-discipline somewhat curiously combined with narcotic indul-
gence. Drug-taking and deep-breathing exercises—it could not
have seemed a very death-defying regimen; yet the fact remains
that when the last of the old monks died, in 1794, Perrault himself was still living.

"It would almost have brought a smile had there been any one
at Shangri-La with a sufficiently distorted sense of humor. The
wrinkled Capuchin, no more decrepit than he had been for a
dozen years, persevered in a secret ritual he had evolved, while
to the folk of the valley he soon became veiled in mystery, a her-
mit of uncanny powers who lived alone on that formidable cliff.
But there was still a tradition of affection for him, and it came to
be regarded as meritorious and luck-bringing to climb to Shangri-
La and leave a simple gift, or perform some manual task that
was needed there. On all such pilgrims Perrault bestowed his
blessing—forgetful, it might be, that they were lost and straying
sheep. For 'Te Deum Laudamus' and 'Om Mane Padme Hum'
were now heard equally in the temples of the valley.

"As the new century approached, the legend grew into a rich and fantastic folklore—it was said that Perrault had become a god, that he worked miracles, and that on certain nights he flew to the summit of Karakal to hold a candle to the sky. There is a paleness always on the mountain at full moon; but I need not assure you that neither Perrault nor any other man has ever climbed there. I mention it, even though it may seem unnecessary, because there is a mass of unreliable testimony that Perrault did and could do all kinds of impossible things. It was supposed, for instance, that he practiced the art of self-levitation, of which so much appears in accounts of Buddhist mysticism; but the more sober truth is that he made many experiments to that end, but entirely without success. He did, however, discover that the impairment of ordinary senses could be somewhat offset by a development of others; he acquired skill in telepathy which was perhaps remarkable, and though he made no claim to any specific powers of healing, there was a quality in his mere presence that was helpful in certain cases.

"You will wish to know how he spent his time during these unprecedented years. His attitude may be summed up by saying that, as he had not died at a normal age, he began to feel that there was no discoverable reason why he either should or should not do so at any definite time in the future. Having already proved himself abnormal, it was as easy to believe that the abnormality might continue as to expect it to end at any moment. And that being so, he began to behave without care for the imminence with which he had been so long preoccupied; he began to live the kind of life that he had always desired, but had so rarely found possible; for he had kept at heart and throughout all vicissitudes the tranquil tastes of a scholar. His memory was astonishing; it appeared to have escaped the trammels of the physical into some upper region of immense clarity; it almost seemed that he could now learn everything with far greater ease than during his student days he had been able to learn *anything*. He was soon, of course, brought up against a need for books, but there were a few he had had with him from the first, and they included, you may be interested to hear, an English grammar and dictionary and Florio's translation of Montaigne. With these to work on he contrived to master the intricacies of your language, and we still possess in our library the manuscript of one of his first linguistic exercises—a translation of Montaigne's essay on Vanity into Tibetan—surely a unique production."

Conway smiled. "I should be interested to see it sometime, if I might."

"With the greatest of pleasure. It was, you may think, a singularly unpractical accomplishment, but recollect that Perrault had reached a singularly unpractical age. He would have been lonely without some such occupation—at any rate until the fourth year of the nineteenth century, which marks an important event in the history of our foundation. For it was then that a second stranger from Europe arrived in the valley of Blue Moon. He was a young Austrian named Henschell who had soldiered against Napoleon in Italy—a youth of noble birth, high culture, and much charm of manner. The wars had ruined his fortunes, and he had wandered across Russia into Asia with some vague intention of retrieving them. It would be interesting to know how exactly he reached the plateau, but he had no very clear idea himself; indeed, he was as near death when he arrived here as Perrault himself had once been. Again the hospitality of Shangri-La was extended, and the stranger recovered—but there the parallel breaks down. For Perrault had come to preach and proselytize, whereas Henschell took a more immediate interest in the gold deposits. His first ambition was to enrich himself and return to Europe as soon as possible.

"But he did not return. An odd thing happened—though one that has happened so often since that perhaps we must now agree that it cannot be very odd after all. The valley, with its peacefulness and its utter freedom from worldly cares, tempted him again and again to delay his departure, and one day, having

heard the local legend, he climbed to Shangri-La and had his
first meeting with Perrault.

"That meeting was, in the truest sense, historic. Perrault, if a
little beyond such human passions as friendship or affection, was
yet endowed with a rich benignity of mind which touched the
youth as water upon a parched soil. I will not try to describe the
association that sprang up between the two; the one gave utmost
adoration, while the other shared his knowledge, his ecstasies,
and the wild dream that had now become the only reality left
for him in the world."

There was a pause, and Conway said very quietly: "Pardon
the interruption, but that is not quite clear to me."

"I know." The whispered reply was completely sympathetic.
"It would be remarkable indeed if it were. It is a matter which I
shall be pleased to explain before our talk is over, but for the
present, if you will forgive me, I will confine myself to simpler
things. A fact that will interest you is that Henschell began our
collections of Chinese art, as well as our library and musical ac-
quisitions. He made a remarkable journey to Pekin and brought
back the first consignment in the year 1809. He did not leave the
valley again, but it was his ingenuity which devised the complicated system by which the lamasery has ever since been able to
obtain anything needful from the outer world."

"I suppose you found it easy to make payment in gold?"

"Yes, we have been fortunate in possessing supplies of a metal
which is held in such high esteem in other parts of the world."

"Such high esteem that you must have been very lucky to escape a gold rush."

The High Lama inclined his head in the merest indication of
agreement. "That, my dear Conway, was always Henschell's
fear. He was careful that none of the porters bringing books and
art treasures should ever approach too closely; he made them
leave their burdens a day's journey outside, to be fetched afterwards by our valley folk themselves. He even arranged for sen-
tries to keep constant watch on the entrance to the defile. But it

soon occurred to him that there was an easier and more final safeguard."

"Yes?" Conway's voice was guardedly tense.

"You see there was no need to fear invasion by an army. That will never be possible, owing to the nature and distances of the country. The most ever to be expected was the arrival of a few half-lost wanderers who, even if they were armed, would probably be so weakened as to constitute no danger. It was decided, therefore, that henceforward strangers might come as freely as they chose—with but one important proviso.

"And, over a period of years, such strangers did come. Chinese merchants, tempted into the crossing of the plateau, chanced occasionally on this one traverse out of so many others possible to them. Nomad Tibetans, wandering from their tribes, strayed here sometimes like weary animals. All were made welcome, though some reached the shelter of the valley only to die. In the year of Waterloo two English missionaries, traveling overland to Pekin, crossed the ranges by an unnamed pass and had the extraordinary luck to arrive as calmly as if they were paying a call. In 1820 a Greek trader, accompanied by sick and famished servants, was found dying at the topmost ridge of the pass. In 1822 three Spaniards, having heard some vague story of gold, reached here after many wanderings and disappointments. Again, in 1830, there was a larger influx. Two Germans, a Russian, an Englishman, and a Swede made the dreaded crossing of the Tian-Shans, impelled by a motive that was to become increasingly common—scientific exploration. By the time of their approach a slight modification had taken place in the attitude of Shangri-La towards its visitors—not only were they now welcomed if they chanced to find their way into the valley, but it had become customary to meet them if they ever ventured within a certain radius. All this was for a reason I shall later discuss, but the point is of importance as showing that the lamasery was no longer hospitably indifferent; it had already both a need and a desire for new arrivals. And indeed in the years to follow it happened that more than one party of explorers, glorying in their first distant glimpse of Karakal, encountered messengers bearing a cordial invitation—and one that was rarely declined.

"Meanwhile the lamasery had begun to acquire many of its present characteristics. I must stress the fact that Henschell was exceedingly able and talented, and that the Shangri-La of to-day owes as much to him as to its founder. Yes, quite as much, I often think. For his was the firm yet kindly hand that every institution needs at a certain stage of its development, and his loss would have been altogether irreparable had he not completed more than a lifework before he died."

Conway looked up to echo rather than question those final words. "*He died!*"

"Yes. It was very sudden. He was killed. It was in the year of your Indian Mutiny. Just before his death a Chinese artist had sketched him, and I can show you that sketch now—it is in this room."

The slight gesture of the hand was repeated, and once again a servant entered. Conway, as a spectator in a trance, watched the man withdraw a small curtain at the far end of the room and leave a lantern swinging amongst the shadows. Then he heard the whisper inviting him to move, and it was extraordinary how hard it was to do so.

He stumbled to his feet and strode across to the trembling circle of light. The sketch was small, hardly more than a miniature in colored inks, but the artist had contrived to give the flesh tones a waxwork delicacy of texture. The features were of great beauty, almost girlish in modeling, and Conway found in their winsomeness a curiously personal appeal, even across the barriers of time, death, and artifice. But the strangest thing of all was one that he realized only after his first gasp of admiration: the face was that of a young man.

He stammered as he moved away: "But—you said—this was done just before his death?"

"Yes. It is a very good likeness."

"Then if he died in the year you said—"

"He did."

"And he came here, you told me, in 1803, when he was a youth?"

"Yes."

Conway did not answer for a moment; presently, with an effort, he collected himself to say: "And he was killed, you were telling me?"

"Yes. An Englishman shot him. It was a few weeks after the Englishman had arrived at Shangri-La. He was another of those explorers."

"What was the cause of it?"

"There had been a quarrel—about some porters. Henschell had just told him of the important proviso that governs our reception of guests. It was a task of some difficulty, and ever since, despite my own enfeeblement, I have felt constrained to perform it myself."

The High Lama made another and longer pause, with just a hint of enquiry in his silence; when he continued, it was to add: "Perhaps you are wondering, my dear Conway, what that proviso may be?"

Conway answered slowly and in a low voice: "I think I can already guess."

"Can you, indeed? And can you guess anything else after this long and curious story of mine?"

Conway dizzied in brain as he sought to answer the question; the room was now a whorl of shadows with that ancient benignity at its center. Throughout the narrative he had listened with an intentness that had perhaps shielded him from realizing the fullest implications of it all; now, with the mere attempt at conscious expression, he was flooded over with amazement, and the gathering certainty in his mind was almost stifled as it sprang to words. "It seems impossible," he stammered. "And yet I can't help thinking of it—it's astonishing—and extraordinary—and quite incredible—and yet not *absolutely* beyond my powers of belief—"

"What is, my *son?*"

And Conway answered, shaken with an emotion for which he knew no reason and which he did not seek to conceal: *"That you are still alive, Father Perrault."*

8

THERE HAD been a pause, imposed by the High Lama's call for
further refreshment; Conway did not wonder at it, for the strain
of such a long recital must have been considerable. Nor was he
himself ungrateful for the respite. He felt that the interval was as
desirable from an artistic as from any other point of view, and
that the bowls of tea, with their accompaniment of conven-
tionally improvised courtesies, fulfilled the same function as a
cadenza in music. This reflection brought out (unless it were
mere coincidence) an odd example of the High Lama's tele-
pathic powers, for he immediately began to talk about music and
to express pleasure that Conway's taste in that direction had not
been entirely unsatisfied at Shangri-La. Conway answered with
suitable politeness and added that he had been surprised to find
the lamasery in possession of such a complete library of European composers. The compliment was acknowledged between
slow sips of tea. "Ah, my dear Conway, we are fortunate in that
one of our number is a gifted musician—he was, indeed, a pupil
of Chopin's—and we have been happy to place in his hands the
entire management of our salon. You must certainly meet him."

"I should like to. Chang, by the way, was telling me that your
favorite Western composer is Mozart."

"That is so," came the reply. "Mozart has an austere elegance
which we find very satisfying. He builds a house which is neither
too big nor too little, and he furnishes it in perfect taste."

The exchange of comments continued until the tea-bowls were taken away; by that time Conway was able to remark quite calmly: "So, to resume our earlier discussion, you intend to keep us? That, I take it, is the important and invariable proviso?"

"You have guessed correctly, my son."

"In other words, we are to stay here for ever?"

"I should greatly prefer to employ your excellent English idiom and say that we are all of us here 'for good.'"

"What puzzles me is why we four, out of all the rest of the world's inhabitants, should have been chosen."

Relapsing into his earlier and more consequential manner, the High Lama responded: "It is an intricate story, if you would care to hear it. You must know that we have always aimed, as far as possible, to keep our numbers in fairly constant recruitment—since, apart from any other reasons, it is pleasant to have with us people of various ages and representative of different periods. Unfortunately, since the recent European War and the Russian Revolution, travel and exploration in Tibet have been almost completely held up; in fact, our last visitor, a Japanese, arrived in 1912, and was not, to be candid, a very valuable acquisition. You see, my dear Conway, we are not quacks or charlatans; we do not and cannot guarantee success; some of our visitors derive no benefit at all from their stay here; others merely live to what might be called a normally advanced age and then die from some trifling ailment. In general we have found that Tibetans, owing to their being inured to both the altitude and other conditions, are much less sensitive than outside races; they are charming people, and we have admitted many of them, but I doubt if more than a few will pass their hundredth year. The Chinese are a little better, but even among them we have a high percentage of failures. Our best subjects, undoubtedly, are the Nordic and Latin races of Europe; perhaps the Americans would be equally adaptable, and I count it our great good fortune that we have at last, in the person of one of your companions, secured a citizen of that nation. But I must continue with the answer to your

question. The position was, as I have been explaining, that for
nearly two decades we had welcomed no newcomers, and as
there had been several deaths during that period, a problem was
beginning to arise. A few years ago, however, one of our number
came to the rescue with a novel idea; he was a young fellow, a
native of our valley, absolutely trustworthy and in fullest sympathy with our aims; but, like all the valley people, he was denied
by nature the chance that comes more fortunately to those from
a distance. It was he who suggested that he should leave us,
make his way to some surrounding country, and bring us addi-
tional colleagues by a method which would have been impossible in an earlier age. It was in many respects a revolutionary
proposal, but we gave our consent after due consideration. For
we must move with the times, you know, even at Shangri-La."

"You mean that he was sent out deliberately to bring some
one back by air?"

"Well, you see, he was an exceedingly gifted and resourceful
youth, and we had great confidence in him. It was his own idea,
and we allowed him a free hand in carrying it out. All we knew
definitely was that the first stage of his plan included a period of
tuition at an American flying-school."

"But how could he manage the rest of it? It was only by
chance that there happened to be that aeroplane at Baskul—"

"True, my dear Conway—many things are by chance. But it
happened, after all, to be just the chance that Talu was looking
for. Had he not found it, there might have been another chance
in a year or two—or perhaps, of course, none at all. I confess I
was surprised when our sentinels gave news of his descent on
the plateau. The progress of aviation is rapid, but it had seemed
likely to me that much more time would elapse before an average machine could make such a crossing of the mountains."

"It wasn't an average machine. It was a rather special one,
made for mountain-flying."

"Again by chance? Our young friend was indeed fortunate. It

is a pity that we cannot discuss the matter with him—we were all grieved at his death. You would have liked him, Conway."

Conway nodded slightly; he felt it very possible. He said, after a silence: "But what's the idea behind it all?"

"My son, your way of asking that question gives me infinite pleasure. In the course of a somewhat long experience it has never before been put to me in tones of such calmness. My revelation has been greeted in almost every conceivable manner— with indignation, distress, fury, disbelief, and hysteria—but never until this night with mere interest. It is, however, an attitude that I most cordially welcome. To-day you are interested; to-morrow you will feel concern; eventually, it may be, I shall claim your devotion."

"That is more than I should care to promise."

"Your very doubt pleases me—it is the basis of profound and significant faith. . . . But let us not argue. You are interested, and that, from you, is much. All I ask in addition is that what I tell you now shall remain, for the present, unknown to your three companions."

Conway was silent.

"The time will come when they will learn, like you, but that moment, for their own sakes, had better not be hastened. I am so certain of your wisdom in this matter that I do not ask for a promise; you will act, I know, as we both think best. . . . Now let me begin by sketching for you a very agreeable picture. You are still, I should say, a youngish man by the world's standards; your life, as people say, lies ahead of you; in the normal course you might expect twenty or thirty years of only slightly and gradually diminishing activity. By no means a cheerless prospect, and I can hardly expect you to see it as I do—as a slender, breathless, and far too frantic interlude. The first quarter-century of your life was doubtless lived under the cloud of being too young for things, while the last quarter-century would normally be shadowed by the still darker cloud of being too old for them; and between those two clouds, what small and narrow sunlight illumines a human lifetime! But you, it may be, are destined to be more fortunate, since by the standards of Shangri-La your sunlit years have scarcely yet begun. It will happen, perhaps, that decades hence you will feel no older than you are to-day—you may preserve, as Henschell did, a long and wondrous youth. But that, believe me, is only an early and superficial phase. There will come a time when you will age like others, though far more slowly, and into a condition infinitely nobler; at eighty you may still climb to the pass with a young man's gait, but at twice that age you must not expect the whole marvel to have persisted. We are not workers of miracles; we have made no conquest of death or even of decay. All we have done and can sometimes do is to slacken the *tempo* of this brief interval that is called life. We do this by methods which are as simple here as they are impossible elsewhere; but make no mistake; the end awaits us all.

"Yet it is, nevertheless, a prospect of much charm that I unfold for you—long tranquillities during which you will observe a sunset as men in the outer world hear the striking of a clock, and with far less care. The years will come and go, and you will pass from fleshly enjoyments into austerer but no less satisfying realms; you may lose the keenness of muscle and appetite, but there will be gain to match your loss; you will achieve calmness and profundity, ripeness and wisdom, and the clear enchantment of memory. And, most precious of all, you will have Time—that rare and lovely gift that your Western countries have lost the more they have pursued it. Think for a moment. You will have time to read—never again will you skim pages to save minutes, or avoid some study lest it prove too engrossing. You have also a taste for music—here, then, are your scores and instruments, with Time, unruffled and unmeasured, to give you their richest savor. And you are also, we will say, a man of good fellowship—does it not charm you to think of wise and serene friendships, a long and kindly traffic of the mind from which death may not call you away with his customary hurry? Or, if it is solitude that you prefer, could you not employ our pavilions to enrich the gentleness of lonely thoughts?"

The voice made a pause which Conway did not seek to fill.

"You make no comment, my dear Conway. Forgive my eloquence—I belong to an age and a nation that never considered it bad form to be articulate. . . . But perhaps you are thinking of wife, parents, children, left behind in the world? Or maybe ambitions to do this or that? Believe me, though the pang may be keen at first, in a decade from now even its ghost will not haunt you. Though in point of fact, if I read your mind correctly, you have no such griefs."

Conway was startled by the accuracy of the judgment. "That's so," he replied. "I'm unmarried; I have few close friends and no ambitions."

"No ambitions? And how have you contrived to escape those widespread maladies?"

For the first time Conway felt that he was actually taking part in a conversation. He said: "It always seemed to me in my profession that a good deal of what passed for success would be rather disagreeable, apart from needing more effort than I felt called upon to make. I was in the Consular Service—quite a subordinate post, but it suited me well enough."

"Yet your soul was not in it?"

"Neither my soul nor my heart nor more than half my energies. I'm naturally rather lazy."

The wrinkles deepened and twisted till Conway realized that the High Lama was very probably smiling. "Laziness in doing stupid things can be a great virtue," resumed the whisper. "In any case, you will scarcely find us exacting in such a matter. Chang, I believe, explained to you our principle of moderation, and one of the things in which we are always moderate is activity. I myself, for instance, have been able to learn ten languages; the ten might have been twenty had I worked immoderately. But I did not. And it is the same in other directions; you will find us neither profligate nor ascetic. Until we reach an age when care is advisable, we gladly accept the pleasures of the table, while—for the benefit of our younger colleagues—the women of the valley have happily applied the principle of moderation to their own chastity. All things considered, I feel sure you will get used to our ways without much effort. Chang, indeed, was very optimistic—and so, after this meeting, am I. But there is, I admit, an odd quality in you that I have never met in any of our visitors hitherto. It is not quite cynicism, still less bitterness; perhaps it is partly disillusionment, but it is also a clarity of mind that I should not have expected in any one younger than—say, a century or so. It is, if I had to put a single word to it, passionlessness."

Conway answered: "As good a word as most, no doubt. I don't know whether you classify the people who come here, but if so, you can label me '1914-1918.' That makes me, I should think, a unique specimen in your museum of antiquities—the other three who arrived along with me don't enter the category. I used up most of my passions and energies during the years I've mentioned, and though I don't talk much about it, the chief thing I've asked from the world since then is to leave me alone. I find in this place a certain charm and quietness that appeals to me, and no doubt, as you remark, I shall get used to things."

"Is that all, my son?"

"I hope I am keeping well to your own rule of moderation."

"You are clever—as Chang told me, you are very clever. But is there nothing in the prospect I have outlined that tempts you to any stronger feeling?"

Conway was silent for an interval and then replied: "I was deeply impressed by your story of the past, but to be candid, your sketch of the future interests me only in an abstract sense. I can't look so far ahead. I should certainly be sorry if I had to leave Shangri-La to-morrow, or next week, or perhaps even next year; but how I shall feel about it if I live to be a hundred isn't a matter to prophesy. I can face it, like any other future, but in order to make me keen it must have a point. I've sometimes doubted whether life itself has any; and if not, long life must be even more pointless."

"My friend, the traditions of this building, both Buddhist and Christian, are very reassuring."

"Maybe. But I'm afraid I still hanker after some more definite reason for envying the centenarian."

"There *is* a reason, and a very definite one indeed. It is the whole reason for this colony of chance-sought strangers living beyond their years. We do not follow an idle experiment, a mere whimsy. We have a dream and a vision. It is a vision that first appeared to old Perrault when he lay dying in this room in the year 1789. He looked back then on his long life, as I have already told you, and it seemed to him that all the loveliest things were transient and perishable, and that war, lust, and brutality might some day crush them until there were no more left in the world. He remembered sights he had seen with his own eyes, and with his mind he pictured others; he saw the nations strengthening, not in wisdom, but in vulgar passions and the will to destroy; he saw their machine power multiplying until a single-weaponed man might have matched a whole army of the Grand Monarque. And he perceived that when they had filled the land and sea with ruin, they would take to the air. . . . Can you say that his vision was untrue?"

"True indeed."

"But that was not all. He foresaw a time when men, exultant in the technique of homicide, would rage so hotly over the world that every precious thing would be in danger, every book and picture and harmony, every treasure garnered through two millenniums, the small, the delicate, the defenseless—all would be lost like the lost books of Livy, or wrecked as the English wrecked the Summer Palace in Pekin."

"I share your opinion of that."

"Of course. But what are the opinions of reasonable men against iron and steel? Believe me, that vision of old Perrault will come true. And that, my son, is why *I* am here, and why *you* are here, and why we may pray to outlive the doom that gathers around on every side."

"To outlive it?"

"There is a chance. It will all come to pass before you are as old as I am."

"And you think that Shangri-La will escape?"

"Perhaps. We may expect no mercy, but we may faintly hope for neglect. Here we shall stay with our books and our music and our meditations, conserving the frail elegancies of a dying age, and seeking such wisdom as men will need when their passions are all spent. We have a heritage to cherish and bequeath. Let us take what pleasure we may until that time comes."

"And then?"

"Then, my son, when the strong have devoured each other, the Christian ethic may at last be fulfilled, and the meek shall inherit the earth."

A shadow of emphasis had touched the whisper, and Conway surrendered to the beauty of it; again he felt the surge of darkness around, but now symbolically, as if the world outside were already brewing for the storm. And then he saw that the High Lama of Shangri-La was actually astir, rising from his chair, standing upright like the half-embodiment of a ghost. In mere politeness Conway made to assist; but suddenly a deeper impulse seized him, and he did what he had never done to any man before—he knelt, and hardly knew why he did.

"I understand you, Father," he said.

He was not perfectly aware of how at last he took his leave; he was in a dream from which he did not emerge till long afterwards. He remembered the night air icy after the heat of those upper rooms, and Chang's presence, a silent serenity, as they crossed the starlit courtyards together. Never had Shangri-La offered more concentrated loveliness to his eyes; the valley lay imaged over the edge of the cliff, and the image was of a deep unrippled pool that matched the peace of his own thoughts. For Conway had passed beyond astonishments. The long talk, with its varying phases, had left him empty of all save a satisfaction that was as much of the mind as of the emotions, and as much of the spirit as of either; even his doubts were now no longer harassing, but part of a subtle harmony. Chang did not speak, and neither did he. It was very late, and he was glad that all the others had gone to bed.

9

In the morning he wondered if all that he could call to mind were part of a waking or a sleeping vision.

He was soon reminded. A chorus of questions greeted him when he appeared at breakfast. "You certainly had a long talk with the boss last night," began the American. "We meant to wait up for you, but we got tired. What sort of guy is he?"

"Did he say anything about the porters?" asked Mallinson eagerly.

"I hope you mentioned to him about having a missionary stationed here," said Miss Brinklow.

The bombardment served to raise in Conway his usual defensive armament. "I'm afraid I'm probably going to disappoint you all," he replied, slipping easily into the mood. "I didn't discuss with him the question of missions; he didn't mention the porters to me at all; and as for his appearance, I can only say that he's a very old man who speaks excellent English and is quite intelligent."

Mallinson cut in with irritation: "The main thing to us is whether he's to be trusted or not. Do you think he means to let us down?"

"He didn't strike me as a dishonorable person."

"Why on earth didn't you worry him about the porters?"

"It didn't occur to me."

Mallinson stared at him incredulously. "I can't understand

you, Conway. You were so damned good in that Baskul affair that I can hardly believe you're the same man. You seem to have gone all to pieces."

"I'm sorry."

"No good being sorry. You ought to buck up and look as if you cared what happens."

"You misunderstand me. I meant that I was sorry to have disappointed you."

Conway's voice was curt, an intended mask to his feelings, which were, indeed, so mixed that they could hardly have been guessed by others. He had slightly surprised himself by the ease with which he had prevaricated; it was clear that he intended to observe the High Lama's suggestion and keep the secret. He was also puzzled by the naturalness with which he was accepting a position which his companions would certainly and with some justification think traitorous; as Mallinson had said, it was hardly the sort of thing to be expected of a hero. Conway felt a sudden half-pitying fondness for the youth; then he steeled himself by reflecting that people who hero-worship must be prepared for disillusionments. Mallinson at Baskul had been far too much the new boy adoring the handsome games-captain, and now the games-captain was tottering if not already fallen from the pedestal. There was always something a little pathetic in the smashing of an ideal, however false; and Mallinson's admiration might have been at least a partial solace for the strain of pretending to be what he was not. But pretense was impossible anyway. There was a quality in the air of Shangri-La—perhaps due to its altitude—that forbade one the effort of counterfeit emotion.

He said: "Look here, Mallinson, it's no use harping continually on Baskul. Of course I was different then—it was a completely different situation."

"And a much healthier one in my opinion. At least we knew what we were up against."

"Murder and rape—to be precise. You can call that healthier if you like."

The youth's voice rose in pitch as he retorted: "Well, I *do* call it healthier—in one sense. It's something I'd rather face than all this mystery business." Suddenly he added: "That Chinese girl, for instance—how did *she* get here? Did the fellow tell you?"

"No. Why should he?"

"Well, why shouldn't he? And why shouldn't you ask, if you had any interest in the matter at all? Is it usual to find a young girl living with a lot of monks?"

That way of looking at it was one that had scarcely occurred to Conway before. "This isn't an ordinary monastery," was the best reply he could give after some thought.

"My God, it isn't!"

There was a silence, for the argument had evidently reached a dead end. To Conway the history of Lo-Tsen seemed rather far from the point; the little Manchu lay so quietly in his mind that he hardly knew she was there. But at the mere mention of her Miss Brinklow had looked up suddenly from the Tibetan grammar which she was studying even over the breakfast table (just as if, thought Conway, with secret meaning, she hadn't all her life for it). Chatter of girls and monks reminded her of those stories of Indian temples that men missionaries told their wives, and that the wives passed on to their unmarried female colleagues. "Of course," she said between tightened lips, "the morals of this place are quite hideous—we might have expected that." She turned to Barnard as if inviting support, but the American only grinned. "I don't suppose you folks'd value my opinion on a matter of morals," he remarked dryly. "But I should say myself that quarrels are just as bad. Since we've gotter be here for some time yet, let's keep our tempers and make ourselves comfortable."

Conway thought this good advice, but Mallinson was still unplacated. "I can quite believe you find it more comfortable than Dartmoor," he said meaningly.

"Dartmoor? Oh, that's your big penitentiary?—I get you. Well, yes, I certainly never did envy the folks in them places. And there's another thing, too—it don't hurt when you chip me about it. Thick-skinned and tender-hearted, that's my mixture."

Conway glanced at him in appreciation, and at Mallinson with some hint of reproof; but then abruptly he had the feeling that they were all acting on a vast stage, of whose background only he himself was conscious; and such knowledge, so incommunicable, made him suddenly want to be alone. He nodded to them and went out into the courtyard. In sight of Karakal misgivings faded, and qualms about his three companions were lost in an uncanny acceptance of the new world that lay so far beyond their guesses. There came a time, he realized, when the strangeness of everything made it increasingly difficult to realize the strangeness of anything; when one took things for granted merely because astonishment would have been as tedious for oneself as for others. Thus far had he progressed at Shangri-La, and he remembered that he had attained a similar though far less pleasant equanimity during his years at the War.

He needed equanimity, if only to accommodate himself to the double life he was compelled to lead. Thenceforward, with his fellow exiles, he lived in a world conditioned by the arrival of porters and a return to India; at all other times the horizon lifted like a curtain; time expanded and space contracted, and the name Blue Moon took on a symbolic meaning, as if the future, so delicately plausible, were of a kind that might happen once in a blue moon only. Sometimes he wondered which of his two lives were the more real, but the problem was not pressing; and again he was reminded of the War, for during heavy bombardments he had had the same comforting sensation that he had many lives, only one of which could be claimed by death.

Chang, of course, now talked to him completely without reserve, and they had many conversations about the rule and routine of the lamasery. Conway learned that during his first five years he would live a normal life, without any special regimen; this was always done, as Chang said, "to enable the body to accustom itself to the altitude, and also to give time for the dispersal of mental and emotional regrets."

Conway remarked with a smile: "I suppose you're certain, then, that no human affection can outlast a five-year absence?"

"It can, undoubtedly," replied the Chinese, "but only as a fragrance whose melancholy we may enjoy."

After the probationary five years, Chang went on to explain, the process of retarding age would begin, and if successful, might give Conway half a century or so at the apparent age of forty—which was not a bad time of life at which to remain stationary.

"What about yourself?" Conway asked. "How did it work out in your case?"

"Ah, my dear sir, I was lucky enough to arrive when I was quite young—only twenty-two. I was a soldier, though you might not have thought it; I had command of troops operating against brigand tribes in the year 1855. I was making what I should have called a reconnaissance if I had ever returned to my superior officers to tell the tale, but in plain truth I had lost my way in the mountains, and of my men only seven out of over a hundred survived the rigors of the climate. When at last I was rescued and brought to Shangri-La I was so ill that extreme youth and virility alone could have saved me."

"Twenty-two," echoed Conway, performing the calculation. "So you're now ninety-seven?"

"Yes. Very soon, if the lamas give their consent, I shall receive full initiation."

"I see. You have to wait for the round figure?"

"No, we are not restricted by any definite age limit, but a century is generally considered to be an age beyond which the passions and moods of ordinary life are likely to have disappeared."

"I should certainly think so. And what happens afterwards? How long do you expect to carry on?"

"There is reason to hope that I shall enter lamahood with such prospects as Shangri-La has made possible. In years, perhaps another century or more."

Conway nodded. "I don't know whether I ought to congratulate you—you seem to have been granted the best of both worlds, a long and pleasant youth behind you, and an equally long and pleasant old age ahead. When did you begin to grow old in appearance?"

"When I was over seventy. That is often the case, though I think I may still claim to look younger than my years."

"Decidedly. And suppose you were to leave the valley now, what would happen?"

"Death, if I remained away for more than a very few days."

"The atmosphere, then, is essential?"

"There is only one valley of Blue Moon, and those who expect to find another are asking too much of nature."

"Well, what would have happened if you had left the valley, say, thirty years ago, during your prolonged youth?"

Chang answered: "Probably I should have died even then. In any case, I should have acquired very quickly the full appearance of my actual age. We had a curious example of that some years ago, though there had been several others before. One of our number had left the valley to look out for a party of travelers whom we had heard might be approaching. This man, a Russian, had arrived here originally in the prime of life, and had taken to our ways so well that at nearly eighty he did not look more than half as old. He should have been absent no longer than a week (which would not have mattered), but unfortunately he was taken prisoner by nomad tribes and carried away some distance. We suspected an accident and gave him up for lost. Three months later, however, he returned to us, having made his escape. But he was a very different man. Every year of his age was in his face and behavior, and he died shortly afterwards, as an old man dies."

Conway made no remark for some time. They were talking in

the library, and during most of the narrative he had been gazing through a window towards the pass that led to the outer world; a little wisp of cloud had drifted across the ridge. "A rather grim story, Chang," he commented at length. "It gives one the feeling that Time is like some balked monster, waiting outside the valley to pounce on the slackers who have managed to evade him longer than they should."

"*Slackers?*" queried Chang. His knowledge of English was extremely good, but sometimes a colloquialism proved unfamiliar.

" 'Slacker,' " explained Conway, "is a slang word meaning a lazy fellow, a good-for-nothing. I wasn't, of course, using it seriously."

Chang bowed his thanks for the information. He took a keen interest in languages, and liked to weigh a new word philosophically. "It is significant," he said after a pause, "that the English regard slackness as a vice. We, on the other hand, should vastly prefer it to tension. Is there not too much tension in the world at present, and might it not be better if more people were slackers?"

"I'm inclined to agree with you," Conway answered with solemn amusement.

During the course of a week or so after the interview with the High Lama, Conway met several others of his future colleagues. Chang was neither eager nor reluctant to make the introductions, and Conway sensed a new and to him rather attractive atmosphere in which urgency did not clamor nor postponement disappoint. "Indeed," as Chang explained, "some of the lamas may not meet you for a considerable time—perhaps years—but you must not be surprised at that. They are prepared to make your acquaintance when it may so happen, and their avoidance of hurry does not imply any degree of unwillingness." Conway, who had often had similar feelings when calling on new arrivals at foreign consulates, thought it a very intelligible attitude.

The meetings he did have, however, were quite successful, and conversation with men thrice his age held none of the social embarrassments that might have obtruded in London or Delhi. His first encounter was with a genial German named Meister, who had entered the lamasery during the 'eighties, as the survivor of an exploring party. He spoke English well, though with an accent. A day or two later a second introduction took place, and Conway enjoyed his first talk with the man whom the High Lama had particularly mentioned—Alphonse Briac, a wiry, small-statured Frenchman who did not look especially old, though he announced himself as a pupil of Chopin. Conway thought that both he and the German would prove agreeable company. Already he was subconsciously analyzing, and after a few further meetings he reached one or two general conclusions; he perceived that though the lamas he met had individual differences, they all possessed that quality for which agelessness was not an outstandingly good name, but the only one he could think of. Moreover, they were all endowed with a calm intelligence which pleasantly overflowed into measured and well-balanced opinions. Conway could give an exact response to that kind of approach, and he was aware that they realized it and were gratified. He found them quite as easy to get on with as any other group of cultured people he might have met, though there was often a sense of oddity in hearing reminiscences so distant and apparently so casual. One white-haired and benevolent-looking person, for instance, asked Conway, after a little conversation, if he were interested in the Brontës. Conway said he was, to some extent, and the other replied: "You see, when I was a curate in the West Riding during the 'forties, I once visited Haworth and stayed at the Parsonage. Since coming here I've made a study of the whole Brontë problem—indeed, I'm writing a book on the subject. Perhaps you might care to go over it with me sometime?"

Conway responded cordially, and afterwards, when he and Chang were left together, commented on the vividness with which the lamas appeared to recollect their pre-Tibetan lives. Chang answered that it was all part of the training. "You see, my dear sir, one of the first steps towards the clarifying of the mind is to obtain a panorama of one's own past, and that, like any other view, is more accurate in perspective. When you have been among us long enough you will find your old life slipping gradually into focus as through a telescope when the lens is adjusted. Everything will stand out still and clear, duly proportioned and with its correct significance. Your new acquaintance, for instance, discerns that the really big moment of his entire life occurred when he was a young man visiting a house in which there lived an old parson and his three daughters."

"So I suppose I shall have to set to work to remember my own big moments?"

"It will not be an effort. They will come to you."

"I don't know that I shall give them much of a welcome," answered Conway moodily.

But whatever the past might yield, he was discovering happiness in the present. When he sat reading in the library, or playing Mozart in the music room, he often felt the invasion of a deep spiritual emotion, as if Shangri-La were indeed a living essence, distilled from the magic of the ages and miraculously preserved against time and death. His talk with the High Lama recurred memorably at such moments; he sensed a calm intelligence brooding gently over every diversion, giving a thousand whispered reassurances to ear and eye. Thus he would listen while Lo-Tsen marshaled some intricate fugue rhythm, and wonder what lay behind the faint impersonal smile that stirred her lips into the likeness of an opening flower. She talked very little, even though she now knew that Conway could speak her language; to Mallinson, who liked to visit the music room sometimes, she was almost dumb. But Conway discerned a charm that was perfectly expressed by her silences.

Once he asked Chang her history, and learned that she came

of royal Manchu stock. "She was betrothed to a prince of Turkestan, and was traveling to Kashgar to meet him when her carriers lost their way in the mountains. The whole party would doubtless have perished but for the customary meeting with our emissaries."

"When did this happen?"

"In 1884. She was eighteen."

"Eighteen *then?*"

Chang bowed. "Yes, we are succeeding very well with her, as you may judge for yourself. Her progress has been consistently excellent."

"How did she take things when she first came?"

"She was, perhaps, a little more than averagely reluctant to accept the situation—she made no protest, but we were aware that she was troubled for a time. It was, of course, an unusual occurrence—to intercept a young girl on the way to her wedding. . . . We were all particularly anxious that she should be happy here." Chang smiled blandly. "I am afraid the excitement of love does not make for an easy surrender, though the first five years proved ample for their purpose."

"She was deeply attached, I suppose, to the man she was to have married?"

"Hardly that, my dear sir, since she had never seen him. It was the old custom, you know. The excitement of her affections was entirely impersonal."

Conway nodded, and thought a little tenderly of Lo-Tsen. He pictured her as she might have been half a century before, statuesque in her decorated chair as the carriers toiled over the plateau, her eyes searching the wind-swept horizons that must have seemed so harsh after the gardens and lotus-pools of the East. "Poor child!" he said, thinking of such elegance held captive over the years. Knowledge of her past increased rather than lessened his content with her stillness and silence; she was like a lovely cold vase, unadorned save by an escaping ray.

He was also content, though less ecstatically, when Briac

talked to him of Chopin, and played the familiar melodies with much brilliance. It appeared that the Frenchman knew several Chopin compositions that had never been published, and as he had written them down, Conway devoted pleasant hours to memorizing them himself. He found a certain piquancy in the reflection that neither Cortot nor Pachmann had been so fortunate. Nor were Briac's recollections at an end; his memory continually refreshed him with some little scrap of tune that the composer had thrown off or improvised on some occasion; he took them all down on paper as they came into his head, and some were very delightful fragments. "Briac," Chang explained, "has not long been initiated, so you must make allowances if he talks a great deal about Chopin. The younger lamas are naturally preoccupied with the past; it is a necessary step to envisaging the future."

"Which is, I take it, the job of the older ones?"

"Yes. The High Lama, for instance, spends almost his entire life in clairvoyant meditation."

Conway pondered a moment and then said: "By the way, when do you suppose I shall see him again?"

"Doubtless at the end of the first five years, my dear sir."

But in that confident prophecy Chang was wrong, for less than a month after his arrival at Shangri-La Conway received a second summons to that torrid upper room. Chang had told him that the High Lama never left his apartments, and that their heated atmosphere was necessary for his bodily existence; and Conway, being thus prepared, found the change less disconcerting than before. Indeed, he breathed easily as soon as he had made his bow and been granted the faintest answering liveliness of the sunken eyes. He felt kinship with the mind beyond them, and though he knew that this second interview following so soon upon the first was an unprecedented honor, he was not in the least nervous or weighed down with solemnity. Age was to him no more an obsessing factor than rank or color; he had never felt debarred from liking people because they were too young or too old. He held the High Lama in most cordial respect, but he did not see why their social relations should be anything less than urbane.

They exchanged the usual courtesies, and Conway answered many polite questions. He said he was finding the life very agreeable and had already made friendships.

"And you have kept our secrets from your three companions?"

"Yes, up to now. It has proved awkward for me at times, but probably less so than if I had told them."

"Just as I surmised; you have acted as you thought best. And the awkwardness, after all, is only temporary. Chang tells me he thinks that two of them will give little trouble."

"I dare say that is so."

"And the third?"

Conway replied: "Mallinson is an excitable youth—he's pretty keen to get back."

"You like him?"

"Yes, I like him very much."

At this point the tea-bowls were brought in, and talk became less serious between sips of the scented liquid. It was an apt convention, enabling the verbal flow to acquire a touch of that almost frivolous fragrance, and Conway was responsive. When the High Lama asked him whether Shangri-La was not unique in his experience, and if the Western world could offer anything in the least like it, he answered with a smile: "Well, yes—to be quite frank, it reminds me very slightly of Oxford, where I used to lecture. The scenery there is not so good, but the subjects of study are often just as impractical, and though even the oldest of the dons is not quite so old, they appear to age in a somewhat similar way."

"You have a sense of humor, my dear Conway," replied the High Lama, "for which we shall all be grateful during the years to come."

10

"Extraordinary," Chang said, when he heard that Conway had seen the High Lama again. And from one so reluctant to employ superlatives, the word was significant. It had never happened before, he emphasized, since the routine of the lamasery became established; never had the High Lama desired a second meeting until the five years' probation had effected a purge of all the exile's likely emotions. "Because, you see, it is a great strain on him to talk to the average newcomer. The mere presence of human passions is an unwelcome and, at his age, an almost unendurable unpleasantness. Not that I doubt his entire wisdom in the matter. It teaches us, I believe, a lesson of great value—that even the fixed rules of our community are only moderately fixed. But it is extraordinary, all the same."

To Conway, of course, it was no more extraordinary than anything else, and after he had visited the High Lama on a third and fourth occasion, he began to feel that it was not very extraordinary at all. There seemed, indeed, something almost preordained in the ease with which their two minds approached each other; it was as if in Conway all secret tensions were relaxed, giving him, when he came away, a sumptuous tranquillity. At times he had the sensation of being completely bewitched by the mastery of that central intelligence, and then, over the little pale blue tea-bowls, the cerebration would contract into a liveliness so gentle and miniature that he had an impression of a theorem dissolving limpidly into a sonnet.

Their talks ranged far and fearlessly; entire philosophies were unfolded; the long avenues of history surrendered themselves for inspection and were given new plausibility. To Conway it was an entrancing experience, but he did not suspend the critical attitude, and once, when he had argued a point, the High Lama replied: "My son, you are young in years, but I perceive that your wisdom has the ripeness of age. Surely some unusual thing has happened to you?"

Conway smiled. "No more unusual than has happened to many others of my generation."

"I have never met your like before."

Conway answered after an interval: "There's not a great deal of mystery about it. That part of me which seems old to you was worn out by intense and premature experience. My years from nineteen to twenty-two were a supreme education, no doubt, but rather exhausting."

"You were very unhappy at the War?"

"Not particularly so. I was excited and suicidal and scared and reckless and sometimes in a tearing rage—like a few million others, in fact. I got mad-drunk and killed and lechered in great style. It was the self-abuse of all one's emotions, and one came through it, if one did at all, with a sense of almighty boredom and fretfulness. That's what made the years afterwards so difficult. Don't think I'm posing myself too tragically—I've had pretty fair luck since, on the whole. But it's been rather like being in a school where there's a bad headmaster—plenty of fun to be got if you feel like it, but nerve-racking off and on, and not really very satisfactory. I think I found that out rather more than most people."

"And your education thus continued?"

Conway gave a shrug. "Perhaps the exhaustion of the passions is the beginning of wisdom, if you care to alter the proverb."

"That also, my son, is the doctrine of Shangri-La."

"I know. It makes me feel quite at home."

He had spoken no less than the truth. As the days and weeks passed he began to feel an ache of contentment uniting mind and body; like Perrault and Henschell and the others, he was falling under the spell. Blue Moon had taken him, and there was no escape. The mountains gleamed around in a hedge of inaccessible purity, from which his eyes fell dazzled to the green depths of the valley; the whole picture was incomparable, and when he heard the harpsichord's silver monotony across the lotus-pool, he felt that it threaded the perfect pattern of sight and sound.

He was, and he knew it, very quietly in love with the little Manchu. His love demanded nothing, not even reply; it was a tribute of the mind, to which his senses added only a flavor. She stood for him as a symbol of all that was delicate and fragile; her stylized courtesies and the touch of her fingers on the keyboard yielded a completely satisfying intimacy. Sometimes he would address her in a way that might, if she had cared, have led to less formal conversation; but her replies never broke through the exquisite privacy of her thoughts, and in a sense he did not wish them to. He had suddenly come to realize a single facet of the promised jewel; he had Time, Time for everything that he wished to happen, such Time that desire itself was quenched in the certainty of fulfillment. A year, a decade hence, there would still be Time. The vision grew on him, and he was happy with it.

Then, at intervals, he stepped into the other life to encounter Mallinson's impatience, Barnard's heartiness, and Miss Brinklow's robust intention. He felt he would be glad when they all knew as much as he; and, like Chang, he could imagine that neither the American nor the missionary would prove difficult cases. He was even amused when Barnard once said: "You know, Conway, I'm not sure that this wouldn't be a nice little place to settle down in. I thought at first I'd miss the newspapers and the movies, but I guess one can get used to anything."

"I guess one can," agreed Conway.

He learned afterwards that Chang had taken Barnard down to the valley, at his own request, to enjoy everything in the way of a "night out" that the resources of the locality could provide. Mallinson, when he heard of this, was rather scornful. "Getting tight, I suppose," he remarked to Conway, and to Barnard himself he commented: "Of course it's none of my business, but you'll want to keep yourself pretty fit for the journey, you know. The porters are due in a fortnight's time, and from what I gather, the return trip won't be exactly a joy ride."

Barnard nodded equably. "I never figgered it would," he answered. "And as for keeping fit, I guess I'm fitter than I've been for years. I get exercise daily, I don't have any worries, and the speakeasies down in the valley don't let you go too far. Moderation, y'know—the motto of the firm."

"Yes, I've no doubt you've been managing to have a moderately good time," said Mallinson acidly.

"Certainly I have. This establishment caters for all tastes—some people like little Chink gels who play the pi-anno, isn't that so? You can't blame anybody for what they fancy."

Conway was not at all put out, but Mallinson flushed like a schoolboy. "You can send them to jail, though, when they fancy other people's property," he snapped, stung to fury that set a raw edge to his wits.

"Sure, if you can catch 'em." The American grinned affably. "And that leads me to something I may as well tell you folks right away, now we're on the subject. I've decided to give those porters a miss. They come here pretty regular, and I'll wait for the next trip, or maybe the next but one. That is, if the monks'll take my word that I'm still good for my hotel expenses."

"You mean you're not coming with us?"

"That's it. I've decided to stop over for a while. It's all very fine for you—you'll have the band playing when *you* get home, but all the welcome I'll get is from a row of cops. And the more I think about it, the more it don't seem good enough."

"In other words, you're just afraid to face the music?"

"Well, I never did like music, anyhow."

Mallinson said with cold scorn: "I suppose it's your own affair. Nobody can prevent you from stopping here all your life if you feel inclined." Nevertheless he looked round with a flash of appeal. "It's not what everybody would choose to do, but ideas differ. What do you say, Conway?"

"I agree. Ideas *do* differ."

Mallinson turned to Miss Brinklow, who suddenly put down her book and remarked: "As a matter of fact, I think I shall stay too."

"*What?*" they all cried together.

She continued, with a bright smile that seemed more an attachment to her face than an illumination of it: "You see, I've been thinking over the way things happened to bring us all here, and there's only one conclusion I can come to. There's a mysterious power working behind the scenes. Don't you think so, Mr. Conway?"

Conway might have found it hard to reply, but Miss Brinklow went on in a gathering hurry: "Who am I to question the dictates of Providence? I was sent here for a purpose, and I shall stay."

"Do you mean you're hoping to start a mission here?" Mallinson asked.

"Not only hoping, but fully intending. I know just how to deal with these people—I shall get my own way, never fear. There's no real grit in any of them."

"And you intend to introduce some?"

"Yes, I do, Mr. Mallinson. I'm strongly opposed to that idea of moderation that we hear so much about. You can call it broadmindedness if you like, but in my opinion it leads to the worst kinds of laxity. The whole trouble with the people here is their so-called broadmindedness, and I intend to fight it with all my powers."

"And they're so broadminded that they're going to let you?" said Conway, smiling.

"Or else she's so strong-minded that they can't stop her," put in Barnard. He added with a chuckle: "It's just what I said—this establishment caters for all tastes."

"Possibly, if you happen to *like* prison," Mallinson snapped.

"Well, there's two ways of looking even at that. My goodness, if you think of all the folks in the world who'd give all they've got to be out of the racket and in a place like this, only they can't *get* out! Are *we* in the prison or are *they?*"

"A comforting speculation for a monkey in a cage," retorted Mallinson; he was still furious.

Afterwards he spoke to Conway alone. "That man still gets on my nerves," he said, pacing the courtyard. "I'm not sorry we shan't have him with us when we go back. You may think me touchy, but being chipped about that Chinese girl didn't appeal to my sense of humor."

Conway took Mallinson's arm. It was becoming increasingly clear to him that he was very fond of the youth, and that their recent weeks in company had deepened the feeling, despite jarring moods. He answered: "I rather took it that *I* was being ragged about her, not you."

"No, I think he intended it for me. He knows I'm interested in her. I am, Conway. I can't make out why she's here, and whether she really likes being here. My God, if I spoke her language as you do, I'd soon have it out with her."

"I wonder if you would. She doesn't say a great deal to any one, you know."

"It puzzles me that you don't badger her with all sorts of questions."

"I don't know that I care for badgering people."

He wished he could have said more, and then suddenly the sense of pity and irony floated over him in a filmy haze; this youth, so eager and ardent, would take things very hardly. "I shouldn't worry about Lo-Tsen if I were you," he added. "She's happy enough."

The decision of Barnard and Miss Brinklow to remain behind seemed to Conway all to the good, though it threw Mallinson and himself into an apparently opposite camp for the time being. It was an extraordinary situation, and he had no definite plans for tackling it.

Fortunately there was no apparent need to tackle it at all. Until the two months were past, nothing much could happen; and afterwards there would be a crisis no less acute for his having tried to prepare himself for it. For this and other reasons he was disinclined to worry over the inevitable, though he did once say: "You know, Chang, I'm bothered about young Mallinson. I'm afraid he'll take things very badly when he finds out."

Chang nodded with some sympathy. "Yes, it will not be easy to persuade him of his good fortune. But the difficulty is, after all, only a temporary one. In twenty years from now our friend will be quite reconciled."

Conway felt that this was looking at the matter almost too philosophically. "I'm wondering," he said, "just how the truth's going to be broached to him. He's counting the days to the arrival of the porters, and if they don't come—"

"But they *will* come."

"Oh? I rather imagined that all your talk about them was just a pleasant fable to let us down lightly."

"By no means. Although we have no bigotry on the point, it is our custom at Shangri-La to be moderately truthful, and I can assure you that my statements about the porters were almost correct. At any rate, we are expecting the men at or about the time I said."

"Then you'll find it hard to stop Mallinson from joining them."

"But we should never attempt to do so. He will merely discover—no doubt by personal experiment—that the porters are reluctantly unable to take any one back with them."

"I see. So that's the method? And what do you expect to happen afterwards?"

"Then, my dear sir, after a period of disappointment, he will—since he is young and optimistic—begin to hope that the next convoy of porters, due in nine or ten months' time, will prove more amenable to his suggestions. And this is a hope which, if we are wise, we shall not at first discourage."

Conway said sharply: "I'm not so sure that he'll do that at all. I should think he's far more likely to try an escape on his own."

"*Escape?* Is that *really* the word that should be used? After all, the pass is open to any one at any time. We have no jailers, save those that Nature herself has provided."

Conway smiled. "Well, you must admit that she's done her job pretty well. But I don't suppose you rely on her in every case, all the same. What about the various exploring parties that have arrived here? Was the pass always equally open to *them* when they wanted to get away?"

It was Chang's turn now to smile. "Special circumstances, my dear sir, have sometimes required special consideration."

"Excellent. So you only allow people the chance of escape when you know they'd be fools to take it? Even so, I expect some of them do."

"Well, it has happened very occasionally, but as a rule the absentees are glad to return after the experience of a single night on the plateau."

"Without shelter and proper clothing? If so, I can quite understand that your mild methods are as effective as stern ones. But what about the less usual cases that don't return?"

"You have yourself answered the question," replied Chang. "They do *not* return." But he made haste to add: "I can assure you, however, that there are few indeed who have been so unfortunate, and I trust your friend will not be rash enough to increase the number."

Conway did not find these responses entirely reassuring, and Mallinson's future remained a preoccupation. He wished it were

possible for the youth to return by consent, and this would not
be unprecedented, for there was the recent case of Talu, the airman. Chang admitted that the authorities were fully empow-
ered to do anything that they considered wise. "But *should* we
be wise, my dear sir, in trusting ourselves and our future entirely
to your friend's feelings of gratitude?"

Conway felt that the question was pertinent, for Mallinson's
attitude left little doubt as to what he would do as soon as he
reached India. It was his favorite theme, and he had often en-
larged upon it.

But all that, of course, was in the mundane world that was
gradually being pushed out of his mind by the rich, pervasive
world of Shangri-La. Except when he thought about Mallinson
he was extraordinarily content; the slowly revealed fabric of this
new environment continued to astonish him by its intricate suita-
bility to his own needs and tastes.

Once he said to Chang: "By the way, how do you people here
fit love into your scheme of things? I suppose it does sometimes
happen that those who come here develop attachments?"

"Quite often," replied Chang with a broad smile. "The lamas,
of course, are immune, and so are most of us when we reach the
riper years, but until then we are as other men, except that I
think we can claim to behave more reasonably. And this gives
me the opportunity, Mr. Conway, of assuring you that the hospitality of Shangri-La is of a comprehensive kind. Your friend Mr.
Barnard has already availed himself of it."

Conway returned the smile. "Thanks," he answered dryly.
"I've no doubt he has, but my own inclinations are not—at the
moment—so assertive. It was the emotional more than the physical aspect that I was curious about."

"You find it easy to separate the two? Is it possible that you
are falling in love with Lo-Tsen?"

Conway was somewhat taken aback, though he hoped he did
not show it. "What makes you ask that?"

"Because, my dear sir, it would be quite suitable if you were to do so—always, of course, in moderation. Lo-Tsen would not respond with any degree of passion—that is more than you could expect—but the experience would be very delightful, I assure you. And I speak with some authority, for I was in love with her myself when I was much younger."

"Were you indeed? And did she respond then?"

"Only by the most charming appreciation of the compliment I paid her, and by a friendship which has grown more precious with the years."

"In other words, she didn't respond?"

"If you prefer it so." Chang added, a little sententiously: "It has always been her way to spare her lovers the moment of satiety that goes with all absolute attainment."

Conway laughed. "That's all very well in your case, and perhaps in mine too—but what about the attitude of a hot-blooded young fellow like Mallinson?"

"My dear sir, it would be the best possible thing that could happen! Not for the first time, I assure you, would Lo-Tsen comfort the sorrowful exile when he learns that there is to be no return."

"*Comfort?*"

"Yes, though you must not misunderstand my use of the term. Lo-Tsen gives no caresses, except such as touch the stricken heart from her very presence. What does your Shakespeare say of Cleopatra?—'She makes hungry where she most satisfies.' A popular type, doubtless, among the passion-driven races, but such a woman, I assure you, would be altogether out of place at Shangri-La. Lo-Tsen, if I might amend the quotation, *removes* hunger where she *least* satisfies. It is a more delicate and lasting accomplishment."

"And one, I assume, which she has much skill in performing?"

"Oh, decidedly—we have had many examples of it. It is her way to calm the throb of desire to a murmur that is no less pleasant when left unanswered."

"In that sense, then, you could regard her as a part of the training equipment of the establishment?"

"*You* could regard her as that, if you wished," replied Chang with deprecating blandness. "But it would be more graceful, and just as true, to liken her to the rainbow reflected in a glass bowl or to the dewdrops on the blossom of the fruit tree."

"I entirely agree with you, Chang. That would be *much* more graceful." Conway enjoyed the measured yet agile repartees which his good-humored ragging of the Chinese very often elicited.

But the next time he was alone with the little Manchu he felt that Chang's remarks had had a great deal of shrewdness in them. There was a fragrance about her that communicated itself to his own emotions, kindling the embers to a glow that did not burn, but merely warmed. And suddenly then he realized that Shangri-La and Lo-Tsen were quite perfect, and that he did not wish for more than to stir a faint and eventual response in all that stillness. For years his passions had been like a nerve that the world jarred on; now at last the aching was soothed, and he could yield himself to love that was neither a torment nor a bore. As he passed by the lotus-pool at night he sometimes pictured her in his arms, but the sense of time washed over the vision, calming him to an infinite and tender reluctance.

He did not think he had ever been so happy, even in the years of his life before the great barrier of the War. He liked the serene world that Shangri-La offered him, pacified rather than dominated by its single tremendous idea. He liked the prevalent mood in which feelings were sheathed in thoughts, and thoughts softened into felicity by their transference into language. Conway, whom experience had taught that rudeness is by no means a guarantee of good faith, was even less inclined to regard a well-turned phrase as a proof of insincerity. He liked the mannered, leisurely atmosphere in which talk was an accomplishment, not a mere habit. And he liked to realize that the idlest things could now be freed from the curse of time-wasting, and the frailest dreams receive the welcome of the mind. Shangri-La was always tranquil, yet always a hive of unpursuing occupations; the lamas lived as if indeed they had time on their hands, but time that was scarcely a feather-weight. Conway met no more of them, but he came gradually to realize the extent and variety of their employments; besides their knowledge of languages, some, it appeared, took to the full seas of learning in a manner that would have yielded big surprises to the Western world. Many were engaged in writing manuscript books of various kinds; one (Chang said) had made valuable researches into pure mathematics; another was co-ordinating Gibbon and Spengler into a vast thesis on the history of European civilization. But this kind of thing was not for them all, nor for any of them always; there were many tideless channels in which they dived in mere waywardness, retrieving, like Briac, fragments of old tunes, or like the English ex-curate, a new theory about *Wuthering Heights*. And there were even fainter impracticalities than these. Once, when Conway made some remark in this connection, the High Lama replied with a story of a Chinese artist in the third century B.C. who, having spent many years in carving dragons, birds, and horses upon a cherry stone, offered his finished work to a royal prince. The prince could see nothing in it at first except a mere stone, but the artist bade him "have a wall built, and make a window in it, and observe the stone through the window in the glory of the dawn." The prince did so, and then perceived that the stone was indeed very beautiful. "Is not that a charming story, my dear Conway, and do you not think it teaches a very valuable lesson?"

Conway agreed; he found it pleasant to realize that the serene purpose of Shangri-La could embrace an infinitude of odd and apparently trivial employments, for he had always had a taste for such things himself. In fact, when he regarded his past, he saw it strewn with images of tasks too vagrant or too taxing ever to have been accomplished; but now they were all possible, even in a mood of idleness. It was delightful to contemplate, and he was not disposed to sneer when Barnard confided in him that he too envisaged an interesting future at Shangri-La.

It seemed that Barnard's excursions to the valley, which had been growing more frequent of late, were not entirely devoted to drink and women. "You see, Conway, I'm telling you this because you're different from Mallinson—he's got his knife into me, as probably you've gathered. But I feel you'll be better at understanding the position. It's a funny thing—you British officials are so darned stiff and starchy at first, but you're the sort a fellow can put his trust in, when all's said and done."

"I wouldn't be too sure," replied Conway, smiling. "And anyhow, Mallinson's just as much a British official as I am."

"Yes, but he's a mere boy. He don't look at things reasonably. You and me are men of the world—we take things as we find them. This joint here, for instance—we still can't understand all the ins and outs of it, and why we've been landed here, but then, isn't that the usual way of things? Do we know why we're in the world at all, for that matter?"

"Perhaps some of us don't, but what's all this leading up to?"

Barnard dropped his voice to a rather husky whisper. "Gold, my lad," he answered with a certain ecstasy. "Just that, and nothing less. There's tons of it—literally—in the valley. I was a mining engineer in my young days and I haven't forgotten what a reef looks like. Believe me, it's as rich as the Rand, and ten times easier to get at. I guess you thought I was on the loose whenever I went down there in my little armchair. Not a bit of it. I knew what I was doing. I'd figgered it out all along, you know, that these guys here couldn't get all their stuff sent in from outside without paying mighty high for it, and what else could they pay with except gold or silver or diamonds or something? Only logic, after all. And when I began to scout round, it didn't take me long to discover the whole bag of tricks."

"You found it out on your own?" asked Conway.

"Well, I won't say that, but I made my guess, and then I put the matter to Chang—straight, mind you, as man to man. And believe me, Conway, that Chink's not as bad a fellow as we might have thought."

"Personally, I never thought him a bad fellow at all."

"Of course, I know you always took to him, so you won't be surprised at the way we got on together. We certainly did hit it off famously. He showed me all over the workings, and it may interest you to know that I've got the full permission of the authorities to prospect in the valley as much as I like and make a comprehensive report. What d'you think of that, my lad? They seemed quite glad to have the services of an expert, especially when I said I could probably give 'em tips on how to increase output."

"I can see you're going to be altogether at home here," said Conway.

"Well, I must say I've found a job, and that's something. And you never know how a thing'll turn out in the end. Maybe the folks at home won't be so keen to jail me when they know I can show 'em the way to a new gold mine. The only difficulty is—would they take my word about it?"

"They might. It's extraordinary what people *will* believe."

Barnard nodded with enthusiasm. "Glad you get the point, Conway. And that's where you and I can make a deal. We'll go fifty-fifty in everything, of course. All you've gotter do is to put your name to my report—British Consul, you know, and all that. It'll carry weight."

Conway laughed. "We'll have to see about it. Make your report first."

It amused him to contemplate a possibility so unlikely to happen, and at the same time he was glad that Barnard had found something that yielded such immediate comfort.

So also was the High Lama, whom Conway began to see more and more frequently. He often visited him in the late evening and stayed for many hours, long after the servants had taken away the last bowls of tea and had been dismissed for the night.

The High Lama never failed to ask him about the progress and welfare of his three companions, and once he enquired particularly as to the kind of careers that their arrival at Shangri-La had so inevitably interrupted.

Conway answered reflectively: "Mallinson might have done quite well in his own line—he's energetic and has ambitions. The two others—" He shrugged his shoulders. "As a matter of fact, it happens to suit them both to stay here—for a while, at any rate."

He noticed a flicker of light at the curtained window; there had been mutterings of thunder as he crossed the courtyards on his way to the now familiar room. No sound could be heard, and the heavy tapestries subdued the lightning into mere sparks of pallor.

"Yes," came the reply, "we have done our best to make both of them feel at home. Miss Brinklow wishes to convert us, and Mr. Barnard would also like to convert us—into a limited liability company. Harmless projects—they will pass the time quite pleasantly for them. But your young friend, to whom neither gold nor religion can offer solace, how about him?"

"Yes, he's going to be the problem."

"I am afraid he is going to be *your* problem."

"Why mine?"

There was no immediate answer, for the tea-bowls were introduced at that moment, and with their appearance the High Lama rallied a faint and desiccated hospitality. "Karakal sends us storms at this time of the year," he remarked, feathering the conversation according to ritual. "The people of Blue Moon believe they are caused by demons raging in the great space beyond the pass. The 'outside,' they call it—perhaps you are aware that in their patois the word is used for the entire rest of the world. Of course they know nothing of such countries as France or England or even India—they imagine the dread altiplano stretching, as it almost does, illimitably. To them, so snug at their warm and windless levels, it appears unthinkable that any one inside the valley should ever wish to leave it; indeed, they picture all unfortunate 'outsiders' as passionately desiring to enter. It is just a question of viewpoint, is it not?"

Conway was reminded of Barnard's somewhat similar remarks, and quoted them. "How very sensible!" was the High Lama's comment. "And he is our first American, too—we are truly fortunate."

Conway found it piquant to reflect that the lamasery's fortune was to have acquired a man for whom the police of a dozen countries were actively searching; and he would have liked to share the piquancy but for feeling that Barnard had better be left to tell his own story in due course. He said: "Doubtless he's quite right, and there are many people in the world nowadays who would be glad enough to be here."

"*Too* many, my dear Conway. We are a single lifeboat riding the seas in a gale; we can take a few chance survivors, but if all the shipwrecked were to reach us and clamber aboard we should go down ourselves. . . . But let us not think of it just now. I hear that you have been associating with our excellent Briac. A delightful fellow countryman of mine, though I do not share his opinion that Chopin is the greatest of all composers. For myself, as you know, I prefer Mozart. . . ."

Not till the tea-bowls were removed and the servant had been finally dismissed, did Conway venture to recall the unanswered question. "We were discussing Mallinson, and you said he was going to be *my* problem. Why mine, particularly?"

Then the High Lama replied very simply: "Because, my son, I am going to die."

It seemed an extraordinary statement, and for a time Conway was speechless after it. Eventually the High Lama continued: "You are surprised? But surely, my friend, we are all mortal—even at Shangri-La. And it is possible that I may still have a few moments left to me—or even, for that matter, a few years. All I announce is the simple truth that already I see the end. It is charming of you to appear so concerned, and I will not pretend that there is not a touch of wistfulness, even at my age, in contemplating death. Fortunately little is left of me that can die physically, and as for the rest, all our religions display a pleasant unanimity of optimism. I am quite content, but I must accustom myself to a strange sensation during the hours that remain—I must realize that I have time for only one thing more. Can you imagine what that is?"

Conway was silent.

"It concerns you, my son."

"You do me a great honor."

"I have in mind to do much more than that."

Conway bowed slightly, but did not speak, and the High Lama, after waiting awhile, resumed: "You know, perhaps, that the frequency of these talks has been unusual here. But it is our tradition, if I may permit myself the paradox, that we are never slaves to tradition. We have no rigidities, no inexorable rules. We do as we think fit, guided a little by the example of the past, but still more by our present wisdom, and by our clairvoyance of the future. And thus it is that I am encouraged to do this final thing."

Conway was still silent.

"I place in your hands, my son, the heritage and destiny of Shangri-La."

At last the tension broke, and Conway felt beyond it the power of a bland and benign persuasion; the echoes swam into silence, till all that was left was his own heartbeat, pounding like a gong. And then, intercepting the rhythm, came the words:

"I have waited for you, my son, for quite a long time. I have sat in this room and seen the faces of newcomers, I have looked into their eyes and heard their voices, and always in hope that some day I might find you. My colleagues have grown old and wise, but you who are still young in years are as wise already. My friend, it is not an arduous task that I bequeath, for our order knows only silken bonds. To be gentle and patient, to care for the riches of the mind, to preside in wisdom and secrecy

while the storm rages without—it will all be very pleasantly simple for you, and you will doubtless find great happiness."

Again Conway sought to reply, but could not, till at length a
vivid lightning-flash paled the shadows and stirred him to exclaim: "The storm . . . this storm you talk of. . . ."

"It will be such a one, my son, as the world has not seen before. There will be no safety by arms, no help from authority, no
answer in science. It will rage till every flower of culture is trampled, and all human things are leveled in a vast chaos. Such was
my vision when Napoleon was still a name unknown; and I see it
now, more clearly with each hour. Do you say I am mistaken?"

Conway answered: "No, I think you may be right. A similar
crash came once before, and then there were the Dark Ages lasting five hundred years."

"The parallel is not quite exact. For those Dark Ages were not
really so very dark—they were full of flickering lanterns, and
even if the light had gone out of Europe altogether, there were
other rays, literally from China to Peru, at which it could have
been rekindled. But the Dark Ages that are to come will cover
the whole world in a single pall; there will be neither escape nor
sanctuary, save such as are too secret to be found or too humble
to be noticed. And Shangri-La may hope to be both of these.
The airman bearing loads of death to the great cities will not
pass our way, and if by chance he should, he may not consider
us worth a bomb."

"And you think all this will come in my time?"

"I believe that you will live through the storm. And after,
through the long age of desolation, you may still live, growing
older and wiser and more patient. You will conserve the fragrance of our history and add to it the touch of your own mind.
You will welcome the stranger, and teach him the rule of age
and wisdom; and one of these strangers, it may be, will succeed
you when you are yourself very old. Beyond that, my vision
weakens, but I see, at a great distance, a new world stirring in
the ruins, stirring clumsily but in hopefulness, seeking its lost

and legendary treasures. And they will all be here, my son, hidden behind the mountains in the valley of Blue Moon, preserved as by miracle for a new Renaissance. . . ."

The speaking finished, and Conway saw the face before him full of a remote and drenching beauty; then the glow faded and there was nothing left but a mask, dark-shadowed, and crumbling like old wood. It was quite motionless, and the eyes were closed. He watched for a while, and presently, as part of a dream, it came to him that the High Lama was dead.

It seemed necessary to rivet the situation to some kind of actuality, lest it become too strange to be believed in; and with instinctive mechanism of hand and eye, Conway glanced at his wrist watch. It was a quarter past midnight. Suddenly, when he crossed the room to the door, it occurred to him that he did not in the least know how or whence to summon help. The Tibetans, he knew, had all been sent away for the night, and he had no idea where to find Chang or any one else. He stood uncertainly on the threshold of the dark corridor; through a window he could see that the sky was clear, though the mountains still blazed in lightning like a silver fresco. And then, in the midst of the still encompassing dream, he felt himself master of Shangri-La. These were his beloved things, all around him, the things of that inner mind in which he lived increasingly, away from the fret of the world. His eyes strayed into the shadows and were caught by golden pinpoints sparkling in rich, undulating lacquers; and the scent of tuberose, so faint that it expired on the very brink of sensation, lured him from room to room. At last he stumbled into the courtyards and by the fringe of the pool; a full moon sailed behind Karakal. It was twenty minutes to two.

Later, he was aware that Mallinson was near him, holding his arm and leading him away in a great hurry. He did not gather what it was all about, but he could hear that the boy was chattering excitedly.

11

THEY REACHED the balconied room where they had meals, Mallinson still clutching his arm and half dragging him along. "Come on, Conway, we've till dawn to pack what we can and get away. Great news, man—I wonder what old Barnard and Miss Brinklow will think in the morning when they find us gone . . . still, it's their own choice to stay, and we'll probably get on far better without them. . . . The porters are about five miles beyond the pass—they came yesterday with loads of books and things . . . tomorrow they begin the journey back. . . . It just shows how these fellows here intended to let us down—they never told us— we should have been stranded here for God knows how much longer. . . . I say, what's the matter? Are you ill?"

Conway had sunk into a chair, and was leaning forward with elbows on the table. He passed his hand across his eyes. "Ill? No, I don't think so. Just—rather—tired."

"Probably the storm. Where were you all the while? I'd been waiting for you for hours."

"I—I was visiting the High Lama."

"Oh, *him!* Well, *that's* for the last time, anyhow, thank God."

"Yes, Mallinson, for the last time."

Something in Conway's voice, and still more in his succeeding silence, roused the youth to irascibility. "Well, I wish you wouldn't sound so deuced leisurely about it—we've got to get a considerable move on, you know."

Conway stiffened for the effort of emerging into keener consciousness. "I'm sorry," he said. Partly to test his nerve and the reality of his sensations he lit a cigarette. He found that both hands and lips were unsteady. "I'm afraid I don't quite follow . . . you say the porters . . ."

"Yes, the porters, man—do pull yourself together."

"You're thinking of going out to them?"

"*Thinking* of it? I'm damn well certain—they're only just over the ridge. And we've got to start immediately."

"*Immediately?*"

"Yes, yes—why not?"

Conway made a second attempt to transfer himself from the one world into the other. He said at length, having partly succeeded: "I suppose you realize that it mayn't be quite as simple as it sounds?"

Mallinson was lacing a pair of knee-high Tibetan mountain-boots as he answered jerkily: "I realize everything, but it's something we've got to do, and we shall do it, with luck, if we don't delay."

"I don't see how—"

"Oh, Lord, Conway, must you fight shy of everything? Haven't you any guts left in you at all?"

The appeal, half passionate and half derisive, helped Conway to collect himself. "Whether I have or haven't isn't the point, but if you want me to explain myself, I will. It's a question of a few rather important details. Suppose you *do* get beyond the pass and find the porters there, how do you know they'll take you with them? What inducement can you offer? Hasn't it struck you that they mayn't be quite so willing as you'd like them to be? You can't just present yourself and demand to be escorted. It all needs arrangement, negotiations beforehand—"

"Or anything else to cause a delay," exclaimed Mallinson bitterly. "God, what a fellow you are! Fortunately I haven't you to rely on for arranging things. Because they *have* been arranged—the porters have been paid in advance, and they've agreed to take us. And here are clothes and equipment for the journey, all ready. So your last excuse disappears. Come on, let's *do* something."

"But—I don't understand. . . ."

"I don't suppose you do, but it doesn't matter."

"Who's been making all these plans?"

Mallinson answered brusquely: "Lo-Tsen, if you're really keen to know. She's with the porters now. She's waiting."

"*Waiting?*"

"Yes. She's coming with us. I assume you've no objection?"

At the mention of Lo-Tsen the two worlds touched and fused suddenly in Conway's mind. He cried sharply, almost contemptuously: "That's nonsense. It's impossible."

Mallinson was equally on edge. "Why is it impossible?"

"Because . . . well, it is. There are all sorts of reasons. Take my word for it; it won't do. It's incredible enough that she should be out there now—I'm astonished at what you say has happened—but the idea of her going any further is just preposterous."

"I don't see that it's preposterous at all. It's as natural for her to want to leave here as for me."

"But she doesn't want to leave. That's where you make the mistake."

Mallinson smiled tensely. "You think you know a good deal more about her than I do, I dare say," he remarked. "But perhaps you don't, for all that."

"What do you mean?"

"There are other ways of getting to understand people without learning heaps of languages."

"For Heaven's sake, what *are* you driving at?" Then Conway added more quietly: "This is absurd. We mustn't wrangle. Tell me, Mallinson, what's it all about? I still don't understand."

"Then why are you making such an almighty fuss?"

"Tell me the truth, *please* tell me the truth."

"Well, it's simple enough. A kid of her age, shut up here with a lot of queer old men—naturally she'll get away if she's given a chance. She hasn't had one up to now."

"Don't you think you may be imagining her position in the light of your own? As I've always told you, she's perfectly happy."

"Then why did she say she'd come?"

"She said that? How could she? She doesn't speak English."

"I asked her—in Tibetan—Miss Brinklow worked out the words. It wasn't a very fluent conversation, but it was quite enough to—to lead to an understanding." Mallinson flushed a little. "Damn it, Conway, don't stare at me like that—any one would think I'd been poaching on *your* preserves."

Conway answered: "No one would think so at all, I hope, but the remark tells me more than you were perhaps intending me to know. I can only say that I'm very sorry."

"And why the devil should you be?"

Conway let the cigarette fall from his fingers. He felt tired, bothered, and full of deep conflicting tendernesses that he would rather not have had aroused. He said gently: "I wish we weren't always at such cross purposes. Lo-Tsen is very charming, I know, but why should we quarrel about it?"

"*Charming?*" Mallinson echoed the word with scorn. "She's a good bit more than that. You mustn't think everybody's as cold-blooded about these things as you are yourself. Admiring her as if she were an exhibit in a museum may be your idea of what she deserves, but mine's more practical, and when I see some one I like in a rotten position I try and *do* something."

"But surely there's such a thing as being too impetuous? Where do you think she'll go to if she does leave?"

"I suppose she must have friends in China or somewhere. Anyhow, she'll be better off than here."

"How can you possibly be so sure of that?"

"Well, I'll see that she's looked after myself, if nobody else will. After all, if you're rescuing people from something quite hellish, you don't usually stop to enquire if they've anywhere else to go to."

"And you think Shangri-La is hellish?"

"Definitely, I do. There's something dark and evil about it. The whole business has been like that, from the beginning—the way we were brought here, without reason at all, by some madman—and the way we've been detained since, on one excuse or another. But the most frightful thing of all—to me—is the effect it's had on you."

"On *me?*"

"Yes, on you. You've just mooned about as if nothing mattered and you were content to stay here for ever. Why, you even admitted you liked the place. . . . Conway, what *has* happened to you? Can't you manage to be your real self again? We got on so well together at Baskul—you were absolutely different in those days."

"My *dear* boy!"

Conway reached his hand towards Mallinson's, and the answering grip was hot and eagerly affectionate. Mallinson went on: "I don't suppose you realize it, but I've been terribly alone these last few weeks. Nobody seemed to be caring a damn about the only thing that was really important—Barnard and Miss Brinklow had reasons of a kind, but it was pretty awful when I found *you* against me."

"I'm sorry."

"You keep on saying that, but it doesn't help."

Conway replied on sudden impulse: "Then let me help, if I can, by telling you something. When you've heard it, you'll understand, I hope, a great deal of what now seems very curious and difficult. At any rate, you'll realize why Lo-Tsen can't possibly go back with you."

"I don't think anything would make me see that. And do cut it as short as you can, because we really haven't time to spare."

Conway then gave, as briefly as he could, the whole story of Shangri-La, as told him by the High Lama, and as amplified by conversation both with the latter and with Chang. It was the last thing he had ever intended to do, but he felt that in the circumstances it was justified and even necessary; it was true enough that Mallinson *was* his problem, to solve as he thought fit. He narrated rapidly and easily, and in doing so came again under the spell of that strange, timeless world; its beauty overwhelmed him as he spoke of it, and more than once he felt himself reading from a page of memory, so clearly had ideas and phrases impressed themselves. Only one thing he withheld—and that to spare himself an emotion he could not yet grapple with—the fact of the High Lama's death that night and of his own succession.

When he approached the end he felt comforted; he was glad to have got it over, and it was the only solution, after all. He looked up calmly when he had finished, confident that he had done well.

But Mallinson merely tapped his fingers on the tabletop and said, after a long wait: "I really don't know what to say, Conway . . . except that you must be completely mad. . . ."

There followed a long silence, during which the two men stared at each other in far differing moods—Conway withdrawn and disappointed, Mallinson in hot, fidgeting discomfort. "So you think I'm mad?" said Conway at length.

Mallinson broke into a nervous laugh. "Well, I should damn well say so, after a tale like that. I mean . . . well, really . . . such utter nonsense . . . it seems to me rather beyond arguing about."

Conway looked and sounded immensely astonished. "You think it's nonsense?"

"Well . . . how else can I look at it? I'm sorry, Conway—it's a pretty strong statement—but I don't see how any sane person could be in any doubt about it."

"So you still hold that we were brought here by blind accident —by some lunatic who made careful plans to run off with an aeroplane and fly it a thousand miles just for the fun of the thing?"

Conway offered a cigarette, and the other took it. The pause was one for which they both seemed grateful. Mallinson answered eventually: "Look here, it's no good arguing the thing point by point. As a matter of fact, your theory that the people here sent some one vaguely into the world to decoy strangers, and that this fellow deliberately learned flying and bided his time until it happened that a suitable machine was due to leave Baskul with four passengers . . . well, I won't say that it's literally impossible, though it does seem to me ridiculously far-fetched. If it stood by itself, it might just be worth considering, but when you tack it on to all sorts of other things that are *absolutely* impossible—all this about the lamas being hundreds of years old, and having discovered a sort of elixir of youth, or whatever you'd call it . . . well, it just makes me wonder what kind of microbe has bitten you, that's all."

Conway smiled. "Yes, I dare say you find it hard to believe. Perhaps I did myself at first—I scarcely remember. Of course it *is* an extraordinary story, but I should think your own eyes have had enough evidence that this is an extraordinary place. Think of all that we've actually seen, both of us—a lost valley in the midst of unexplored mountains, a monastery with a library of European books—"

"Oh, yes, and a central heating plant, and modern plumbing, and afternoon tea, and everything else—it's all very marvelous, I know."

"Well, then, what do you make of it?"

"Damn little, I admit. It's a complete mystery. But that's no reason for accepting tales that are physically impossible. Believing in hot baths because you've had them is different from believing in people hundreds of years old just because they've told you they are." He laughed again, still uneasily. "Look here, Conway, it's got on your nerves, this place, and I really don't wonder at it. Pack up your things and let's quit. We'll finish this argument a month or two hence after a jolly little dinner at Maiden's."

Conway answered quietly: "I've no desire to go back to that life at all."

"What life?"

"The life you're thinking of . . . dinners . . . dances . . . polo . . . all that. . . ."

"But I never said anything about dances and polo! Anyhow, what's wrong with them? D'you mean that you're not coming with me? You're going to stay here like the other two? Then at least you shan't stop *me* from clearing out of it!" Mallinson threw down his cigarette and sprang towards the door with eyes blazing. "You're off your head!" he cried wildly. "You're mad, Conway, that's what's the matter with you! I know you're always calm, and I'm always excited, but I'm sane, at any rate, and you're not! They warned me about it before I joined you at Baskul, and I thought they were wrong, but now I can see they weren't—"

"What did they warn you of?"

"They said you'd been blown up in the War, and you'd been queer at times ever since. I'm not reproaching you—I know it was nothing you could help—and Heaven knows I hate talking like this. . . . Oh, I'll go. It's all frightful and sickening, but I must go. I gave my word."

"To Lo-Tsen?"

"Yes, if you want to know."

Conway got up and held out his hand. "Good-by, Mallinson."

"For the last time, you're not coming?"

"I can't."

"Good-by, then."

They shook hands, and Mallinson left.

Conway sat alone in the lantern-light. It seemed to him, in a phrase engraved on memory, that all the loveliest things were transient and perishable, that the two worlds were finally beyond reconciliation, and that one of them hung, as always, by a thread. After he had pondered for some time he looked at his watch; it was ten minutes to three.

He was still at the table, smoking the last of his cigarettes, when Mallinson returned. The youth entered with some commotion, and on seeing him, stood back in the shadows as if to gather his wits. He was silent, and Conway began, after waiting a moment: "Hullo, what's happened? Why are you back?"

The complete naturalness of the question fetched Mallinson forward; he pulled off his heavy sheepskins and sat down. His face was ashen and his whole body trembled. "I hadn't the nerve," he cried, half sobbing. "That place where we were all roped—you remember? I got as far as that. . . . I couldn't manage it. I've no head for heights, and in moonlight it looked fearful. Silly, isn't it?" He broke down completely and was hysterical until Conway pacified him. Then he added: "They needn't worry, these fellows here—nobody will ever threaten them by land. But, my God, I'd give a good deal to fly over with a load of bombs!"

"Why would you like to do that, Mallinson?"

"Because the place wants smashing up, whatever it is. It's unhealthy and unclean—and for that matter, if your impossible yarn were true, it would be more hateful still! A lot of wizened old men crouching here like spiders for any one who comes near . . . it's filthy . . . who'd want to live to an age like that, anyhow? And as for your precious High Lama, if he's half as old as you say he is, it's time some one put him out of his misery. . . . Oh, why *don't* you come away with me, Conway? I hate imploring you for my own sake, but damn it all, I'm young and we've been pretty good friends together—does my whole life mean nothing to you compared with the lies of these awful creatures? And Lo-Tsen, too—*she's* young—doesn't *she* count at all?"

"Lo-Tsen is not young," said Conway.

Mallinson looked up and began to titter hysterically. "Oh, no, not young—not young at all, of course. She looks about seventeen, but I suppose you'll tell me she's really a well-preserved ninety."

"Mallinson, she came here in 1884."

"You're raving, man!"

"Her beauty, Mallinson, like all other beauty in the world, lies at the mercy of those who do not know how to value it. It is a fragile thing that can only live where fragile things are loved. Take it away from this valley and you will see it fade like an echo."

Mallinson laughed harshly, as if his own thoughts gave him confidence. "I'm not afraid of that. It's here that she's only an echo, if she's one anywhere at all." He added after a pause: "Not that this sort of talk gets us anywhere. We'd better cut out all the poetic stuff and come down to realities. Conway, I want to help you—it's all the sheerest nonsense, I know, but I'll argue it out if it'll do you any good. I'll pretend it's something possible that you've told me, and that it really does need examining. Now tell me, seriously, what evidence have you for this story of yours?"

Conway was silent.

"Merely that some one spun you a fantastic rigmarole. Even from a thoroughly reliable person whom you'd known all your life, you wouldn't accept that sort of thing without proof. And what proofs have you in this case? None at all, so far as I can see. Has Lo-Tsen ever told you her history?"

"No, but—"

"Then why believe it from some one else? And all this longevity business—can you point to a single outside fact in support of it?"

Conway thought a moment and then mentioned the unknown Chopin works that Briac had played.

"Well, that's a matter that means nothing to me—I'm not a musician. But even if they're genuine, isn't it possible that he could have got hold of them in some way without his story being true?"

"Quite possible, no doubt."

"And then this method that you say exists—of preserving youth and so on. What is it? You say it's a sort of drug—well, I want to know *what* drug? Have you ever seen it or tried it? Did any one ever give you any positive facts about the thing at all?"

"Not in detail, I admit."

"And you never asked for details? It didn't strike you that such a story needed any confirmation at all? You just swallowed it whole?" Pressing his advantage, he continued: "How much do you actually know of this place, apart from what you've been told? You've seen a few old men—that's all it amounts to. Apart from that, we can only say that the place is well fitted up, and seems to be run on rather highbrow lines. How and why it came into existence we've no idea, and why they want to keep us here, if they do, is equally a mystery, but surely all that's hardly an excuse for believing any old legend that comes along! After all, man, you're a critical sort of person—you'd hesitate to believe all you were told even in an English monastery—I really can't see why you should jump at everything just because you're in Tibet!"

Conway nodded. Even in the midst of far keener perceptions he could not restrain approval of a point well made. "That's an acute remark, Mallinson. I suppose the truth is that when it comes to believing things without actual evidence, we all incline to what we find most attractive."

"Well, I'm dashed if I can see anything attractive about living till you're half dead. Give me a short life and a gay one, for choice. And this stuff about a future war—it all sounds pretty thin to me. How does any one know when the next war's going to be or what it'll be like? Weren't all the prophets wrong about the last war?" He added, when Conway did not reply: "Anyhow, I don't believe in saying things are inevitable. And even if they were, there's no need to get into a funk about them. Heaven knows I'd most likely be scared stiff if I had to fight in a war, but I'd rather face up to it than bury myself here."

Conway smiled. "Mallinson, you have a superb knack of misunderstanding me. When we were at Baskul you thought I was a hero—now you take me for a coward. In point of fact, I'm neither

—though of course it doesn't matter. When you get back to India you can tell people, if you like, that I decided to stay in a Tibetan monastery because I was afraid there'd be another war. It isn't my reason at all, but I've no doubt it'll be believed by the people who already think me mad."

Mallinson answered rather sadly: "It's silly, you know, to talk like that. Whatever happens, I'd never say a word against you. You can count on that. I don't understand you—I admit that—but —but—I wish I did. Oh, I wish I did. Conway, can't I possibly help you? Isn't there anything I can say or do?"

There was a long silence after that, which Conway broke at last by saying: "There's just a question I'd like to ask—if you'll forgive me for being terribly personal."

"Yes?"

"Are you in love with Lo-Tsen?"

The youth's pallor changed quickly to a flush. "I dare say I am. I know you'll say it's absurd and unthinkable, and probably it is, but I can't help my feelings."

"I don't think it's absurd at all."

The argument seemed to have sailed into a harbor after many buffetings, and Conway added: "I can't help *my* feelings either. You and that girl happen to be the two people in the world I care most about . . . though you may think it odd of me." Abruptly he got up and paced the room. "We've said all we *can* say, haven't we?"

"Yes, I suppose we have." But Mallinson went on, in a sudden rush of eagerness: "Oh, what stupid nonsense it all is—about her not being young! And foul and horrible nonsense, too. Conway, you *can't* believe it! It's just too ridiculous. How can it really mean anything?"

"How can you really know that she's young?"

Mallinson half turned away, his face lit with a grave shyness. "Because I *do* know. . . . Perhaps you'll think less of me for it . . . but I *do* know. I'm afraid you never properly understood her, Conway. She was cold on the surface, but that was the result of living here—it had frozen all the warmth. But the warmth was there."

"To be unfrozen?"

"Yes . . . that would be one way of putting it."

"And she's *young*, Mallinson—you are so *sure* of that?"

Mallinson answered softly: "God, yes—she's just a girl. I was terribly sorry for her, and we were both attracted, I suppose. I don't see that it's anything to be ashamed of. In fact in a place like this I should think it's about the decentest thing that's ever happened. . . ."

Conway went to the balcony and gazed at the dazzling plume of Karakal; the moon was riding high in a waveless ocean. It came to him that a dream had dissolved, like all too lovely things, at the first touch of reality; that the whole world's future, weighed in the balance against youth and love, would be light as air. And he knew, too, that his mind dwelt in a world of its own, Shangri-La in microcosm, and that this world also was in peril. For even as he nerved himself, he saw the corridors of his imagination twist and strain under impact; the pavilions were toppling; all was about to be in ruins. He was only partly unhappy, but he was infinitely and rather sadly perplexed. He did not know whether he had been mad and was now sane, or had been sane for a time and was now mad again.

When he turned, there was a difference in him; his voice was keener, almost brusque, and his face twitched a little; he looked much more the Conway who had been a hero at Baskul. Clenched for action, he faced Mallinson with a suddenly new alertness. "Do you think you could manage that tricky bit with a rope if I were with you?" he asked.

Mallinson sprang forward. "*Conway!*" he cried chokingly. "You mean you'll *come?* You've made up your mind at last?"

They left as soon as Conway had prepared himself for the journey. It was surprisingly simple to leave—a departure rather than an escape; there were no incidents as they crossed the bars of moonlight and shadow in the courtyards. One might have thought there was no one there at all, Conway reflected; and immediately the idea of such emptiness became an emptiness in himself; while all the time, though he hardly heard him, Mallinson was chattering about the journey. How strange that their long argument should have ended thus in action, that this secret sanctuary should be forsaken by one who had found in it such happiness! For indeed, less than an hour later, they halted breathlessly at a curve of the track and saw the last of Shangri-La. Deep below them the valley of Blue Moon was like a cloud, and to Conway the scattered roofs had a look of floating after him through the haze. Now, at that moment, it was farewell. Mallinson, whom the steep ascent had kept silent for a time, gasped out: "Good man, we're doing fine—carry on!"

Conway smiled, but did not reply; he was already preparing the rope for the knife-edge traverse. It was true, as the youth had said, that he had made up his mind; but it was only what was left of his mind. That small and active fragment now dominated; the rest comprised an absence hardly to be endured. He was a wanderer between two worlds and must ever wander; but for the present, in a deepening inward void, all he felt was that he liked Mallinson and must help him; he was doomed, like millions, to flee from wisdom and be a hero.

Mallinson was nervous at the precipice, but Conway got him over in traditional mountaineering fashion, and when the trial was past, they leaned together over Mallinson's cigarettes. "Conway, I must say it's damned good of you. . . . Perhaps you guess how I feel. . . . I can't tell you how glad I am. . . ."

"I wouldn't try, then, if I were you."

After a long pause, and before they resumed the journey, Mallinson added: "But I *am* glad—not only for my own sake, but for yours as well. . . . It's fine that you can realize now that all that stuff was sheer nonsense . . . it's just wonderful to see you your real self again. . . ."

"Not at all," responded Conway with a wryness that was for his own private comforting.

Towards dawn they crossed the divide, unchallenged by sentinels, even if there were any; though it occurred to Conway that the route, in the true spirit, might only be moderately well watched. Presently they reached the plateau, picked clean as a bone by roaring winds, and after a gradual descent the encampment of porters came in sight. Then all was as Mallinson had foretold; they found the men ready for them, sturdy fellows in furs and sheepskins, crouching under the gale and eager to begin the journey to Tatsien-Fu—eleven hundred miles eastward on the China border.

"He's coming with us!" Mallinson cried excitedly when they met Lo-Tsen. He forgot that she knew no English; but Conway translated.

It seemed to him that the little Manchu had never looked so radiant. She gave him a most charming smile, but her eyes were all for the boy.

EPILOGUE

It was in Delhi that I met Rutherford again. We had been
guests at a Viceregal dinner-party, but distance and ceremonial
kept us apart until the turbaned flunkeys handed us our hats afterwards. "Come back to my hotel and have a drink," he invited.

We shared a cab along the arid miles between the Lutyens
still-life and the warm, palpitating motion picture of Old Delhi. I
knew from the newspapers that he had just returned from Kashgar. His was one of those well-groomed reputations that get the
most out of everything; any unusual holiday acquires the character of an exploration, and though the explorer takes care to do
nothing really original, the public does not know this, and he
capitalizes the full value of a hasty impression. It had not
seemed to me, for instance, that Rutherford's journey, as re-
ported in the press, had been particularly epoch-making; the
buried cities of Khotan were old stuff, if any one remembered
Stein and Sven Hedin. I knew Rutherford well enough to chaff
him about this, and he laughed. "Yes, the truth would have
made a better story," he admitted cryptically.

We went to his hotel room and drank whisky. "So you *did*
search for Conway?" I suggested when the moment seemed pro-
pitious.

"Search is much too strong a word," he answered. "You can't
search a country half as big as Europe for one man. All I can say
is that I visited places where I was prepared to come across him

or to get news of him. His last message, you remember, was that he had left Bangkok for the northwest. There were traces of him up-country for a little way, and my own opinion is that he probably made for the tribal districts on the Chinese border. I don't think he'd have cared to enter Burma, where he might have run up against British officials. Anyhow, the definite trail, you may say, peters out somewhere in Upper Siam, but of course I never expected to follow it far that end."

"You thought it might be easier to look for the valley of Blue Moon?"

"Well, it did seem as if it might be a more fixed proposition. I suppose you glanced at that manuscript of mine?"

"Much more than glanced at it. I should have returned it, by the way, but you left no address."

Rutherford nodded. "I wonder what you made of it?"

"I thought it very remarkable—assuming, of course, that it's all quite genuinely based on what Conway told you."

"I give you my solemn word for that. I invented nothing at all —indeed, there's even less of my own language in it than you might think. I've a good memory, and Conway always had a way of describing things. Don't forget that we had about twenty-four hours of practically continuous talk."

"Well, as I said, it's all very remarkable."

He leaned back and smiled. "If that's all you're going to say, I can see I shall have to speak for myself. I suppose you consider me a rather credulous person. I don't really think I am. People make mistakes in life through believing too much, but they have a damned dull time if they believe too little. I was certainly taken with Conway's story—in more ways than one—and that was why I felt interested enough to put as many tabs on it as I could —apart from the chance of running up against the man himself."

He went on, after lighting a cigar: "It meant a good deal of odd journeying, but I like that sort of thing, and my publishers can't object to a travel book once in a while. Altogether I must have done some thousands of miles—Baskul, Bangkok, Chung-

Kiang, Kashgar—I visited them all, and somewhere inside the area between them the mystery lies. But it's a pretty big area, you know, and all my investigations didn't touch more than the fringe of it—or of the mystery either, for that matter. Indeed, if you want the actual downright facts about Conway's adventures, so far as I've been able to verify them, all I can tell you is that he left Baskul on the twentieth of May and arrived in Chung-Kiang on the fifth of October. And the last we know of him is that he left Bangkok again on the third of February. All the rest is probability, possibility, guesswork, myth, legend, whatever you like to call it."

"So you didn't find anything in Tibet?"

"My dear fellow, I never got into Tibet at all. The people up at Government House wouldn't hear of it; it's as much as they'll do to sanction an Everest expedition, and when I said I thought of wandering about the Kuen-Luns on my own, they looked at me rather as if I'd suggested writing a life of Gandhi. As a matter of fact, they knew more than I did. Strolling about Tibet isn't a one-man job; it needs an expedition properly fitted out and run by some one who knows at least a word or two of the language. I remember when Conway was telling me his story I kept wondering why there was all that fuss about waiting for porters—why didn't they all simply walk off? I wasn't very long in discovering. The Government people were quite right—all the passports in the world couldn't have got me over the Kuen-Luns. I actually went as far as seeing them in the distance, on a very clear day— perhaps fifty miles off. Not many Europeans can claim even that."

"Are they so very forbidding?"

"They looked just like a white frieze on the horizon, that was all. At Yarkand and Kashgar I questioned every one I met about them, but it was extraordinary how little I could discover. I should think they must be the least-explored range in the world. I had the luck to meet an American traveler who had once tried to cross them, but he'd been unable to find a pass. There *are* passes, he said, but they're terrifically high and unmapped. I asked him if he thought it possible for a valley to exist of the kind Conway described, and he said he wouldn't call it impossible, but he thought it not very likely—on geological grounds, at any rate. Then I asked if he had ever heard of a cone-shaped mountain almost as high as the highest of the Himalayas, and his answer to that was rather intriguing. There was a legend, he said, about such a mountain, but he thought himself there could be no foundation for it. There were even rumors, he added, about mountains actually higher than Everest, but he didn't himself give credit to them. 'I doubt if any peak in the Kuen-Luns is more than twenty-five thousand feet, if that,' he said. But he admitted that they had never been properly surveyed.

"Then I asked him what he knew about Tibetan lamaseries—he'd been in the country several times—and he gave me just the usual accounts that one can read in all the books. They weren't beautiful places, he assured me, and the monks in them were generally corrupt and dirty. 'Do they live long?' I asked, and he said, yes, they often did, if they didn't die of some filthy disease. Then I went boldly to the point and asked if he'd ever heard legends of extreme longevity among the lamas. 'Heaps of them,' he answered; 'it's one of the stock yarns you hear everywhere, but you can't verify them. You're told that some foul-looking creature has been walled up in a cell for a hundred years, and he certainly looks as if he might have been, but of course you can't demand his birth certificate.' I asked him if he thought they had any occult or medicinal way of prolonging life or preserving youth, and he said they were supposed to have a great deal of very curious knowledge about such things, but he suspected that if you came to look into it, it was rather like the Indian rope trick—always something that somebody else had seen. He did say, however, that the lamas appeared to have odd powers of bodily control. 'I've watched them,' he said, 'sitting by the edge of a frozen lake, stark naked, with a temperature below zero and in a tearing wind, while their servants break the ice and wrap sheets round them that have been dipped in the water. They do this a dozen times or more, and the lamas dry the sheets on their own bodies. Keeping warm by will power, so one imagines, though that's a poor sort of explanation.'"

Rutherford helped himself to more drink. "But of course, as my American friend admitted, all that had nothing much to do with longevity. It merely showed that the lamas had somber tastes in self-discipline. . . . So there we were, and probably you'll agree with me that all the evidence, so far, was less than you'd hang a dog on."

I said it was certainly inconclusive, and asked if the names "Karakal" and "Shangri-La" had meant anything to the American.

"Not a thing—I tried him with them. After I'd gone on questioning him for a time, he said: 'Frankly, I'm not keen on monasteries—indeed, I once told a fellow I met in Tibet that if I went out of my way at all, it would be to avoid them, not pay them a visit.' That chance remark of his gave me a curious idea, and I asked him when this meeting in Tibet had taken place. 'Oh, a long time ago,' he answered, 'before the War—in nineteen-eleven, I think it was.' I badgered him for further details, and he gave them, as well as he could remember. It seemed that he'd been traveling then for some American geographical society, with several colleagues, porters, and so on—in fact, a pukka expedition. Somewhere near the Kuen-Luns he met this other man, a Chinese who was being carried in a chair by native bearers. The fellow turned out to speak English quite well, and strongly recommended them to visit a certain lamasery in the neighborhood —he even offered to be the guide there. The American said they hadn't time and weren't interested, and that was that." Rutherford went on, after an interval: "I don't suggest that it means a great deal. When a man tries to remember a casual incident that happened twenty years ago, you can't build *too* much on it. But it offers an attractive speculation."

"Yes, though if a well-equipped expedition had accepted the

invitation, I don't see how they could have been detained at the lamasery against their will."

"Oh, quite. And perhaps it wasn't Shangri-La at all."

We thought it over, but it seemed too hazy for argument, and I went on to ask if there had been any discoveries at Baskul.

"Baskul was hopeless, and Peshawur was worse. Nobody could tell me anything, except that the kidnaping of the aeroplane did undoubtedly take place. They weren't keen even to admit that—it's an episode they're not proud of."

"And nothing was heard of the plane afterwards?"

"Not a word or a rumor, or of its four passengers either. I verified, however, that it was capable of climbing high enough to cross the ranges. I also tried to trace that fellow Barnard, but I found his past history so mysterious that I wouldn't be at all surprised if he really were Chalmers Bryant, as Conway said. After all, Bryant's complete disappearance in the midst of the big hue and cry was rather amazing."

"Did you try to find anything about the actual kidnaper?"

"I did, but again it was hopeless. The Air Force man whom the fellow had knocked out and impersonated had since been killed, so one promising line of enquiry was closed. I even wrote to a friend of mine in America who runs an aviation school, asking if he had had any Tibetan pupils lately, but his reply was prompt and disappointing. He said he couldn't differentiate Tibetans from Chinese, and he had had about fifty of the latter—all training to fight the Japs. Not much chance there, you see. But I did make one rather quaint discovery—and which I could have made just as easily without leaving London. There was a German professor at Jena about the middle of the last century who took to globe-trotting and visited Tibet in 1887. He never came back, and there was some story about him having been drowned in fording a river. His name was Friedrich Meister."

"Good heavens—one of the names Conway mentioned!"

"Yes—though it may only have been coincidence. It doesn't

prove the whole story, by any means, because the Jena fellow
was born in 1845. Nothing very exciting about that."

"But it's odd," I said.

"Oh, yes, it's odd enough."

"Did you succeed in tracing any of the others?"

"No. It's a pity I hadn't a longer list to work on. I couldn't find
any record of a pupil of Chopin's called Briac, though of course
that doesn't prove that there wasn't one. Conway was pretty spar-
ing with his names, when you come to think about it—out of
fifty-odd lamas supposed to be on the premises he only gave us
one or two. Perrault and Henschell, by the way, proved equally
impossible to trace."

"How about Mallinson?" I asked. "Did you try to find out
what had happened to him? And that girl—the Chinese girl?"

"My dear fellow, of course I did. The awkward part was, as
you perhaps gathered from the manuscript, that Conway's story
ended at the moment of leaving the valley with the porters.
After that he either couldn't or wouldn't tell me what happened
—perhaps he might have done, mind you, if there'd been more
time. I feel that we can guess at some sort of tragedy. The
hardships of the journey would be perfectly appalling, apart
from the risk of brigandage or even treachery among their own
escorting party. Probably we shall never know exactly what did
occur, but it seems tolerably certain that Mallinson never
reached China. I made all sorts of enquiries, you know. First of
all I tried to trace details of books, et cetera, sent in large con-
signments across the Tibetan frontier, but at all the likely
places, such as Shanghai and Pekin, I drew complete blanks.
That, of course, doesn't count for much, since the lamas would
doubtless see that their methods of importation were kept secret.
Then I tried at Tatsien-Fu. It's a weird place, a sort of world's-
end market town, deuced difficult to get at, where the Chinese
coolies from Yunnan transfer their loads of tea to the Tibetans.
You can read about it in my new book when it comes out. Europeans don't often get as far. I found the people quite civil and

courteous, but there was absolutely no record of Conway's party arriving at all."

"So how Conway himself reached Chung-Kiang is still unexplained?"

"The only conclusion is that he wandered there, just as he might have wandered anywhere else. Anyhow, we're back in the realm of hard facts when we get to Chung-Kiang, that's something. The nuns at the mission hospital were genuine enough, and so, for that matter, was Sieveking's excitement on the ship when Conway played that pseudo-Chopin." Rutherford paused and then added reflectively: "It's really an exercise in the balancing of probabilities, and I must say the scales don't bump very emphatically either way. Of course if you don't accept Conway's story, it means that you doubt either his veracity or his sanity—one may as well be frank."

He paused again, as if inviting a comment, and I said: "As you know, I never saw him after the War, but people said he was a good deal changed by it."

Rutherford answered: "Yes, and he was, there's no denying the fact. You can't subject a mere boy to three years of intense physical and emotional stress without tearing something to tatters. People would say, I suppose, that he came through without a scratch. But the scratches were there—on the inside."

We talked for a little time about the War and its effects on various people, and at length he went on: "But there's just one more point that I must mention—and perhaps in some ways the oddest of all. It came out during my enquiries at the mission. They all did their best for me there, as you can guess, but they couldn't recollect much, especially as they'd been so busy with a fever epidemic at the time. One of the questions I put was about the manner Conway had reached the hospital first of all—whether he had presented himself alone, or had been found ill and been taken there by some one else. They couldn't exactly remember—after all, it was a long while back—but suddenly, when I was on the point of giving up the cross-examination, one of the nuns remarked quite casually, 'I think the doctor said he was brought here by a woman.' That was all she could tell me, and as the doctor himself had left the mission, there was no confirmation to be had on the spot.

"But having got so far, I wasn't in any mood to give up. It appeared that the doctor had gone to a bigger hospital in Shanghai, so I took the trouble to get his address and call on him there. It was just after the Jap air-raiding, and things were pretty grim. I'd met the man before during my first visit to Chung-Kiang, and he was very polite, though terribly overworked—yes, terribly's the word, for, believe me, the air raids on London by the Germans were just nothing to what the Japs did to the native parts of Shanghai. Oh, yes, he said instantly, he remembered the case of the Englishman who had lost his memory. Was it true he had been brought to the mission hospital by a woman? I asked. Oh, yes, certainly, by a woman, a Chinese woman. Did he remember anything about her? Nothing, he answered, except that she had been ill of the fever herself, and had died almost immediately. . . . Just then there was an interruption—a batch of wounded were carried in and packed on stretchers in the corridors—the wards were all full—and I didn't care to go on taking up the man's time, especially as the thudding of the guns at Woosung was a reminder that he would still have plenty to do. When he came back to me, looking quite cheerful even amidst such ghastliness, I just asked him one final question, and I dare say you can guess what it was. 'About that Chinese woman,' I said. 'Was she young?'"

Rutherford flicked his cigar as if the narration had excited him quite as much as he hoped it had me. Continuing, he said: "The little fellow looked at me solemnly for a moment, and then answered in that funny clipped English that the educated Chinese have—'Oh, no, she was most old—most old of any one I have ever seen.'"

We sat for a long time in silence, and then talked again of Conway as I remembered him, boyish and gifted and full of charm, and of the War that had altered him, and of so many mysteries of time and age and of the mind, and of the little Manchu who had been "most old," and of the strange ultimate dream of Blue Moon. "Do you think he will ever find it?" I asked.

WOODFORD GREEN
April, 1933

Good-bye, Mr. Chips

FOREWORD

JAMES HILTON was not only a very good novelist, he was a very good talker. Though he was English-born, he lived for the latter part of his life in California, and on my visits to the Coast I always looked forward to having a leisurely dinner with him, in the course of which we would compare notes about everything under the sun. I remember well our last meeting, for it occurred shortly after we had learned for sure that the Russians had perfected, far ahead of schedule, their atomic bomb. Jimmie was depressed by the news, for in his farsighted way he saw at once that this would involve us in the most dangerous armament race in human history.

I knew that he was at work on a new novel and at a favorable opening I asked how it was going. "I have made four beginnings," he said. "I think I have got a good idea and for about a week I'll start off each morning at the typewriter with a feeling of confidence. And then just after I have passed page fifty, it is as if the words 'So what!' suddenly stood out in capitals on the page. We haven't got the confidence we once had, now that we know about those bombs. It is a hard time in which to try to write fiction."

Good-bye, Mr. Chips, Hilton's most successful novel, and surely the most endearing portrait of a schoolteacher in our time, was written in another kind of desperation. In November, 1933, James Hilton was struggling to meet his deadline for a story for the Christmas issue of the *British Weekly*. He needed the fifty pounds (then two hundred and fifty dollars) he would be paid for the story; and he hadn't an idea. After a sleepless night, he rose and went for a bicycle ride in the foggy dawn. When he returned, ravenous, for breakfast he had his lead, and *Mr. Chips* was written in longhand and almost without alteration in the four days that followed. It was published with little notice in London, but when it appeared in the *Atlantic* the following April, the American acclaim woke up the English. Everywhere you went you heard people talking about Mr. Chips as if he were someone they had known. Bishop William A. Lawrence spoke of *Mr. Chips* in a sermon at Trinity Church in Boston; William Lyon Phelps, the most quoted professor in New Haven, said it was "a masterpiece and ought to be so regarded a hundred years from now"; and Alexander Woollcott, who as the Town Crier had a more stimulating effect on readers at that period than any other single person, devoted a whole broadcast to *Mr. Chips,* which he called "the most profoundly moving story that has passed this way in several years."

To Jimmie Hilton the theme was as natural as breathing. His father was a headmaster, and at the boarding school where Jimmie was sent, he was happy. Had he cared more for athletics he might have been less observant of his teachers. But he was a roly-poly, good tempered, and no good at games. His mind was inquiring and responsive: he wrote poems about the Russian Revolution and the sinking of the *Lusitania,* and broke all speed records for reciting the long Latin grace.

Mr. Chips, as Hilton drew him, is a composite; he has the wise and sweetening influence of Jimmie's father, the discipline and idiosyncrasy of his Latin teacher, and the unsparing devotion which the profession demands of all. And this was why people wrote him from all parts of the globe to say that they had been taught by the original Mr. Chips. He was thirty-three when he wrote this story, but it established him for life.

Edward Weeks

PREFACE

GOOD-BYE, MR. CHIPS was written in London during a foggy week of November 1933. I am chary of using the word "inspiration," which is too often something nonexistent that a writer waits for when he is lazy; but, as a matter of record, *Good-bye, Mr. Chips* was written more quickly, more easily, and with fewer subsequent alterations than anything I had ever written before, or have ever written since.

It was first published in the Christmas number of the *British Weekly*, in December 1933; after which, with a certain wild abandon, I had it sent to the *Atlantic Monthly*—a magazine which I had long held as a secret pinnacle of ambition. The *Atlantic* printed the story in its issue of April 1934, and about the same time proposed its publication as a book. This publication took place on June 8. Four months later *Good-bye, Mr. Chips* first appeared as a book in England, from Messrs. Hodder and Stoughton. Thus one may summarize that, having been written and first printed in its native land, it was discovered by America, and later came back to England with the success that America had given it. And now, again in America, it appears in this new and sumptuous dress.

If I recount these details with pride, I do so also with modesty, for I know how few are the writers to whom such romances happen, and that, with no matter how much or little merit, a portion of luck must be distilled. But I do take pride in the reception that America has given to my very English book; certainly no author could ever have enjoyed his correspondence more than I have during the past year. One feature has been the discovery of the original Mr. Chips in so many different parts of the world; and I believe those letters from readers have told the whole truth, and that my tribute to a great profession has fitted a great many members of it everywhere.

J. H.

Wanstead, London
March 1935

GOOD-BYE, MR. CHIPS

1

WHEN you are getting on in years (but not ill, of course), you get very sleepy at times, and the hours seem to pass like lazy cattle moving across a landscape. It was like that for Chips as the autumn term progressed and the days shortened till it was actually dark enough to light the gas before call-over. For Chips, like some old sea captain, still measured time by the signals of the past; and well he might, for he lived at Mrs. Wickett's, just across the road from the School. He had been there more than a decade, ever since he finally gave up his mastership; and it was Brookfield far more than Greenwich time that both he and his landlady kept. "Mrs. Wickett," Chips would sing out, in that jerky, high-pitched voice that had still a good deal of sprightliness in it, "you might bring me a cup of tea before prep, will you?"

When you are getting on in years it is nice to sit by the fire and drink a cup of tea and listen to the School bell sounding dinner, call-over, prep, and lights-out. Chips always wound up the clock after that last bell; then he put the wire guard in front of the fire, turned out the gas, and carried a detective novel to bed. Rarely did he read more than a page of it before sleep came swiftly and peacefully, more like a mystic intensifying of perception than any changeful entrance into another world. For his days and nights were equally full of dreaming.

He was getting on in years (but not ill, of course); indeed, as

Doctor Merivale said, there was really nothing the matter with him. "My dear fellow, you're fitter than I am," Merivale would say, sipping a glass of sherry when he called every fortnight or so. "You're past the age when people get these horrible diseases; you're one of the few lucky ones who're going to die a really natural death. That is, of course, if you die at all. You're such a remarkable old boy that one never knows." But when Chips had a cold or when east winds roared over the fenlands, Merivale would sometimes take Mrs. Wickett aside in the lobby and whisper: "Look after him, you know. His chest . . . it puts a strain on his heart. Nothing really wrong with him—only anno domini, but that's the most fatal complaint of all, in the end."

Anno domini . . . by Jove, yes. Born in 1848, and taken to the Great Exhibition as a toddling child—not many people still alive could boast a thing like that. Besides, Chips could even remember Brookfield in Wetherby's time. A phenomenon, that was. Wetherby had been an old man in those days—1870—easy to remember because of the Franco-Prussian War. Chips had put in for Brookfield after a year at Melbury, which he hadn't liked, because he had been ragged there a good deal. But Brookfield he *had* liked, almost from the beginning. He remembered that day of his preliminary interview—sunny June, with the air full of flower scents and the plick-plock of cricket on the pitch. Brookfield was playing Barnhurst, and one of the Barnhurst boys, a chubby little fellow, made a brilliant century. Queer that a thing like that should stay in the memory so clearly. Wetherby himself was very fatherly and courteous; he must have been ill then, poor chap, for he died during the summer vacation, before Chips began his first term. But the two had seen and spoken to each other, anyway.

Chips often thought, as he sat by the fire at Mrs. Wickett's: I am probably the only man in the world who has a vivid recollection of old Wetherby. . . . Vivid, yes; it was a frequent picture in his mind, that summer day with the sunlight filtering through the dust in Wetherby's study. "You are a young man,

Mr. Chipping, and Brookfield is an old foundation. Youth and age often combine well. Give your enthusiasm to Brookfield, and Brookfield will give you something in return. And don't let any-one play tricks with you. I—er—gather that discipline was not al-ways your strong point at Melbury?"

"Well, no, perhaps not, sir."

"Never mind; you're full young; it's largely a matter of experi-ence. You have another chance here. Take up a firm attitude from the beginning—that's the secret of it."

Perhaps it was. He remembered that first tremendous ordeal of taking prep; a September sunset more than half a century ago; Big Hall full of lusty barbarians ready to pounce on him as their legitimate prey. His youth, fresh-complexioned, high-collared, and side-whiskered (odd fashions people followed in those days), at the mercy of five hundred unprincipled ruffians to whom the baiting of new masters was a fine art, an exciting sport, and something of a tradition. Decent little beggars indi-vidually, but, as a mob, just pitiless and implacable. The sudden hush as he took his place at the desk on the dais; the scowl he assumed to cover his inward nervousness; the tall clock ticking behind him, and the smells of ink and varnish; the last blood-red rays slanting in slabs through the stained-glass windows. Some-one dropped a desk lid. Quickly, he must take everyone by sur-prise; he must show that there was no nonsense about him. "You there in the fifth row—you with the red hair—what's your name?" "Colley, sir." "Very well, Colley, you have a hundred lines." No trouble at all after that. He had won his first round.

And years later, when Colley was an alderman of the City of London and a baronet and various other things, he sent his son (also red-haired) to Brookfield, and Chips would say: "Colley, your father was the first boy I ever punished when I came here twenty-five years ago. He deserved it then, and you deserve it now." How they all laughed; and how Sir Richard laughed when his son wrote home the story in next Sunday's letter!

And again, years after that, many years after that, there was an even better joke. For another Colley had just arrived—son of the Colley who was a son of the first Colley. And Chips would say, punctuating his remarks with that little "umph-um" that had by then become a habit with him: "Colley, you are—umph—a splendid example of—umph—inherited traditions. I remember your grandfather—umph—he could never grasp the Ablative Absolute. A stupid fellow, your grandfather. And your father, too—umph—I remember him—he used to sit at that far desk by the wall—he wasn't much better, either. But I do believe—my dear Colley—that you are—umph—the biggest fool of the lot!" Roars of laughter.

A great joke, this growing old—but a sad joke, too, in a way. And as Chips sat by his fire with autumn gales rattling the windows, the waves of humor and sadness swept over him very often until tears fell, so that when Mrs. Wickett came in with his cup of tea she did not know whether he had been laughing or crying. And neither did Chips himself.

2

Across the road behind a rampart of ancient elms lay Brookfield, russet under its autumn mantle of creeper. A group of eighteenth-century buildings centred upon a quadrangle, and there were acres of playing fields beyond; then came the small dependent village and the open fen country. Brookfield, as Wetherby had said, was an old foundation; established in the reign of Elizabeth, as a grammar school, it might, with better luck, have become as famous as Harrow. Its luck, however, had been not so good; the School went up and down, dwindling almost to nonexistence at one time, becoming almost illustrious at another. It was during one of these latter periods, in the reign of the first George, that the main structure had been rebuilt and large additions made. Later, after the Napoleonic Wars and until mid-Victorian days, the School declined again, both in numbers and in repute. Wetherby, who came in 1840, restored its fortunes somewhat; but its subsequent history never raised it to front-rank status. It was, nevertheless, a good school of the second rank. Several notable families supported it; it supplied fair samples of the history-making men of the age—judges, members of parliament, colonial administrators, a few peers and bishops. Mostly, however, it turned out merchants, manufacturers, and professional men, with a good sprinkling of country squires and parsons. It was the sort of school which, when mentioned, would sometimes

make snobbish people confess that they rather thought they had
heard of it.

But if it had not been this sort of school it would probably not
have taken Chips. For Chips, in any social or academic sense,
was just as respectable, but no more brilliant, than Brookfield itself.

It had taken him some time to realize this, at the beginning.
Not that he was boastful or conceited, but he had been, in his
early twenties, as ambitious as most other young men at such an
age. His dream had been to get a headship eventually, or at any
rate a senior mastership in a really first-class school; it was only
gradually, after repeated trials and failures, that he realized the
inadequacy of his qualifications. His degree, for instance, was
not particularly good, and his discipline, though good enough
and improving, was not absolutely reliable under all conditions.
He had no private means and no family connections of any importance. About 1880, after he had been at Brookfield a decade,
he began to recognize that the odds were heavily against his
being able to better himself by moving elsewhere; but about that
time, also, the possibility of staying where he was began to fill a
comfortable niche in his mind. At forty, he was rooted, settled,
and quite happy. At fifty, he was the doyen of the staff. At sixty,
under a new and youthful Head, he *was* Brookfield—the guest of
honor at Old Brookfeldian dinners, the court of appeal in all
matters affecting Brookfield history and traditions. And in 1913,
when he turned sixty-five, he retired, was presented with a check
and a writing desk and a clock, and went across the road to live
at Mrs. Wickett's. A decent career, decently closed; three cheers
for old Chips, they all shouted, at that uproarious end-of-term
dinner.

Three cheers, indeed; but there was more to come, an un-
guessed epilogue, an encore played to a tragic audience.

3

It was a small but very comfortable and sunny room that Mrs. Wickett let to him. The house itself was ugly and pretentious; but that didn't matter. It was convenient—that was the main thing. For he liked, if the weather were mild enough, to stroll across to the playing fields in an afternoon and watch the games. He liked to smile and exchange a few words with the boys when they touched their caps to him. He made a special point of getting to know all the new boys and having them to tea with him during their first term. He always ordered a walnut cake with pink icing from Reddaway's, in the village, and during the winter term there were crumpets, too—a little pile of them in front of the fire, soaked in butter so that the bottom one lay in a little shallow pool. His guests found it fun to watch him make tea—mixing careful spoonfuls from different caddies. And he would ask the new boys where they lived, and if they had family connections at Brookfield. He kept watch to see that their plates were never empty, and punctually at five, after the session had lasted an hour, he would glance at the clock and say: "Well—umph—it's been very delightful—umph—meeting you like this—I'm sorry—umph—you can't stay. . . ." And he would smile and shake hands with them in the porch, leaving them to race across the road to the School with their comments. "Decent old boy, Chips. Gives you a jolly good tea, anyhow, and you *do* know when he wants you to push off. . . ."

And Chips also would be making his comments—to Mrs. Wickett when she entered his room to clear away the remains of the party. "A most—umph—interesting time, Mrs. Wickett. Young Branksome tells me—umph—that his uncle was Major Collingwood—the Collingwood we had here in—umph—nought-two, I think it was. Dear me, I remember Collingwood very well. I once thrashed him—umph—for climbing on to the gymnasium roof—to get a ball out of the gutter. Might have—umph—broken his neck, the young fool. Do you remember him, Mrs. Wickett? He must have been in your time."

Mrs. Wickett, before she saved money, had been in charge of the linen room at the School.

"Yes, I knew 'im, sir. Cheeky, 'e was to me, gener'ly. But we never 'ad no bad words between us. Just cheeky-like. 'E never meant no harm. That kind never does, sir. Wasn't it 'im that got the medal, sir?"

"Yes, a D.S.O."

"Will you be wanting anything else, sir?"

"Nothing more now—umph—till chapel time. He was killed—in Egypt, I think. . . . Yes—umph—you can bring my supper about then."

"Very good, sir."

A pleasant, placid life, at Mrs. Wickett's. He had no worries; his pension was adequate, and there was a little money saved up besides. He could afford everything and anything he wanted. His room was furnished simply and with schoolmasterly taste: a few bookshelves and sporting trophies; a mantelpiece crowded with fixture cards and signed photographs of boys and men; a worn Turkey carpet; big easy-chairs; pictures on the wall of the Acropolis and the Forum. Nearly everything had come out of his old housemaster's room in School House. The books were chiefly classical, the classics having been his subject; there was, however, a seasoning of history and belles-lettres. There was also a bottom shelf piled up with cheap editions of detective novels. Chips enjoyed these. Sometimes he took down Vergil or Xenophon and read for a few moments, but he was soon back again with Doctor Thorndyke or Inspector French. He was not, despite his long years of assiduous teaching, a very profound classical scholar; indeed, he thought of Latin and Greek far more as dead languages from which English gentlemen ought to know a few quotations than as living tongues that had ever been spoken by living people. He liked those short leading articles in the *Times* that introduced a few tags that he recognized. To be among the dwindling number of people who understood such things was to him a kind of secret and valued freemasonry; it represented, he felt, one of the chief benefits to be derived from a classical education.

So there he lived, at Mrs. Wickett's, with his quiet enjoyments of reading and talking and remembering; an old man, white-haired and only a little bald, still fairly active for his years, drinking tea, receiving callers, busying himself with corrections for the next edition of the Brookfeldian Directory, writing his occasional letters in thin, spidery, but very legible script. He had new masters to tea, as well as new boys. There were two of them that autumn term, and as they were leaving after their visit one of them commented: "Quite a character, the old boy, isn't he? All that fuss about mixing the tea—a typical bachelor, if ever there was one."

Which was oddly incorrect; because Chips was not a bachelor at all. He had married; though it was so long ago that none of the staff at Brookfield could remember his wife.

4

THERE came to him, stirred by the warmth of the fire and the gentle aroma of tea, a thousand tangled recollections of old times. Spring—the spring of 1896. He was forty-eight—an age at which a permanence of habits begins to be predictable. He had just been appointed housemaster; with this and his classical forms, he had made for himself a warm and busy corner of life. During the summer vacation he went up to the Lake District with Rowden, a colleague; they walked and climbed for a week, until Rowden had to leave suddenly on some family business. Chips stayed on alone at Wasdale Head, where he boarded in a small farmhouse.

One day, climbing on Great Gable, he noticed a girl waving excitedly from a dangerous-looking ledge. Thinking she was in difficulties, he hastened toward her, but in doing so slipped himself and wrenched his ankle. As it turned out, she was not in difficulties at all, but was merely signaling to a friend farther down the mountain; she was an expert climber, better even than Chips, who was pretty good. Thus he found himself the rescued instead of the rescuer; and neither rôle was one for which he had much relish. For he did not, he would have said, care for women; he never felt at home or at ease with them; and that monstrous creature beginning to be talked about, the New Woman of the nineties, filled him with horror. He was a quiet, conventional person, and the world, viewed from the haven of

Brookfield, seemed to him full of distasteful innovations; there
was a fellow named Bernard Shaw who had the strangest and
most reprehensible opinions; there was Ibsen, too, with his dis-
turbing plays; and there was this new craze for bicycling which
was being taken up by women equally with men. Chips did not
hold with all this modern newness and freedom. He had a vague
notion, if he ever formulated it, that nice women were weak,
timid, and delicate, and that nice men treated them with a polite
but rather distant chivalry. He had not, therefore, expected to
find a woman on Great Gable; but, having encountered one who
seemed to need masculine help, it was even more terrifying that
she should turn the tables by helping him. For she did. She and
her friend had to. He could scarcely walk, and it was a hard job
getting him down the steep track to Wasdale.

Her name was Katherine Bridges; she was twenty-five—young
enough to be Chips's daughter. She had blue, flashing eyes and
freckled cheeks and smooth straw-colored hair. She too was staying at a farm, on holiday with a girl friend, and as she considered herself responsible for Chips's accident, she used to bicycle
along the side of the lake to the house in which the quiet, middle-aged, serious-looking man lay resting.

That was how she thought of him at first. And he, because she
rode a bicycle and was unafraid to visit a man alone in a farmhouse sitting room, wondered vaguely what the world was coming to. His sprain put him at her mercy, and it was soon revealed
to him how much he might need that mercy. She was a govern-
ess out of a job, with a little money saved up; she read and admired Ibsen; she believed that women ought to be admitted to
the universities; she even thought they ought to have a vote. In
politics she was a radical, with leanings toward the views of people like Bernard Shaw and William Morris. All her ideas and
opinions she poured out to Chips during those summer after-
noons at Wasdale Head; and he, because he was not very articulate, did not at first think it worth while to contradict them. Her
friend went away, but she stayed; what *could* you do with such

a person, Chips thought. He used to hobble with sticks along a footpath leading to the tiny church; there was a stone slab on the wall, and it was comfortable to sit down, facing the sunlight and the green-brown majesty of the Gable and listening to the chatter of—well, yes, Chips had to admit it—a very beautiful girl.

He had never met anyone like her. He had always thought that the modern type, this "new woman" business, would repel him; and here she was, making him positively look forward to the glimpse of her safety bicycle careering along the lakeside road. And she, too, had never met anyone like *him*. She had always thought that middle-aged men who read the *Times* and disapproved of modernity were terrible bores; yet here he was, claiming her interest and attention far more than youths of her own age. She liked him, initially, because he was so hard to get to know, because he had gentle and quiet manners, because his opinions dated from those utterly impossible seventies and eighties and even earlier—yet were, for all that, so thoroughly honest; and because—because his eyes were brown and he looked charming when he smiled. "Of course, *I* shall call you Chips, too," she said, when she learned that was his nickname at school.

Within a week they were head over heels in love; before Chips could walk without a stick, they considered themselves engaged; and they were married in London a week before the beginning of the autumn term.

5

WHEN Chips, dreaming through the hours at Mrs. Wickett's, recollected those days, he used to look down at his feet and wonder which one it was that had performed so signal a service. That, the trivial cause of so many momentous happenings, was the one thing of which details evaded him. But he resaw the glorious hump of the Gable (he had never visited the Lake District since), and the mouse-gray depths of Wastwater under the Screes; he could resmell the washed air after heavy rain, and refollow the ribbon of the pass across to Sty Head. So clearly it lingered, that time of dizzy happiness, those evening strolls by the waterside, her cool voice and her gay laughter. She had been a very happy person, always.

They had both been so eager, planning a future together; but he had been rather serious about it, even a little awed. It would be all right, of course, her coming to Brookfield; other housemasters were married. And she liked boys, she told him, and would enjoy living among them. "Oh, Chips, I'm so glad you are what you are. I was afraid you were a solicitor or a stockbroker or a dentist or a man with a big cotton business in Manchester. When I first met you, I mean. Schoolmastering's so different, so important, don't you think? To be influencing those who are going to grow up and matter to the world . . ."

Chips said he hadn't thought of it like that—or, at least, not often. He did his best; that was all anyone could do in any job.

"Yes, of course, Chips. I do love you for saying simple things like that."

And one morning—another memory gem-clear when he turned to it—he had for some reason been afflicted with an acute desire to depreciate himself and all his attainments. He had told her of his only mediocre degree, of his occasional difficulties of discipline, of the certainty that he would never get a promotion, and of his complete ineligibility to marry a young and ambitious girl. And at the end of it all she had laughed in answer.

She had no parents and was married from the house of an aunt in Ealing. On the night before the wedding, when Chips left the house to return to his hotel, she said, with mock gravity: "This is an occasion, you know—this last farewell of ours. I feel rather like a new boy beginning his first term with you. Not scared, mind you—but just, for once, in a thoroughly respectful mood. Shall I call you 'sir'—or would 'Mr. Chips' be the right thing? 'Mr. Chips,' I think. Good-bye, then—good-bye, Mr. Chips. . . ."

(A hansom clop-clopping in the roadway; green-pale gas lamps flickering on a wet pavement; newsboys shouting something about South Africa; Sherlock Holmes in Baker Street.)

"Good-bye, Mr. Chips. . . ."

6

THERE HAD followed then a time of such happiness that Chips,
remembering it long afterward, hardly believed it could ever
have happened before or since in the world. For his marriage
was a triumphant success. Katherine conquered Brookfield as she
had conquered Chips; she was immensely popular with boys and
masters alike. Even the wives of the masters, tempted at first to
be jealous of one so young and lovely, could not long resist her
charms.

But most remarkable of all was the change she made in Chips.
Till his marriage he had been a dry and rather neutral sort of
person; liked and thought well of by Brookfield in general, but
not of the stuff that makes for great popularity or that stirs great
affection. He had been at Brookfield for over a quarter of a century, long enough to have established himself as a decent fellow
and a hard worker; but just too long for anyone to believe him
capable of ever being much more. He had, in fact, already
begun to sink into that creeping dry rot of pedagogy which is
the worst and ultimate pitfall of the profession; giving the same
lessons year after year had formed a groove into which the other
affairs of his life adjusted themselves with insidious ease. He
worked well; he was conscientious; he was a fixture that gave
service, satisfaction, confidence, everything except inspiration.

And then came this astonishing girl-wife whom nobody had
expected—least of all Chips himself. She made him, to all ap-

pearances, a new man; though most of the newness was really a warming to life of things that were old, imprisoned, and un-guessed. His eyes gained sparkle; his mind, which was ade-quately if not brilliantly equipped, began to move more adven-turously. The one thing he had always had, a sense of humor, blossomed into a sudden richness to which his years lent matu-rity. He began to feel a greater sureness; his discipline improved to a point at which it could become, in a sense, less rigid; he be-came more popular. When he had first come to Brookfield he had aimed to be loved, honored, and obeyed—but obeyed, at any rate. Obedience he had secured, and honor had been granted him; but only now came love, the sudden love of boys for a man who was kind without being soft, who understood them well enough, but not too much, and whose private happiness linked them with their own. He began to make little jokes, the sort that schoolboys like—mnemonics and puns that raised laughs and at the same time imprinted something in the mind. There was one that never failed to please, though it was only a sample of many others. Whenever his Roman History forms came to deal with the Lex Canuleia, the law that permitted patricians to marry plebeians, Chips used to add: "So that, you see, if Miss Plebs wanted Mr. Patrician to marry her, and he said he couldn't, she probably replied: 'Oh yes, you can, you liar!'" Roars of laughter.

And Kathie broadened his views and opinions, also, giving him an outlook far beyond the roofs and turrets of Brookfield, so that he saw his country as something deep and gracious to which Brookfield was but one of many feeding streams. She had a cleverer brain than his, and he could not confute her ideas even if and when he disagreed with them; he remained, for instance, a Conservative in politics, despite all her radical-socialist talk. But even where he did not accept, he absorbed; her young idealism worked upon his maturity to produce an amalgam very gentle and wise.

Sometimes she persuaded him completely. Brookfield, for ex-ample, ran a mission in East London, to which boys and parents contributed generously with money but rarely with personal contact. It was Katherine who suggested that a team from the mission should come up to Brookfield and play one of the School's elevens at soccer. The idea was so revolutionary that from anyone but Katherine it could not have survived its first frosty reception. To introduce a group of slum boys to the serene pleasaunces of better-class youngsters seemed at first a wanton stirring of all kinds of things that had better be left untouched. The whole staff was against it, and the School, if its opinion could have been taken, was probably against it too. Everyone was certain that the East End lads would be hooligans, or else that they would be made to feel uncomfortable; anyhow, there would be "incidents," and everyone would be confused and upset. Yet Katherine persisted.

"Chips," she said, "they're wrong, you know, and I'm right. I'm looking ahead to the future, they and you are looking back to the past. England isn't always going to be divided into officers and 'other ranks.' And those Poplar boys are just as important—to England—as Brookfield is. You've got to have them here, Chips. You can't satisfy your conscience by writing a check for a few guineas and keeping them at arm's length. Besides, they're proud of Brookfield—just as you are. Years hence, maybe, boys of that sort will be coming here—a few of them, at any rate. Why not? Why ever not? Chips, dear, remember this is eighteen-ninety-seven—not sixty-seven, when you were up at Cambridge. You got your ideas well stuck in those days, and good ideas they were too, a lot of them. But a few—just a few, Chips—want unsticking. . . ."

Rather to her surprise, he gave way and suddenly became a keen advocate of the proposal, and the *volte-face* was so complete that the authorities were taken unawares and found themselves consenting to the dangerous experiment. The boys from Poplar arrived at Brookfield one Saturday afternoon, played soccer with the School's second team, were honorably defeated by seven goals to five, and later had high tea with the School team in the Dining Hall. They then met the Head and were shown over the School, and Chips saw them off at the railway station in the evening. Everything had passed without the slightest hitch of any kind, and it was clear that the visitors were taking away with them as fine an impression as they had left behind.

They took back with them also the memory of a charming woman who had met them and talked to them; for once, years later, during the War, a private stationed at a big military camp near Brookfield called on Chips and said he had been one of that first visiting team. Chips gave him tea and chatted with him, till at length, shaking hands, the man said: "And 'ow's the missus, sir? I remember her very well."

"Do you?" Chips answered, eagerly. "Do you remember her?"

"Rather. I should think anyone would."

And Chips replied: "They don't, you know. At least, not here. Boys come and go; new faces all the time; memories don't last. Even masters don't stay forever. Since last year—when old Gribble retired—he's—um—the School butler—there hasn't been anyone here who ever saw my wife. She died, you know, less than a year after your visit. In ninety-eight."

"I'm real sorry to 'ear that, sir. There's two or three o' my pals, anyhow, who remember 'er clear as anything, though we did only see 'er that wunst. Yes, we remember 'er, all right."

"I'm very glad. . . . That was a grand day we all had—and a fine game, too."

"One o' the best days aht I ever 'ad in me life. Wish it was then and not nah—straight, I do. I'm off to Frawnce to-morrer."

A month or so later Chips heard that he had been killed at Passchendaele.

7

AND so it stood, a warm and vivid patch in his life, casting a radiance that glowed in a thousand recollections. Twilight at Mrs. Wickett's, when the School bell clanged for call-over, brought them back to him in a cloud—Katherine scampering along the stone corridors, laughing beside him at some "howler" in an essay he was marking, taking the cello part in a Mozart trio for the School concert, her creamy arm sweeping over the brown sheen of the instrument. She had been a good player and a fine musician. And Katherine furred and muffed for the December house matches, Katherine at the Garden Party that followed Speech Day Prize-giving, Katherine tendering her advice in any little problem that arose. Good advice, too—which he did not always take, but which always influenced him.

"Chips, dear, I'd let them off if I were you. After all, it's nothing very serious."

"I know. I'd like to let them off, but if I do I'm afraid they'll do it again."

"Try telling them that, frankly, and give them the chance."

"I might."

And there were other things, occasionally, that *were* serious.

"You know, Chips, having all these hundreds of boys cooped up here is really an unnatural arrangement, when you come to think about it. So that when anything does occur that oughtn't to, don't you think it's a bit unfair to come down on them as if it were their own fault for being here?"

"Don't know about that, Kathie, but I do know that for everybody's sake we have to be pretty strict about this sort of thing. One black sheep can contaminate others."

"After he himself has been contaminated to begin with. After all, that's what probably *did* happen, isn't it?"

"Maybe. We can't help it. Anyhow, I believe Brookfield is better than a lot of other schools. All the more reason to keep it so."

"But this boy, Chips . . . you're going to sack him?"

"The Head probably will, when I tell him."

"And you're going to tell the Head?"

"It's a duty, I'm afraid."

"Couldn't you think about it a bit . . . talk to the boy again . . . find out how it began . . . After all—apart from this business —isn't he rather a nice boy?"

"Oh, he's all right."

"Then, Chips dear, don't you think there *ought* to be some other way . . ."

And so on. About once in ten times he was adamant and wouldn't be persuaded. In about half of these exceptional cases he afterward rather wished he had taken her advice. And years later, whenever he had trouble with a boy, he was always at the mercy of a softening wave of reminiscence; the boy would stand there, waiting to be told his punishment, and would see, if he were observant, the brown eyes twinkle into a shine that told him all was well. But he did not guess that at such a moment Chips was remembering something that had happened long before he was born; that Chips was thinking: Young ruffian, I'm hanged if *I* can think of any reason to let him off, but I'll bet *she* would have done!

But she had not always pleaded for leniency. On rather rare occasions she urged severity where Chips was inclined to be forgiving. "I don't like his type, Chips. He's too cocksure of himself. If he's looking for trouble I should certainly let him have it."

What a host of little incidents, all deep-buried in the past—problems that had once been urgent, arguments that had once been keen, anecdotes that were funny only because one remembered the fun. Did any emotion really matter when the last trace of it had vanished from human memory; and if that were so, what a crowd of emotions clung to him as to their last home before annihilation! He must be kind to them, must treasure them in his mind before their long sleep. That affair of Archer's resignation, for instance—a queer business, that was. And that affair about the rat that Dunster put in the organ loft while old Ogilvie was taking choir practice. Ogilvie was dead and Dunster drowned at Jutland; of others who had witnessed or heard of the incident, probably most had forgotten. And it had been like that, with other incidents, for centuries. He had a sudden vision of thousands and thousands of boys, from the age of Elizabeth onward; dynasty upon dynasty of masters; long epochs of Brookfield history that had left not even a ghostly record. Who knew why the old fifth-form room was called "the Pit"? There was probably a reason, to begin with; but it had since been lost—lost like the lost books of Livy. And what happened at Brookfield when Cromwell fought at Naseby, near by? How did Brookfield react to the great scare of the "Forty-Five"? Was there a whole holiday when news came of Waterloo? And so on, up to the earliest time that he himself could remember—1870, and Wetherby saying, by way of small talk after their first and only interview: "Looks as if we shall have to settle with the Prussians ourselves one of these fine days, eh?"

When Chips remembered things like this he often felt that he would write them down and make a book of them; and during his years at Mrs. Wickett's he sometimes went even so far as to make desultory notes in an exercise book. But he was soon brought up against difficulties—the chief one being that writing tired him, both mentally and physically. Somehow, too, his recollections lost much of their flavor when they were written down; that story about Rushton and the sack of potatoes, for instance—

it would seem quite tame in print, but Lord, how funny it had been at the time! It was funny, too, to remember it; though perhaps if you didn't remember Rushton . . . and who would, anyway, after all those years? It was such a long time ago . . . Mrs. Wickett, did you ever know a fellow named Rushton? Before your time, I dare say . . . went to Burma in some government job . . . or was it Borneo? . . . Very funny fellow, Rushton. . . .

And there he was, dreaming again before the fire, dreaming of times and incidents in which he alone could take secret interest. Funny and sad, comic and tragic, they all mixed up in his mind, and some day, however hard it proved, he *would* sort them out and make a book of them. . . .

8

AND THERE was always in his mind that spring day in ninety-eight when he had paced through Brookfield village as in some horrifying nightmare, half struggling to escape into an outside world where the sun still shone and where everything had happened differently. Young Faulkner had met him there in the lane outside the School. "Please, sir, may I have the afternoon off? My people are coming up."

"Eh? What's that? Oh yes, yes. . . ."

"Can I miss Chapel, too, sir?"

"Yes . . . yes . . ."

"And may I go to the station to meet them?"

He nearly answered: "You can go to blazes for all I care. My wife is dead and my child is dead, and I wish I were dead myself."

Actually he nodded and stumbled on. He did not want to talk to anybody or to receive condolences; he wanted to get used to things, if he could, before facing the kind words of others. He took his fourth form as usual after call-over, setting them grammar to learn by heart while he himself stayed at his desk in a cold, continuing trance. Suddenly someone said: "Please, sir, there are a lot of letters for you."

So there were; he had been leaning his elbows on them; they were all addressed to him by name. He tore them open one after the other, but each contained nothing but a blank sheet of paper.

He thought in a distant way that it was rather peculiar, but he made no comment; the incident gave hardly an impact upon his vastly greater preoccupations. Not till days afterward did he realize that it had been a piece of April foolery.

They had died on the same day, the mother and the child just born; on April 1, 1898.

9

Chips changed his more commodious apartments in School House for his old original bachelor quarters. He thought at first he would give up his housemastership, but the Head persuaded him otherwise; and later he was glad. The work gave him something to do, filled up an emptiness in his mind and heart. He was different; everyone noticed it. Just as marriage had added something, so did bereavement; after the first stupor of grief he became suddenly the kind of man whom boys, at any rate, unhesitatingly classed as "old." It was not that he was less active; he could still knock up a half century on the cricket field; nor was it that he had lost any interest or keenness in his work. Actually, too, his hair had been graying for years; yet now, for the first time, people seemed to notice it. He was fifty. Once, after some energetic fives, during which he had played as well as many a fellow half his age, he overheard a boy saying: "Not half bad for an old chap like him."

Chips, when he was over eighty, used to recount that incident with many chuckles. "Old at fifty, eh? Umph—it was Naylor who said that, and Naylor can't be far short of fifty himself by now! I wonder if he still thinks that fifty's such an age? Last I heard of him, he was lawyering, and lawyers live long—look at Halsbury—umph—Chancellor at eighty-two, and died at ninety-nine. There's an—umph—age for you! Too old at fifty—why, fellows like that are too *young* at fifty. . . . I was myself . . . a mere infant. . . ."

And there was a sense in which it was true. For with the new century there settled upon Chips a mellowness that gathered all his developing mannerisms and his oft-repeated jokes into a single harmony. No longer did he have those slight and occasional disciplinary troubles, or feel diffident about his own work and worth. He found that his pride in Brookfield reflected back, giving him cause for pride in himself and his position. It was a service that gave him freedom to be supremely and completely himself. He had won, by seniority and ripeness, an uncharted no-man's-land of privilege; he had acquired the right to those gentle eccentricities that so often attack schoolmasters and parsons. He wore his gown till it was almost too tattered to hold together; and when he stood on the wooden bench by Big Hall steps to take call-over, it was with an air of mystic abandonment to ritual. He held the School List, a long sheet curling over a board; and each boy, as he passed, spoke his own name for Chips to verify and then tick off on the list. That verifying glance was an easy and favorite subject of mimicry throughout the School—steel-rimmed spectacles slipping down the nose, eyebrows lifted, one a little higher than the other, a gaze half rapt, half quizzical. And on windy days, with gown and white hair and School List fluttering in uproarious confusion, the whole thing became a comic turn sandwiched between afternoon games and the return to classes.

Some of those names, in little snatches of a chorus, recurred to him ever afterward without any effort of memory. . . . Ainsworth, Attwood, Avonmore, Babcock, Baggs, Barnard, Bassenthwaite, Battersby, Beccles, Bedford-Marshall, Bentley, Best . . .

Another one:—

. . . Unsley, Vailes, Wadham, Wagstaff, Wallington, Waters Primus, Waters Secundus, Watling, Waveney, Webb . . .

And yet another that comprised, as he used to tell his fourth-form Latinists, an excellent example of a hexameter:—

. . . Lancaster, Latton, Lemare, Lytton-Bosworth, MacGonigall, Mansfield . . .

Where had they all gone to, he often pondered; those threads he had once held together, how far had they scattered, some to break, others to weave into unknown patterns? The strange randomness of the world beguiled him, that randomness which never would, so long as the world lasted, give meaning to those choruses again.

And behind Brookfield, as one may glimpse a mountain behind another mountain when the mist clears, he saw the world of change and conflict; and he saw it, more than he realized, with the remembered eyes of Kathie. She had not been able to bequeath him all her mind, still less the brilliance of it; but she had left him with a calmness and a poise that accorded well with his own inward emotions. It was typical of him that he did not share the general jingo bitterness against the Boers. Not that he was a pro-Boer—he was far too traditional for that, and he disliked the kind of people who *were* pro-Boers; but still, it did cross his mind at times that the Boers were engaged in a struggle that had a curious similarity to those of certain English history-book heroes—Hereward the Wake, for instance, or Caractacus. He once tried to shock his fifth form by suggesting this, but they only thought it was one of his little jokes.

However heretical he might be about the Boers, he was orthodox about Mr. Lloyd George and the famous Budget. He did not care for either of them. And when, years later, L.G. came as the guest of honor to a Brookfield Speech Day, Chips said, on being presented to him: "Mr. Lloyd George, I am nearly old enough—umph—to remember you as a young man, and—umph—I confess that you seem to me—umph—to have improved—umph—a great deal." The Head, standing with them, was rather aghast; but L.G. laughed heartily and talked to Chips more than to anyone else during the ceremonial that followed.

"Just like Chips," was commented afterward. "He gets away with it. I suppose at that age anything you say to anybody is all right. . . ."

10

In 1900 old Meldrum, who had succeeded Wetherby as Head and had held office for three decades, died suddenly from pneumonia; and in the interval before the appointment of a successor, Chips became Acting Head of Brookfield. There was just the faintest chance that the Governors might make the appointment a permanent one; but Chips was not really disappointed when they brought in a youngster of thirty-seven, glittering with Firsts and Blues and with the kind of personality that could reduce Big Hall to silence by the mere lifting of an eyebrow. Chips was not in the running with that kind of person; he never had been and never would be, and he knew it. He was an altogether milder and less ferocious animal.

Those years before his retirement in 1913 were studded with sharply remembered pictures.

A May morning; the clang of the School bell at an unaccustomed time; everyone summoned to assemble in Big Hall. Ralston, the new Head, very pontifical and aware of himself, fixing the multitude with a cold, presaging severity. "You will all be deeply grieved to hear that His Majesty King Edward the Seventh died this morning. . . . There will be no school this afternoon, but a service will be held in the Chapel at four-thirty."

A summer morning on the railway line near Brookfield. The railwaymen were on strike, soldiers were driving the engines, stones had been thrown at trains. Brookfield boys were patrolling the line, thinking the whole business great fun. Chips, who was in charge, stood a little way off, talking to a man at the gate of a cottage. Young Cricklade approached. "Please, sir, what shall we do if we meet any strikers?"

"Would you like to meet one?"

"I—I don't know, sir."

God bless the boy—he talked of them as if they were queer animals out of a zoo! "Well, here you are, then—umph—you can meet Mr. Jones—he's a striker. When he's on duty he has charge of the signal box at the station. You've put your life in his hands many a time."

Afterward the story went round the School: There was Chips, talking to a striker. Talking to a striker. Might have been quite friendly, the way they were talking together.

Chips, thinking it over a good many times, always added to himself that Kathie would have approved, and would also have been amused.

Because always, whatever happened and however the avenues of politics twisted and curved, he had faith in England, in English flesh and blood, and in Brookfield as a place whose ultimate worth depended on whether she fitted herself into the English scene with dignity and without disproportion. He had been left a vision that grew clearer with each year—of an England for which days of ease were nearly over, of a nation steering into channels where a hair's breadth of error might be catastrophic. He remembered the Diamond Jubilee; there had been a whole holiday at Brookfield, and he had taken Kathie to London to see the procession. That old and legendary lady, sitting in her carriage like some crumbling wooden doll, had symbolized impressively so many things that, like herself, were nearing an end. Was it only the century, or was it an epoch?

And then that frenzied Edwardian decade, like an electric lamp that goes brighter and whiter just before it burns itself out.

Strikes and lockouts, champagne suppers and unemployed marchers, Chinese labor, tariff reform, *H.M.S. Dreadnought*,

Marconi, Home Rule for Ireland, Doctor Crippen, suffragettes, the lines of Chatalja. . . .

An April evening, windy and rainy; the fourth form construing Vergil, not very intelligently, for there was exciting news in the papers; young Grayson, in particular, was careless and preoccupied. A quiet, nervous boy.

"Grayson, stay behind—umph—after the rest."

Then:—

"Grayson, I don't want to be—umph—severe, because you are generally pretty good—umph—in your work, but to-day—you don't seem—umph—to have been trying at all. Is anything the matter?"

"N-no, sir."

"Well—umph—we'll say no more about it, but—umph—I shall expect better things next time."

Next morning it was noised around the School that Grayson's father had sailed on the *Titanic*, and that no news had yet come through as to his fate.

Grayson was excused lessons; for a whole day the School centred emotionally upon his anxieties. Then came news that his father had been among those rescued.

Chips shook hands with the boy. "Well, umph—I'm delighted, Grayson. A happy ending. You must be feeling pretty pleased with life."

"Y-yes, sir."

A quiet, nervous boy. And it was Grayson Senior, not Junior, with whom Chips was destined later to condole.

11

AND THEN the row with Ralston. Funny thing, Chips had never liked him; he was efficient, ruthless, ambitious, but not, somehow, very likable. He had, admittedly, raised the status of Brookfield as a school, and for the first time in memory there was a longish waiting list. Ralston was a live wire; a fine power transmitter, but you had to beware of him.

Chips had never bothered to beware of him; he was not attracted by the man, but he served him willingly enough and quite loyally. Or, rather, he served Brookfield. He knew that Ralston did not like him, either; but that didn't seem to matter. He felt himself sufficiently protected by age and seniority from the fate of other masters whom Ralston had failed to like.

Then suddenly, in 1908, when he had just turned sixty, came Ralston's urbane ultimatum. "Mr. Chipping, have you ever thought you would like to retire?"

Chips stared about him in that book-lined study, startled by the question, wondering why Ralston should have asked it. He said, at length: "No—umph—I can't say that—umph—I have thought much about it—umph—yet."

"Well, Mr. Chipping, the suggestion is there for you to consider. The Governors would, of course, agree to your being adequately pensioned."

Abruptly Chips flamed up. "But—umph—I don't want—to retire. I don't—umph—need to consider it."

"Nevertheless, I suggest that you do."

"But—umph—I don't see—why—I should!"

"In that case, things are going to be a little difficult."

"Difficult? Why—difficult?"

And then they set to, Ralston getting cooler and harder, Chips getting warmer and more passionate, till at last Ralston said, icily: "Since you force me to use plain words, Mr. Chipping, you shall have them. For some time past, you haven't been pulling your weight here. Your methods of teaching are slack and old-fashioned; your personal habits are slovenly; and you ignore my instructions in a way which, in a younger man, I should regard as rank insubordination. It won't do, Mr. Chipping, and you must ascribe it to my forbearance that I have put up with it so long."

"But—" Chips began, in sheer bewilderment; and then he took up isolated words out of that extraordinary indictment. "*Slovenly*—umph—you said—?"

"Yes, look at the gown you're wearing. I happen to know that that gown of yours is a subject of continual amusement throughout the School."

Chips knew it, too, but it had never seemed to him a very regrettable matter.

He went on: "And—you also said—umph—something about—*insubordination*—?"

"No, I didn't. I said that in a younger man I should have regarded it as that. In your case it's probably a mixture of slackness and obstinacy. This question of Latin pronunciation, for instance—I think I told you years ago that I wanted the new style used throughout the School. The other masters obeyed me; you prefer to stick to your old methods, and the result is simply chaos and inefficiency."

At last Chips had something tangible that he could tackle. "Oh, *that!*" he answered scornfully. "Well, I—umph—I admit that I don't agree with the new pronunciation. I never did. Umph—a lot of nonsense, in my opinion. Making boys say 'Kickero' at school when—umph—for the rest of their lives they'll say 'Cicero'—if they ever—umph—say it at all. And instead of 'vicissim'—God bless my soul—you'd make them say, 'We kiss 'im'! Umph—umph!" And he chuckled momentarily, forgetting that he was in Ralston's study and not in his own friendly form room.

"Well, there you are, Mr. Chipping—that's just an example of what I complain of. You hold one opinion and I hold another, and, since you decline to give way, there can't very well be any alternative. I aim to make Brookfield a thoroughly up-to-date school. I'm a science man myself, but for all that I have no objection to the classics—provided that they are taught efficiently. Because they are dead languages is no reason why they should be dealt with in a dead educational technique. I understand, Mr. Chipping, that your Latin and Greek lessons are exactly the same as they were when I began here ten years ago?"

Chips answered, slowly and with pride: "For that matter—umph—they are the same as when your predecessor—Mr. Meldrum—came here, and that—umph—was thirty-eight years ago. We began here, Mr. Meldrum and I—in—umph—in 1870. And it was—um—Mr. Meldrum's predecessor, Mr. Wetherby—who first approved my syllabus. 'You'll take the Cicero for the fourth,' he said to me. Cicero, too—not Kickero!"

"Very interesting, Mr. Chipping, but once again it proves my point—you live too much in the past, and not enough in the present and future. Times are changing, whether you realize it or not. Modern parents are beginning to demand something more for their three years' school fees than a few scraps of languages that nobody speaks. Besides, your boys don't learn even what they're supposed to learn. None of them last year got through the Lower Certificate."

And suddenly, in a torrent of thoughts too pressing to be put into words, Chips made answer to himself. These examinations and certificates and so on—what did they matter? And all this efficiency and up-to-dateness—what did *that* matter, either? Ralston was trying to run Brookfield like a factory—a factory for turning out a snob culture based on money and machines. The old gentlemanly traditions of family and broad acres were changing, as doubtless they were bound to; but instead of widening them to form a genuine inclusive democracy of duke and dustman, Ralston was narrowing them upon the single issue of a fat banking account. There never had been so many rich men's sons at Brookfield. The Speech Day Garden Party was like Ascot. Ralston met these wealthy fellows in London clubs and persuaded them that Brookfield was *the* coming school, and, since they couldn't buy their way into Eton or Harrow, they greedily swallowed the bait. Awful fellows, some of them—though others were decent enough. Financiers, company promoters, pill manufacturers. One of them gave his son five pounds a week pocket money. Vulgar . . . ostentatious . . . all the hectic rotten-ripeness of the age. . . . And once Chips had got into trouble because of some joke he had made about a boy's name. The boy wrote home about it, and his father sent an angry letter to Ralston. Touchy, no sense of humor, no sense of proportion—that was the matter with them, these new fellows. . . . No sense of proportion. And it was a sense of proportion, above all things, that Brookfield ought to teach—not so much Latin or Greek or Chemistry or Mechanics. And you couldn't expect to test that sense of proportion by setting papers and granting certificates. . . .

All this flashed through his mind in an instant of protest and indignation, but he did not say a word of it. He merely gathered his tattered gown together and with an "umph—umph" walked a few paces away. He had had enough of the argument. At the door he turned and said: "I don't—umph—intend to resign—and you can—umph—do what you like about it!"

Looking back upon that scene in the calm perspective of a quarter of a century, Chips could find it in his heart to feel a little sorry for Ralston. Particularly when, as it happened, Ralston had been in such complete ignorance of the forces he was dealing with. So, for that matter, had Chips himself. Neither had correctly estimated the toughness of Brookfield tradition, and its readiness to defend itself and its defenders. For it had so chanced that a small boy, waiting to see Ralston that morning, had been listening outside the door during the whole of the interview; he had been thrilled by it, naturally, and had told his friends. Some of these, in a surprisingly short time, had told their parents; so that very soon it was common knowledge that Ralston had insulted Chips and had demanded his resignation. The amazing result was a spontaneous outburst of sympathy and partisanship such as Chips, in his wildest dreams, had never envisaged. He found, rather to his astonishment, that Ralston was thoroughly unpopular; he was feared and respected, but not liked; and in this issue of Chips the dislike rose to a point where it conquered fear and demolished even respect. There was talk of having some kind of public riot in the School if Ralston succeeded in banishing Chips. The masters, many of them young men who agreed that Chips was hopelessly old-fashioned, rallied around him nevertheless because they hated Ralston's slave driving and saw in the old veteran a likely champion. And one day the Chairman of the Governors, Sir John Rivers, visited Brookfield, ignored Ralston, and went direct to Chips. "A fine fellow, Rivers," Chips would say, telling the story to Mrs. Wickett for the dozenth time. "Not—umph—a very brilliant boy in class. I remember he could never—umph—master his verbs. And now—umph—I see in the papers—they've made him—umph—a baronet. It just shows you—umph—it just shows you."

Sir John had said, on that morning in 1908, taking Chips by the arm as they walked round the deserted cricket pitches: "Chips, old boy, I hear you've been having the deuce of a row with Ralston. Sorry to hear about it, for your sake—but I want you to know that the Governors are with you to a man. We don't like the fellow a great deal. Very clever and all that, but a bit too clever, if you ask me. Claims to have doubled the School's endowment funds by some monkeying on the Stock Exchange. Dare say he has, but a chap like that wants watching. So if he starts chucking his weight about with you, tell him very politely he can go to the devil. The Governors don't want you to resign. Brookfield wouldn't be the same without you, and they know it. We all know it. You can stay here till you're a hundred if you feel like it—indeed, it's our hope that you will."

And at that—both then and often when he recounted it afterward—Chips broke down.

12

So HE stayed on at Brookfield, having as little to do with Ralston
as possible. And in 1911 Ralston left, "to better himself"; he was
offered the headship of one of the greater public schools. His
successor was a man named Chatteris, whom Chips liked; he
was even younger than Ralston had been—thirty-four. He was
supposed to be very brilliant; at any rate, he was modern (Natural Sciences Tripos), friendly, and sympathetic. Recognizing in
Chips a Brookfield institution, he courteously and wisely accepted the situation.

In 1913 Chips had had bronchitis and was off duty for nearly
the whole of the winter term. It was that which made him decide to resign that summer, when he was sixty-five. After all, it
was a good, ripe age; and Ralston's straight words had, in some
ways, had an effect. He felt that it would not be fair to hang on
if he could not decently do his job. Besides, he would not sever
himself completely. He would take rooms across the road, with
the excellent Mrs. Wickett who had once been linen-room maid;
he could visit the School whenever he wanted, and could still, in a
sense, remain a part of it.

At that final end-of-term dinner, in July 1913, Chips received
his farewell presentations and made a speech. It was not a very
long speech, but it had a good many jokes in it, and was made
twice as long, perhaps, by the laughter that impeded its progress. There were several Latin quotations in it, as well as a refer-

ence to the Captain of the School, who, Chips said, had been guilty of exaggeration in speaking of his (Chips's) services to Brookfield. "But then—umph—he comes of an—umph—exaggerating family. I—um—remember—once—having to thrash his father—for it. [Laughter] I gave him one mark—umph—for a Latin translation, and he—umph—exaggerated the one into a seven! Umph—umph!" Roars of laughter and tumultuous cheers! A typical Chips remark, everyone thought.

And then he mentioned that he had been at Brookfield for forty-two years, and that he had been very happy there. "It has been my life," he said, simply. *"O mihi praeteritos referat si Jupiter annos. . . .* Umph—I need not—of course—translate. . . ." Much laughter. "I remember lots of changes at Brookfield. I remember the—um—the first bicycle. I remember when there was no gas or electric light and we used to have a member of the domestic staff called a lamp-boy—he did nothing else but clean and trim and light lamps throughout the School. I remember when there was a hard frost that lasted for seven weeks in the winter term—there were no games, and the whole School learned to skate on the fens. Eighteen-eighty-something, that was. I remember when two thirds of the School went down with German measles and Big Hall was turned into a hospital ward. I remember the great bonfire we had on Mafeking night. It was lit too near the pavilion and we had to send for the fire brigade to put it out. And the firemen were having their own celebrations and most of them were—um—in a regrettable condition. [Laughter] I remember Mrs. Brool, whose photograph is still in the tuckshop; she served there until an uncle in Australia left her a lot of money. In fact, I remember so much that I often think I ought to write a book. Now what should I call it? 'Memories of Rod and Lines'—eh? [Cheers and laughter. That was a good one, people thought—one of Chips's best.] Well, well, perhaps I shall write it, some day. But I'd rather tell you about it, really. I remember . . . I remember . . . but chiefly I remember all your faces. I never forget them. I have thousands of

faces in my mind—the faces of boys. If you come and see me
again in years to come—as I hope you all will—I shall try to
remember those older faces of yours, but it's just possible I shan't
be able to—and then some day you'll see me somewhere and I
shan't recognize you and you'll say to yourself, 'The old boy
doesn't remember me.' [Laughter] But I *do* remember you—as
you are *now*. That's the point. In my mind you never grow up at
all. Never. Sometimes, for instance, when people talk to me
about our respected Chairman of the Governors, I think to myself, 'Ah yes, a jolly little chap with hair that sticks up on top—
and absolutely no idea whatever about the difference between a
Gerund and a Gerundive.' [Loud laughter] Well, well, I mustn't
go on—umph—all night. Think of me sometimes as I shall certainly think of you. *Haec olim meminisse juvabit* . . . again I
need not translate." Much laughter and shouting and prolonged
cheers.

August 1913. Chips went for a cure to Wiesbaden, where he
lodged at the home of the German master at Brookfield, Herr
Staefel, with whom he had become friendly. Staefel was thirty
years his junior, but the two men got on excellently. In September, when term began, Chips returned and took up residence at
Mrs. Wickett's. He felt a great deal stronger and fitter after his
holiday, and almost wished he had not retired. Nevertheless, he
found plenty to do. He had all the new boys to tea. He watched
all the important matches on the Brookfield ground. Once a term
he dined with the Head, and once also with the masters. He took
on the preparation and editing of a new Brookfeldian Directory.
He accepted presidency of the Old Boys' Club and went to dinners in London. He wrote occasional articles, full of jokes and
Latin quotations, for the Brookfield terminal magazine. He read
his *Times* every morning—very thoroughly; and he also began to
read detective stories—he had been keen on them ever since the
first thrills of Sherlock. Yes, he was quite busy, and quite happy,
too.

A year later, in 1914, he again attended the end-of-term dinner. There was a lot of war talk—civil war in Ulster, and trouble between Austria and Serbia. Herr Staefel, who was leaving for Germany the next day, told Chips he thought the Balkan business wouldn't come to anything.

13

THE War years.

The first shock, and then the first optimism. The Battle of the Marne, the Russian steam-roller, Kitchener.

"Do you think it will last long, sir?"

Chips, questioned as he watched the first trial game of the season, gave quite a cheery answer. He was, like thousands of others, hopelessly wrong; but, unlike thousands of others, he did not afterward conceal the fact. "We ought to have—um—finished it—um—by Christmas. The Germans are already beaten. But why? Are you thinking of—um—joining up, Forrester?"

Joke—because Forrester was the smallest new boy Brookfield had ever had—about four feet high above his muddy football boots. (But not so much a joke, when you came to think of it afterward; for he was killed in 1918—shot down in flames over Cambrai.) But one didn't guess what lay ahead. It seemed tragically sensational when the first Old Brookfeldian was killed in action—in September. Chips thought, when that news came: A hundred years ago boys from the School were fighting *against* the French. Strange, in a way, that the sacrifices of one generation should so cancel out those of another. He tried to express this to Blades, the Head of School House; but Blades, eighteen years old and already in training for a cadetship, only laughed. What had all that history stuff to do with it, anyhow? Just old Chips with one of his queer ideas, that's all.

1915. Armies clenched in deadlock from the sea to Switzerland. The Dardanelles. Gallipoli. Military camps springing up quite near Brookfield; soldiers using the playing fields for sports and training; swift developments of Brookfield O.T.C. Most of the younger masters gone or in uniform. Every Sunday night, in the Chapel after evening service, Chatteris read out the names of old boys killed, together with short biographies. Very moving; but Chips, in the back pew under the gallery, thought: They are only names to him; he doesn't see their faces as I do. . . .

1916. . . . The Somme Battle. Twenty-three names read out one Sunday evening.

Toward the close of that catastrophic July, Chatteris talked to Chips one afternoon at Mrs. Wickett's. He was overworked and overworried and looked very ill. "To tell you the truth, Chipping, I'm not having too easy a time here. I'm thirty-nine, you know, and unmarried, and lots of people seem to think they know what I ought to do. Also, I happen to be diabetic, and couldn't pass the blindest M.O., but I don't see why I should pin a medical certificate on my front door."

Chips hadn't known anything about this; it was a shock to him, for he liked Chatteris.

The latter continued: "You see how it is. Ralston filled the place up with young men—all very good, of course—but now most of them have joined up and the substitutes are pretty dreadful, on the whole. They poured ink down a man's neck in prep one night last week—silly fool—got hysterical. I have to take classes myself, take prep for fools like that, work till midnight every night, and get cold-shouldered as a slacker on top of everything. I can't stand it much longer. If things don't improve next term I shall have a breakdown."

"I do sympathize with you," Chips said.

"I hoped you would. And that brings me to what I came here to ask you. Briefly, my suggestion is that—if you felt equal to it and would care to—how about coming back here for a while? You look pretty fit, and, of course, you know all the ropes. I don't mean a lot of hard work for you—you needn't take anything strenuously—just a few odd jobs here and there, as you choose. What I'd like you for more than anything else is not for the actual work you'd do—though that, naturally, would be very valuable—but for your help in other ways—in just *belonging* here. There's nobody ever been more popular than you were, and are still—you'd help to hold things together if there were any danger of them flying to bits. And perhaps there *is* that danger. . . ."

Chips answered, breathlessly and with a holy joy in his heart: "I'll come. . . ."

14

HE STILL kept on his rooms with Mrs. Wickett; indeed, he still lived there; but every morning, about half-past ten, he put on his coat and muffler and crossed the road to the School. He felt very fit, and the actual work was not taxing. Just a few forms in Latin and Roman History—the old lessons—even the old pronunciation. The same joke about the Lex Canuleia—there was a new generation that had not heard it, and he was absurdly gratified by the success it achieved. He felt a little like a music-hall favorite returning to the boards after a positively last appearance.

They all said how marvelous it was that he knew every boy's name and face so quickly. They did not guess how closely he had kept in touch from across the road.

He was a grand success altogether. In some strange way he did, and they all knew and felt it, help things. For the first time in his life he felt *necessary*—and necessary to something that was nearest his heart. There is no sublimer feeling in the world, and it was his at last.

He made new jokes, too—about the O.T.C. and the food-rationing system and the anti-air-raid blinds that had to be fitted on all the windows. There was a mysterious kind of rissole that began to appear on the School menu on Mondays, and Chips called it *abhorrendum*—"meat to be abhorred." The story went round—heard Chips's latest?

Chatteris fell ill during the winter of '17, and again, for the second time in his life, Chips became Acting Head of Brookfield. Then in April Chatteris died, and the Governors asked Chips if he would carry on "for the duration." He said he would, if they would refrain from appointing him officially. From that last honor, within his reach at last, he shrank instinctively, feeling himself in so many ways unequal to it. He said to Rivers: "You see, I'm not a young man and I don't want people to—um—expect a lot from me. I'm like all these new colonels and majors you see everywhere—just a war-time fluke. A ranker—that's all I am really."

1917. 1918. Chips lived through it all. He sat in the headmaster's study every morning, handling problems, dealing with plaints and requests. Out of vast experience had emerged a kindly, gentle confidence in himself. To keep a sense of proportion, that was the main thing. So much of the world was losing it; as well keep it where it had, or ought to have, a congenial home.

On Sundays in Chapel it was he who now read out the tragic list, and sometimes it was seen and heard that he was in tears over it. Well, why not, the School said; he was an old man; they might have despised anyone else for the weakness.

One day he got a letter from Switzerland, from friends there; it was heavily censored, but conveyed some news. On the following Sunday, after the names and biographies of old boys, he paused a moment and then added:—

"Those few of you who were here before the War will remember Max Staefel, the German master. He was in Germany, visiting his home, when war broke out. He was popular while he was here, and made many friends. Those who knew him will be sorry to hear that he was killed last week, on the Western Front."

He was a little pale when he sat down afterward, aware that he had done something unusual. He had consulted nobody about it, anyhow; no one else could be blamed. Later, outside the Chapel, he heard an argument:—

"On the Western Front, Chips said. Does that mean he was fighting for the Germans?"

"I suppose it does."

"Seems funny, then, to read his name out with all the others. After all, he was an *enemy*."

"Oh, just one of Chips's ideas, I expect. The old boy still has 'em."

Chips, in his room again, was not displeased by the comment. Yes, he still had 'em—those ideas of dignity and generosity that were becoming increasingly rare in a frantic world. And he thought: Brookfield will take them, too, from me; but it wouldn't from anyone else.

Once, asked for his opinion of bayonet practice being carried on near the cricket pavilion, he answered, with that lazy, slightly asthmatic intonation that had been so often and so extravagantly imitated: "It seems—to me—umph—a very vulgar way of killing people."

The yarn was passed on and joyously appreciated—how Chips had told some big brass hat from the War Office that bayonet fighting was vulgar. Just like Chips. And they found an adjective for him—an adjective just beginning to be used: he was pre-War.

15

AND ONCE, on a night of full moonlight, the air-raid warning was given while Chips was taking his lower fourth in Latin. The guns began almost instantly, and, as there was plenty of shrapnel falling about outside, it seemed to Chips that they might just as well stay where they were, on the ground floor of School House. It was pretty solidly built and made as good a dugout as Brookfield could offer; and as for a direct hit, well, they could not expect to survive that, wherever they were.

So he went on with his Latin, speaking a little louder amid the reverberating crashes of the guns and the shrill whine of anti-aircraft shells. Some of the boys were nervous; few were able to be attentive. He said, gently: "It may possibly seem to you, Robertson—at this particular moment in the world's history— umph—that the affairs of Caesar in Gaul some two thousand years ago—are—umph—of somewhat secondary importance—and that—umph—the irregular conjugation of the verb *tollo* is—umph —even less important still. But believe me—umph—my dear Robertson—that is not really the case." Just then there came a particularly loud explosion—quite near. "You cannot—umph—judge the importance of things—umph—by the noise they make. Oh dear me, no." A little chuckle. "And these things—umph—that have mattered—for thousands of years—are not going to be— snuffed out—because some stink merchant—in his laboratory—invents a new kind of mischief." Titters of nervous laughter; for

Buffles, the pale, lean, and medically unfit science master, was nicknamed the Stink Merchant. Another explosion—nearer still. "Let us—um—resume our work. If it is fate that we are soon to be —umph—interrupted, let us be found employing ourselves in something—umph—really appropriate. Is there anyone who will volunteer to construe?"

Maynard, chubby, dauntless, clever, and impudent, said: "I will, sir."

"Very good. Turn to page forty and begin at the bottom line."

The explosions still continued deafeningly; the whole building shook as if it were being lifted off its foundations. Maynard found the page, which was some way ahead, and began, shrilly:—

"*Genus hoc erat pugnae*—this was the kind of fight—*quo se Germani exercuerant*—in which the Germans busied themselves. Oh, sir, that's good—that's really very funny indeed, sir—one of your very best—"

Laughing began, and Chips added: "Well—umph—you can see—now—that these dead languages—umph—can come to life again—sometimes—eh? Eh?"

Afterward they learned that five bombs had fallen in and around Brookfield, the nearest of them just outside the School grounds. Nine persons had been killed.

The story was told, retold, embellished. "The dear old boy never turned a hair. Even found some old tag to illustrate what was going on. Something in Caesar about the way the Germans fought. You wouldn't think there were things like that in Caesar, would you? And the way Chips laughed . . . you know the way he *does* laugh . . . the tears all running down his face . . . never seen him laugh so much. . . ."

He was a legend.

With his old and tattered gown, his walk that was just beginning to break into a stumble, his mild eyes peering over the steel-rimmed spectacles, and his quaintly humorous sayings, Brookfield would not have had an atom of him different.

November 11, 1918.

News came through in the morning; a whole holiday was decreed for the School, and the kitchen staff were implored to provide as cheerful a spread as war-time rationing permitted. There was much cheering and singing, and a bread fight across the Dining Hall. When Chips entered in the midst of the uproar there was an instant hush, and then wave upon wave of cheering; everyone gazed on him with eager, shining eyes, as on a symbol of victory. He walked to the dais, seeming as if he wished to speak; they made silence for him, but he shook his head after a moment, smiled, and walked away again.

It had been a damp, foggy day, and the walk across the quadrangle to the Dining Hall had given him a chill. The next day he was in bed with bronchitis, and stayed there till after Christmas. But already, on that night of November 11, after his visit to the Dining Hall, he had sent in his resignation to the Board of Governors.

When school reassembled after the holidays he was back at Mrs. Wickett's. At his own request there were no more farewells or presentations, nothing but a handshake with his successor and the word "acting" crossed out on official stationery. The "duration" was over.

16

AND NOW, fifteen years after that, he could look back upon it all
with a deep and sumptuous tranquillity. He was not ill, of course
—only a little tired at times, and bad with his breathing during
the winter months. He would not go abroad—he had once tried
it, but had chanced to strike the Riviera during one of its care-
fully unadvertised cold spells. "I prefer—um—to get my chills—
umph—in my own country," he used to say, after that. He had to
take care of himself when there were east winds, but autumn
and winter were not really so bad; there were warm fires, and
books, and you could look forward to the summer. It was the
summer that he liked best, of course; apart from the weather,
which suited him, there were the continual visits of old boys.
Every week-end some of them motored up to Brookfield and
called at his house. Sometimes they tired him, if too many came
at once; but he did not really mind; he could always rest and
sleep afterward. And he enjoyed their visits—more than anything
else in the world that was still to be enjoyed. "Well, Gregson—
umph—I remember you—umph—always late for everything—eh—
eh? Perhaps you'll be late in growing old—umph—like me—umph
—eh?" And later, when he was alone again and Mrs. Wickett
came in to clear away the tea things: "Mrs. Wickett, young
Gregson called—umph—you remember him, do you? Tall boy
with spectacles. Always late. Umph. Got a job with the—umph

—League of Nations—where—I suppose—his—um—dilatoriness— won't be noticeable—eh?"

And sometimes, when the bell rang for call-over, he would go to the window and look across the road and over the School fence and see, in the distance, the thin line of boys filing past the bench. New times, new names . . . but the old ones still remained . . . Jefferson, Jennings, Jolyon, Jupp, Kingsley Primus, Kingsley Secundus, Kingsley Tertius, Kingston . . . where are you all, where have you all gone to? . . . Mrs. Wickett, bring me a cup of tea just before prep, will you, please?

The post-War decade swept through with a clatter of change and maladjustments; Chips, as he lived through it, was profoundly disappointed when he looked abroad. The Ruhr, Chanak, Corfu; there was enough to be uneasy about in the world. But near him, at Brookfield, and even, in a wider sense, in England, there was something that charmed his heart because it was old—and had survived. More and more he saw the rest of the world as a vast disarrangement for which England had sacrificed enough—and perhaps too much. But he was satisfied with Brookfield. It was rooted in things that had stood the test of time and change and war. Curious, in this deeper sense, how little it *had* changed. Boys were a politer race; bullying was nonexistent; there was more swearing and cheating. There was a more genuine friendliness between master and boy—less pomposity on the one side, less unctuousness on the other. One of the new masters, fresh from Oxford, even let the Sixth call him by his Christian name. Chips didn't hold with that; indeed, he was just a little bit shocked. "He might as well—umph—sign his terminal reports—umph—'yours affectionately'—eh—eh?" he told somebody.

During the General Strike of 1926, Brookfield boys loaded motor vans with foodstuffs. When it was all over, Chips felt stirred emotionally as he had not been since the War. Something had happened, something whose ultimate significance had yet to be reckoned. But one thing was clear: England had burned her fire in her own grate again. And when, at a Speech Day function that year, an American visitor laid stress on the vast sums that the strike had cost the country, Chips answered: "Yes, but—umph—advertisement—always *is* costly."

"Advertisement?"

"Well, wasn't it—umph—advertisement—and very fine advertisement—too? A whole week of it—umph—and not a life lost—not a shot fired! Your country would have—umph—spilt more blood in—umph—raiding a single liquor saloon!"

Laughter . . . laughter . . . wherever he went and whatever he said, there was laughter. He had earned the reputation of being a greater jester, and jests were expected of him. Whenever he rose to speak at a meeting, or even when he talked across a table, people prepared their minds and faces for the joke. They listened in a mood to be amused and it was easy to satisfy them. They laughed sometimes before he came to the point. "Old Chips was in fine form," they would say, afterward. "Marvelous the way he can always see the funny side of things. . . ."

After 1929, Chips did not leave Brookfield—even for Old Boys' dinners in London. He was afraid of chills, and late nights began to tire him too much. He came across to the School, however, on fine days; and he still kept up a wide and continual hospitality in his room. His faculties were all unimpaired, and he had no personal worries of any kind. His income was more than he needed to spend, and his small capital, invested in gilt-edged stocks, did not suffer when the slump set in. He gave a lot of money away—to people who called on him with a hard-luck story, to various School funds, and also to the Brookfield mission. In 1930 he made his will. Except for legacies to the mission and to Mrs. Wickett, he left all he had to found an open scholarship to the School.

1931. . . . 1932. . . .

"What do you think of Hoover, sir?"

"Do you think we shall ever go back to gold?"

"How d'you feel about things in general, sir? See any break in the clouds?"

"When's the tide going to turn, Chips, old boy? You ought to know, with all your experience of things."

They all asked him questions, as if he were some kind of prophet and encyclopaedia combined—more even than that, for they liked their answer dished up as a joke. He would say:—

"Well, Henderson, when I was—umph—a much younger man— there used to be someone who—um—promised people ninepence for fourpence. I don't know that anybody—umph—ever got it, but—umph—our present rulers seem—um—to have solved the problem how to give—umph—fourpence for ninepence."

Laughter.

Sometimes, when he was strolling about the School, small boys of the cheekier kind would ask him questions, merely for the fun of getting Chips's "latest" to retail.

"Please, sir, what about the Five-Year Plan?"

"Sir, do you think Germany wants to fight another war?"

"Have you been to the new cinema, sir? I went with my people the other day. Quite a grand affair for a small place like Brookfield. They've got a Wurlitzer."

"And what—umph—on earth—is a Wurlitzer?"

"It's an organ, sir—a cinema organ."

"Dear me. . . . I've seen the name on the hoardings, but I always—umph—imagined—it must be some kind of—umph— sausage."

Laughter. . . . Oh, there's a new Chips joke, you fellows, a perfectly lovely one. I was gassing to the old boy about the new cinema, and . . .

17

HE SAT in his front parlor at Mrs. Wickett's on a November afternoon in thirty-three. It was cold and foggy, and he dared not go out. He had not felt too well since Armistice Day; he fancied he might have caught a slight chill during the Chapel service. Merivale had been that morning for his usual fortnightly chat. "Everything all right? Feeling hearty? That's the style—keep indoors this weather—there's a lot of flu about. Wish I could have your life for a day or two."

His life . . . and what a life it had been! The whole pageant of it swung before him as he sat by the fire that afternoon. The things he had done and seen: Cambridge in the sixties; Great Gable on an August morning; Brookfield at all times and seasons throughout the years. And, for that matter, the things he had *not* done, and would never do now that he had left them too late—he had never traveled by air, for instance, and he had never been to a talkie-show. So that he was both more and less experienced than the youngest new boy at the School might well be; and that, that paradox of age and youth, was what the world called progress.

Mrs. Wickett had gone out, visiting relatives in a neighboring village; she had left the tea things ready on the table, with bread and butter and extra cups laid out in case anybody called. On such a day, however, visitors were not very likely; with the fog thickening hourly outside, he would probably be alone.

But no. About a quarter to four a ring came, and Chips, answering the front door himself (which he oughtn't to have done), encountered a rather small boy wearing a Brookfield cap and an expression of anxious timidity. "Please, sir," he began, "does Mr. Chips live here?"

"Umph—you'd better come inside," Chips answered. And in his room a moment later he added: "I am—umph—the person you want. Now what can I—umph—do for you?"

"I was told you wanted me, sir."

Chips smiled. An old joke—an old leg-pull, and he, of all people, having made so many old jokes in his time, ought not to complain. And it amused him to cap their joke, as it were, with one of his own; to let them see that he could keep his end up, even yet. So he said, with eyes twinkling: "Quite right, my boy. I wanted you to take tea with me. Will you—umph—sit down by the fire? Umph—I don't think I have seen your face before. How is that?"

"I've only just come out of the sanatorium, sir—I've been there since the beginning of term with measles."

"Ah, that accounts for it."

Chips began his usual ritualistic blending of tea from the different caddies; luckily there was half a walnut cake with pink icing in the cupboard. He found out that the boy's name was Linford, that he lived in Shropshire, and that he was the first of his family at Brookfield.

"You know—umph—Linford—you'll like Brookfield—when you get used to it. It's not half such an awful place—as you imagine. You're a bit afraid of it—um, yes—eh? So was I, my dear boy—at first. But that was—um—a long time ago. Sixty-three years ago—umph—to be precise. When I—um—first went into Big Hall and—um—I saw all those boys—I tell you—I was quite scared. Indeed—umph—I don't think I've ever been so scared in my life. Not even when—umph—the Germans bombed us—during the War. But—umph—it didn't last long—the scared feeling, I mean. I soon made myself—um—at home."

"Were there a lot of other new boys that term, sir?" asked Linford shyly.

"Eh? But—God bless my soul—I wasn't a boy at all—I was a man—a young man of twenty-two! And the next time you see a young man—a new master—taking his first prep in Big Hall—umph—just think—what it feels like!"

"But if you were twenty-two then, sir—"

"Yes? Eh?"

"You must be—very old—now, sir."

Chips laughed quietly and steadily to himself. It was a good joke.

"Well—umph—I'm certainly—umph—no chicken."

He laughed quietly to himself for a long time.

Then he talked of other matters, of Shropshire, of schools and school life in general, of the news in that day's papers. "You're growing up into—umph—a very cross sort of world, Linford. Maybe it will have got over some of its—umph—crossness—by the time you're ready for it. Let's hope so—umph—at any rate. . . . Well . . ." And with a glance at the clock he delivered himself of his old familiar formula. "I'm—umph—sorry—you can't stay . . ."

At the front door he shook hands.

"Good-bye, my boy."

And the answer came, in a shrill treble: "Good-bye, Mr. Chips. . . ."

Chips sat by the fire again, with those words echoing along the corridors of his mind. "Good-bye, Mr. Chips. . . ." An old leg-pull, to make new boys think that his name was really Chips; the joke was almost traditional. He did not mind. "Good-bye, Mr. Chips. . . ." He remembered that on the eve of his wedding day Kathie had used that same phrase, mocking him gently for the seriousness he had had in those days. He thought: Nobody would call me serious to-day, that's very certain. . . .

Suddenly the tears began to roll down his cheeks—an old man's failing; silly, perhaps, but he couldn't help it. He felt very tired; talking to Linford like that had quite exhausted him. But he was glad he had met Linford. Nice boy. Would do well.

Over the fog-laden air came the bell for call-over, tremulous and muffled. Chips looked at the window, graying into twilight; it was time to light up. But as soon as he began to move he felt that he couldn't; he was too tired; and, anyhow, it didn't matter. He leaned back in his chair. No chicken—eh, well—that was true enough. And it had been amusing about Linford. A neat score off the jokers who had sent the boy over. Good-bye, Mr. Chips . . . odd, though, that he should have said it just like that. . . .

18

WHEN he awoke, for he seemed to have been asleep, he found himself in bed; and Merivale was there, stooping over him and smiling. "Well, you old ruffian—feeling all right? That was a fine shock you gave us!"

Chips murmured, after a pause, and in a voice that surprised him by its weakness: "Why—um—what—what has happened?"

"Merely that you threw a faint. Mrs. Wickett came in and found you—lucky she did. You're all right now. Take it easy. Sleep again if you feel inclined."

He was glad someone had suggested such a good idea. He felt so weak that he wasn't even puzzled by the details of the business—how they had got him upstairs, what Mrs. Wickett had said, and so on. But then, suddenly, at the other side of the bed, he saw Mrs. Wickett. She was smiling. He thought: God bless my soul, what's she doing up here? And then, in the shadows behind Merivale, he saw Cartwright, the new Head (he thought of him as "new," even though he had been at Brookfield since 1919), and old Buffles, commonly called "Roddy." Funny, the way they were all here. He felt: Anyhow, I can't be bothered to wonder why about anything. I'm going to go to sleep.

But it wasn't sleep, and it wasn't quite wakefulness, either; it was a sort of in-between state, full of dreams and faces and voices. Old scenes and old scraps of tunes: a Mozart trio that Kathie had once played in—cheers and laughter and the sound of guns—and, over it all, Brookfield bells, Brookfield bells. "So you see, if Miss Plebs wanted Mr. Patrician to marry her . . . yes, you can, you liar. . . ." Joke . . . Meat to be abhorred. . . . Joke . . . That you, Max? Yes, come in. What's the news from the Fatherland? . . . *O mihi praeteritos* . . . Ralston said I was slack and inefficient—but they couldn't manage without me. . . . *Obile heres ago fortibus es in aro* . . . Can you translate that, any of you? . . . It's a joke. . . .

Once he heard them talking about him in the room.

Cartwright was whispering to Merivale. "Poor old chap—must have lived a lonely sort of life, all by himself."

Merivale answered: "Not always by himself. He married, you know."

"Oh, did he? I never knew about that."

"She died. It must have been—oh, quite thirty years ago. More, possibly."

"Pity. Pity he never had any children."

And at that, Chips opened his eyes as wide as he could and sought to attract their attention. It was hard for him to speak out loud, but he managed to murmur something, and they all looked round and came nearer to him.

He struggled, slowly, with his words. "What—was that—um—you were saying—about me—just now?"

Old Buffles smiled and said: "Nothing at all, old chap—nothing at all—we were just wondering when you were going to wake out of your beauty sleep."

"But—umph—I heard you—you *were* talking about me—"

"Absolutely nothing of any consequence, my dear fellow—really, I give you my word. . . ."

"I thought I heard you—one of you—saying it was a pity—umph—a pity I never had—any children . . . eh? . . . But I have, you know . . . I have . . ."

The others smiled without answering, and after a pause Chips began a faint and palpitating chuckle.

"Yes—umph—I have," he added, with quavering merriment. "Thousands of 'em . . . thousands of 'em . . . and all boys."

And then the chorus sang in his ears in final harmony, more grandly and sweetly than he had ever heard it before, and more comfortingly too. . . . Pettifer, Pollett, Porson, Potts, Pullman, Purvis, Pym-Wilson, Radlett, Rapson, Reade, Reaper, Reddy Primus . . . come round me now, all of you, for a last word and a joke. . . . Harper, Haslett, Hatfield, Hatherley . . . my last joke . . . did you hear it? . . . Did it make you laugh? . . . Bone, Boston, Bovey, Bradford, Bradley, Bramhall-Anderson . . . wherever you are, whatever has happened, give me this moment with you . . . this last moment . . . my boys . . .

And soon Chips was asleep.

He seemed so peaceful that they did not disturb him to say good-night; but in the morning, as the School bell sounded for breakfast, Brookfield had the news. "Brookfield will never forget his lovableness," said Cartwright, in a speech to the School. Which was absurd, because all things are forgotten in the end. But Linford, at any rate, will remember and tell the tale: "I said good-bye to Chips the night before he died. . . ."